Bake *My* Day

A Maple Falls Novel

SHANNON GRAUPMAN

Bake My Day

ISBN 978-0-9982151-0-5

Cover design by Paper and Sage Design

Printed in the United States of America

For my four beautiful children: Erica, Joseph, Emily, and Jaxson.
I hope you always follow your dreams no matter
how long it may take you to reach them.
I hope I have shown you that you
can do anything you put your mind to.

After 33 years of wanting to be an author, it is finally here.
Never give up. I will always support your dreams.

ACKNOWLEDGMENTS

I would like to thank my dear husband, Chuck, for supporting this journey I have been on to finally finish my book. Thank you for allowing me time away at the library to write, for entertaining the kids so I could write just one more chapter. It is no easy task keeping them busy, but for that I will always be thankful.

To my children, Erica, Joseph, Emily, and Jaxson for allowing me to sneak away and write. I hope you will always remember that hard work pays off and to always believe in yourself.

Thank you to my parents, Bob and Rene, for always believing in me, teaching me to go for my dreams, encouraging me along the way, and helping me to believe that I could do this.

To my siblings, Jen, Lisa, and Bobby for always supporting one another along all of our adventures and for always offering advice and encouragement to start new projects and live out our passions in life. Thank you for all of your support in chasing mine. To my sisters for their input on anything that I got stuck on along the way.

A huge thank you to my best friend, Christina, for keeping me going when I thought I couldn't. For the many text messages, phone calls, and emails to check on my progress almost daily. For saying, "You got this," even when I wasn't sure I did. For reading each chapter along the way and giving me your advice. It means the world to me.

And thank you to the rest of my family (and all of the Henry's) and my friends who have been so supportive along the way. It means more to me than you will ever know. I am so blessed to have each and every one of you in my life.

Chapter One

The apartment didn't feel the same to me anymore; not that it truly ever felt like my home since the day I moved in. There was nothing left here that was mine. A few things we accumulated together but nothing I wanted to take with me that would remind me of him, or even worse us. Once again, my entire life was packed up in my car in the many boxes I'd been collecting over the past two weeks.

I didn't start packing them right away, holding onto hope that Chris would change his mind and want me to stay. I started slowly at first, removing clothes from my closet that I didn't wear much or were out of season that I would not need right away if he asked me to stay. Having never owned much in my life, there really wasn't a lot to pack anyway so most of it was left until yesterday when I finally decided it was time. It was finally clear to me that he wasn't going to change his mind and there was nothing I could do about that. Nothing, that is, unless I wanted to stay in this one-sided, dead-end relationship that was not only not moving forwards, but had somehow began to go backwards.

It wasn't as if I was a stranger to starting over, but I thought this was finally it. I thought this relationship would last; that Chris was the one I was supposed to marry and start the family with that I so longed to have. It was a huge piece of my life that was still missing. It has been just me since my grandmother passed twelve years ago. She took me in when I had nowhere else to go after my mother left. She taught me so much about life and to follow my dreams no matter who told me they would never come true and to always keep reaching for the stars.

When my grandmother was younger, she baked at a local bakery in her hometown. She taught me everything she knew about baking, including all of her secret ingredients. I've wanted to be a baker just like her ever since. The closest I ever got was working for the bakery here in the city as a frosting artist. It wasn't as lame as it sounded, or maybe I just tried to make it seem like a more important job than it was. Yesterday was my last day and I am secretly hoping that I will be missed and hard to replace. My signature swirl will definitely be hard to duplicate. I'm sure they've already hired someone who is doing just fine, but it still made me feel better to think that.

I lifted the last box stacked by the front door and carried it down the hall to the stairwell. Most of my floor was still at work this time of day, making it the perfect time to move. The sound of the elderly neighbor's TV was blaring, filling the usually quiet hall with noise. The lights in the stairwell flickered, making a zapping sound like an electric bug zapper outside in the summer, reminding me of a scary movie as I walked down the steps. Every time I went down them, I was just waiting for a scary man in a mask to be around the corner.

I turned around, pushing the door open with my back, and trying to fight against the pressure of the wind blowing up against it. The dry fall leaves blew across the ground in front of me, crunching under my feet as I walked down the sidewalk towards my car. Dark clouds had begun to roll in, moving quickly in the breeze, covering the pink and orange streaks that stretched across the horizon.

I slid the last box into the only remaining space in the back seat of my Ford Focus. It benefited me to not own much or else I would have to buy a bigger car. I wedged the box in tight like a game of Tetris and slammed the back door shut, giving it an extra nudge with my hip to ensure it closed tightly. I listened for the honk as I locked the car behind me, heading back upstairs to take one more look around the apartment.

As I opened the door, my heart began to race, feeling a tightening in my chest, knowing this was the last time I would be in this apartment. Deep in my heart I knew this was the right thing to do, that there was nothing I could do to change it, but I was still sad. I held onto the hope that he might take a break from work to come home and say goodbye to me, but I must have been asking too much. It was probably better this way anyway. If I were to see him one more time I would try to convince myself to stay, to give it another month that things would change, that he would change. But in my heart I knew that was never going to happen. He is who he is and I have to accept that he is not the one for me.

I walked through the bedroom and bathroom one last time, checking the closet and drawers again to be sure I grabbed everything, ending in the kitchen to raid some snacks for the road. I grabbed three bottles of water, an apple, and some crackers and placed them into my oversized purse, losing them almost immediately among the piles of junk already inside. I pulled my keys out of my back pocket, turning the key ring until the apartment key came loose. Placing it on the counter, I walked to the door, turned the lock on the door handle, and pulled it shut behind me. Taking a deep breath, I pulled my shoulders back, flipped my hair, and walked with purpose down the hallway for the last time.

I slid into the front seat, slamming the door quickly and turning the key, cranking the heat up to high. I reached up to adjust the mirror, trying to see over the mound of boxes stuffed in the back seat. Luckily I was tall enough to angle it up pretty far. Still unsure of my next move, I pushed the scroll button on the radio, searching for a distraction from the deafening silence that was closing in around me. On the third push, the radio stopped on a classical station, something I would not normally listen to, but that seemed to bring an instant calm over me.

Reaching deep into my purse, I pulled out my cell phone to text Chris and let him know that I was all packed up, ready to go, but he already knew. I needed to realize that he didn't care, that he couldn't even find the time to come and say goodbye to me before I left. All the text would do was give him the satisfaction that he won and I left, if he even bothered to read it at all. Part of me, deep, deep down hoped he was going to miss me. That he would be reminded of me every time he came through the front door. Why I even cared anymore, I wasn't sure. Maybe if I had made more of an effort in the beginning of our relationship it would be different, but it seemed so good back then that I didn't see a need.

I placed my phone back in my purse.

Somewhere over the past three years we moved from happy couple to slightly less happy couple to basically roommates. When I first moved in, he would leave me sweet notes on the counter in the morning before he left for work. He opened the doors for me, pulled out my chair, and took me out to dinner. Over the last six months, I couldn't remember a time where we even ate dinner together. His excuse was always the same; working late or he had a business meeting that I wasn't allowed to join him at.

When he was at home, it was usually a quick conversation to either ask if he had clean laundry or if I had gone to the grocery store. It was nothing too out of the ordinary for me as I had always had those responsibilities for myself, but it seemed like that was all I was there for. I knew relationships took time and effort, so that is what I gave it. Probably more time than I should have, but I've never been a person to give up on things easily.

Two weeks ago, when I woke up to find a chore list waiting for me on the counter where he had once put love notes, I decided I was done. Part of me was in shock that our relationship had come to this and the other part of me felt ripped off. The least he could have done was leave me an allowance for completing my chores. It had gotten to be almost laughable, or maybe I just laughed to keep myself from crying.

The following day, I gave my notice at the bakery. In the back of my mind I knew this day would eventually come. When I moved in with Chris, he paid for all of the rent so I tucked a lot of extra money away into my savings in case I needed it some day. As it turned out, today was that day. Today was the day that I was going to finally stand up for myself and take my life back.

Today was the day that I was going to take my grandmother's advice and follow my dreams and reach for the stars. Back to a life I wanted to live; back to the person I used to be. The past three years I was not living a life I loved. I no longer had my friends around me, and I wasn't truly happy in the place I was working. I want more for myself and I am not going to stop this time until I find it. I am not going to settle for good enough again.

Checking the clock on my dashboard, I hadn't realized how much time it took to pack the car; rush hour was about to begin. Having worked in the cities for the past few years, I knew the majority of the traffic would head north. With that in mind, I took it as my first official sign of where to go—or at least in which direction I should drive.

With another quick check of my mirrors, I turned up the music a notch or two and backed out of my parking spot. As I approached the stop sign at the end of the block, the last ray of sunlight shone through the clouds on the road in front of me. It was proof that there was a bright future ahead of me. As I drove through the ray of light, the sun warmed my face, and the view behind me was dark. My dark, lonely past was now behind me and my future was anywhere I wanted to go.

A steady stream of bright headlights passed me on the freeway as I drove south out of town. After leaving work last night, I stopped at the gas station to fill my gas tank and grab a map, tucking it into my glove box just in case. I knew that the days of the paper map were pretty much behind us, but it just didn't feel like a real road trip without one. For all I know, I would end up in some place in the middle of nowhere without cell service and it could totally save the day.

As the hours passed and the sun sunk lower into the sky, the classical music was making me sleepy and was starting to go in and out. Not really knowing where I was, I began to scan the stations again for something different. On the fourth push, a woman's voice came on the air, catching my attention. She had one of those calm radio voices that drew people in. I bet her ratings were probably high because of the tone of her voice more than the content of her show. Either way, it worked on me. I shifted my weight back and forth straightening up in my seat. I cracked the front window to let in some fresh cool air and leaned back to listen.

"Good evening, listeners. We are just about to begin our *Starting Over with Faith* segment. I am Faith and I will be happy to take your calls this evening." The voice of the woman was so soft and soothing: one of a best friend you have had for years.

She greeted the first caller, "Hello, thank you for joining us tonight. Please tell me what I can help you with tonight."

There was a short pause on the line, followed by a deep breath.

"Hi, Faith. I am calling in tonight to ask for advice about my new apartment I just rented. I've always had a roommate and I am a bit nervous leaving that comfort and going out on my own."

"I see," Faith began, and I pictured her nodding on the other end, "That is a very common feeling when people leave the nest, if you will, even if it was with a friend. There is a lot of responsibility that comes along with that and you should be proud of yourself for taking that on."

I listened to her advice until the next freeway exit. Spotting a well lit gas station near the bottom of the ramp, I turned on my signal and got off the freeway, desperately needing to stretch my legs. I pulled into a parking spot close to the front door. Not being familiar with this place, I didn't want to walk too far alone. The door chimed overhead as I entered the gas station, alerting the clerk. The only employee I saw working looked up for a second from her book and returned back to it just as quickly. I assume they don't get much business at this hour of the night.

I quickly used the restroom and politely waved to the clerk on my way out, wanting to get back in the car as fast as I could, before the next caller.

"Thank you again for joining us tonight. You are listening to *Starting Over with Faith* and we are coming back to you with a caller who recently ended their relationship and is trying to move on with her life. She is in her thirties and fears that she is too old to start over again. Please, share your story with us."

"Oh my gosh! That's me!" I shouted at the dashboard, turning the volume up a few more turns.

"Hello, Faith, my name is Amy. I just broke up with my

7

boyfriend that I had been dating for about four years, because I didn't feel like it was going anywhere. But now, I'm single again. Can people in their thirties still find men that aren't already divorced or have children?"

I paused in silence, hoping for Faith to reassure us that it was possible.

"Of course, there are tons of men still out there. You have to remember Amy that women mature a lot quicker then men do, so men in their thirties are just starting to settle down. You definitely have not missed the boat; he is still out there looking for you. You just have to open yourself up to meeting him."

There was silence on the line followed by a sigh of relief. I wasn't sure whose sigh was louder; Amy's or mine. I knew that I wasn't ready to date right now, but it was a nice feeling to know that there was still time.

"You are so right," Amy agreed, "I feel so much better. Sometimes you just need to hear from someone other than your skeptical friends who just fill your head with doubts."

After the caller hung up, the show went to another commercial break. I reached down to take a sip of water as I came to a stop sign. Placing it back into the holder, I realized I missed the freeway entrance a few blocks back while listening to Amy's story. I looked in my rearview mirror at the light from the gas station and the passing cars on the freeway. Not knowing where I was and having driven for seven hours, I was suddenly very tired and my eyes started to burn.

At this point I had two options, pull over somewhere and sleep in my car, or drive a little further to see if I could find a hotel. As tempting as sleeping in my car sounded, the backseat was too full of boxes and my seat wouldn't recline. I continued through the stop sign, driving four more blocks, coming to another four-way stop. To the left was dark and mostly residential; to the right looked like the town's main street. I flipped on my turn signal and turned right, making my way slowly down the street.

The store fronts were dark and closed for the night, each one with a different colored striped awning above the entrance. The street lights along the sidewalk gave off a hazy glow in the mist filled sky. On the first block, there was a bank, a coffee shop, and a hair salon mixed in with a few vacant buildings in between.

The next block had a sign strung over the street that read "Maple Falls Festival October 13-15." Now that the sleeping town finally had a name, I pulled over to an empty parking spot on the side of the street, reaching in the glove box for my map.

"I knew this would come in handy," I whispered to myself, unfolding it in my lap.

I found where I had started on the map, running my finger south along the freeway until Maple Falls appeared. It wasn't a town I had ever heard of before, but seemed to be a good distance from my old life. As I folded the map back up, Faith came back on the air.

"Good evening, listeners. Before I go tonight, I want to leave you with something." She paused for a moment for dramatic effect, "Are you a believer in signs? They are all around you, guiding you in your life. Open yourself up to see them and you will find your way."

I feel like Faith was speaking to me this whole time. I knew there were signs around me, around everybody, but I am sometimes too stubborn to really see them. I grazed my leg along the side of the door as I returned the map to the glove box, knocking a bunch of wrappers onto the floor that I stuffed in there along the way. The street was fairly dark despite the streetlights, but I spotted a trash can on the sidewalk a few stores down. Gathering as much as I could fit in my arms, I decided to make a run for it. Dark, misty streets were about as creepy in my book as the flickering light in my old apartment stairwell. But, I survived them all these years, so I would certainly be fine running fifty feet away.

I glanced around all sides of me to make sure there wasn't anyone creepy hiding in the shadows and made a run for it. I opened the door so hard to get off and running, that it whipped back closed on its own.

As I loaded the trash into the bin, being extra careful not liter, I look up and saw a For Sale sign propped in the front window of a shop. The building was painted a light green with large display windows covering the entire storefront. As I walked closer to it, I see that the windows have been draped in white sheets making it impossible to see what was on the other side. Taking a step back, I looked for a sign above the door, but there was nothing. Whatever had been there previously had been removed. Walking closer to the door, the glow of the street light reflected off of a window decal on the front door, catching my eye. It was a tiny chocolate cupcake with pink glitter frosting.

Just as I reached up to touch it, I was startled by a bright spotlight shining on me. Gasping, I jumped back, dropping the last bit of trash I still had in my arms. I turned around to see a police car parked behind my car, moving his spotlight back and forth from me to my car. I looked behind me to see if I had accidentally parked in a no parking zone or a handicap spot.

The officer turned off the spotlight and climbed out of the car, turning on his flash light instead that he pulled from his belt. He shined the light through my car windows as he walked by, joining me on the sidewalk. I wasn't sure if I should speak first or let him. In the shadows he looked bigger than he did now as he got closer, still a bulky build and broad shoulders, but less intimidating in the light. The look on his face was serious and hard to read; his nostrils flared slightly.

"Is everything okay, ma'am?" he asked politely.

I let out a huge breath I wasn't even aware I was holding in.

"Yes, everything is fine. I pulled over to grab my map and see where I was and then I saw that I had a lot of garbage in the side of my door and I got out so I could throw it away and then I dropped it when you shined the light on me because you scared me." Realizing that I said all of that in one breath, he probably thought I was a crazy person.

He shined his flashlight at the garbage that was still lying on the sidewalk. I quickly leaned down to pick it up before I got into trouble for littering.

"That's a lot of boxes you have there in your car. Are you moving?" he asked, turning the light back on my car.

I joined his glance, shadows of boxes filling the back seat. "Yes, I am, actually. I think I have driven about as far as I can for one night. Is there a hotel near by?"

I waited for his response, but all I was getting was the serious stare again. His eyebrows veered downwards, causing a slight wrinkle between his eyes.

"Moving across the country? How far are you planning on driving?"

My honest response would be as far as I could possibly drive with as many tanks of gas as I could afford, but looking at him I knew that answer wouldn't suffice. He moved his flashlight down to my license plate to confirm where I was coming from.

"I'm not too sure, honestly." That wasn't a complete lie; I still had no destination in mind. "Maple Falls looks pretty nice. I know the town is dark and everything is closed for the night, but it seems to have that inviting feel I'm looking for."

His look still hadn't changed. Looking closer, I wasn't even sure I had seen him blink. He clicked off his flashlight, returning it to his belt.

He lifted his arm up into the air. "If you follow this road for another eight blocks or so, you will find a hotel up there on the left. There is a stone fountain in the middle of a turnaround out front. You can't miss it. If you do, you'll drive into the lake."

I smiled at his joke, hoping to change his expression, but it didn't. "Thank you, I've been in the car most of the day and could use a warm bath and a good night's rest."

The streetlight caught the reflection of his name badge above the right pocket: B. Harper.

"Phil will be working at the front desk. He'll see to it that you have everything you need for the night. Be sure to lock your doors before going inside. It's a pretty safe town, but all of these boxes could tempt someone." He nodded and turned back towards his squad car. I watched as he walked, his toffee brown hair combed perfectly back.

"Thank you again, Officer Harper," I shouted as he pulled open his car door.

I climbed back into my car, cranking the heat back up to warm my hands. Barely having the strength in my frozen fingers to hold a pen, I jotted down the address and phone number for the building for sale, tucking it inside my purse. Buckling my seat belt, I put my car into drive, slowly pulling back out onto the main street. Officer Harper sat in his car behind me until I pulled away.

I counted the blocks as I drove, seeing a bright light coming from the left up ahead as I approached block number seven. I pulled into the front turnaround, spotting the fountain the officer described. The front of the building was beautiful brick from top to bottom, accompanied with flower boxes resting underneath each window. A few of the rooms were still lit, but for the most part, the rooms were dark.

The parking lot was half full as I pulled in, finding a spot near the front. Reaching into the backseat, I placed a blanket over the pile of boxes thinking back to what Officer Harper had said. I grabbed my overnight bag off the seat next to me, looped my arm through the handle of my purse, and climbed out of the car. The wind had picked up even more since I was down the street a few minutes ago. The hotel was near the lake, catching the brisk gusts coming this way along with the crashing waves along the shoreline.

The rod iron handles were as cold as ice as I wrapped my hands around them, opening the front door, feeling a warm rush of air warm my face. The fireplace crackled in the corner of the lobby; the stacked stone surround glowing from the flames. The seating area around the fireplace was deserted, not a guest in sight. A man with silver hair was sitting behind the counter reading the newspaper, a warm smile on his face.

"Good evening, miss. How can I help you on this cold fall night?" he asked as he rose from his chair, resting his forearms on the counter.

"Hi, you must be Phil," I replied holding my hand out, catching him by surprise.

"Yes, I am; have we met before?" he asked with a puzzled look, his hand meeting mine.

I laughed, "No, I met a kind officer in town and he told me where I could find you. I was hoping you had an available room for the night." I tucked my hands back into my pockets trying to warm them.

"You must have been talking to Officer Harper." He smiled as he began typing on his computer.

"That would be him. He stopped to check on me in town when I stopped to throw a few things away. I had been driving in the car all day and needed a place to throw away a few snack wrappers I collected." I watched him as he tapped his fingers on the keys, still hoping for a room.

He politely listened to my stories as he continued on the computer. "All day, huh? Where are you headed?" he asked, clicking the mouse a few more times.

I placed my purse on the top of the counter and began searching for my wallet. "I'm not really sure yet," I replied, still digging, "I'm looking for a new start and I am open to just about anything at this point. Aha!" I shouted, pulling my wallet out from the bottom corner.

"That sounds exciting. Is there any specific type of room you were looking for tonight? Smoking? Non-Smoking?" He pushed his glasses back up his nose, peering at the screen.

"Anything you have with a comfortable bed and hot bath water. Honestly, I could probably sleep on the floor right now, but a bed would be preferable." I pulled my credit card and driver's license out of my wallet and slid them across the counter.

Scrolling the mouse a little further down the screen, he finally found one. "It looks like I have a non-smoking king bed available overlooking the lake. How does that sound?" He picked up my cards and began typing my information into the computer.

"It sounds so wonderful. I may never leave." I glanced around the lobby as he finished entering in my credit card numbers, checking them over again to be sure they were correct. "This is a beautiful place; are you the owner?"

He pulled the receipt off of the printer and activated my room key. "Yes, my wife and I bought this place about thirty years ago. It's the only one in town so we get to meet a lot of new people who are passing through, and also some friendly faces from around town that stop by periodically to say hello."

He handed me my room key and I tucked it inside of my sweatshirt pocket, still trying to warm my hands. Pulling them out of my sleeves, I walked over to the fireplace held them up to the fire, the warm heat radiating against my skin.

"Well, you have definitely done well here. I cannot wait to see the town tomorrow in daylight. Everything was closed when I came through town tonight." Checking my watch I was stating the obvious. "Do you have breakfast here in the morning?"

Phil nodded, pointing down the hall. "We have a continental breakfast every morning starting at six o'clock in the first room there on the right. My wife Nancy will be down here to make sure everything is out and fresh coffee is brewed. Most mornings all you have to do is follow the smell of waffle batter all the way down here," he laughed. "It ends at ten thirty so you will have plenty of time to sleep in and still get down here."

When the feeling returned to my fingers and my cheeks began to feel hot, I turned my backside to the fire, warming my back and legs.

"That's perfect; I will definitely try to sleep in for a while. On the off chance that I really sleep in, is there a bakery in town I can grab something at?" I was still thinking about that building in town that was for sale. If Phil had been living here for the past thirty years, he should know everything there was to know about Maple Falls.

"There was, but it's closed now." Before he could say any more, the phone rang at the desk. "Please excuse me, I have to answer this. Your room is near the end of the hall on your right. I hope you find it to your liking." He excused himself and returned back behind the desk to answer the call.

I pulled the key out of my pocket as I made my way down the hall. I waited for the door light to turn green, turning the handle. The room was spacious and inviting. The bathroom was immediately to the left with complimentary toiletries on the counter and two racks stacked with fluffy, white, terry cloth towels. A tiny hall entrance continued, opening up to a larger room. The bed was freshly made, covered in an off white down comforter. There was a TV resting at the end on a console with a mini refrigerator tucked under one side. A small desk and chair, upholstered in a green velvet fabric were positioned under a window, takeout menus placed neatly on the desktop.

I grabbed my book out of my purse, placing it on the night stand and turned on the lamp. Getting more exhausted with each passing minute, a warm bath seemed out of the question. I put my pajamas on from my overnight bag, washed my face, and brushed my teeth, unwrapping the paper cover from the cup in the bathroom. I pulled the covers back on the king size bed, slowly climbing in and opened my book. Before I could finish the first paragraph, my eyes were closed and I was fast asleep.

Chapter
Two

I was woken the next morning by voices outside of my door and feet stomping up and down the hallway. A young child squealed as he ran by, followed by his mother shouting at him to quiet down, which was probably louder than the child's voice. Rubbing the sleep out of my eyes, it took me a moment to get my bearings and realize where I was waking up. Last night had been the first night in a long time I didn't wake up countless times throughout the night worrying about one thing or another.

The clock on the nightstand read eight thirty as I pulled back the covers and slid out of bed. The wooden floors were cold on my feet as I stepped lightly over to the patio door, pulling the curtains open and filling the room with the warm sunlight. After a moment of blinking and adjusting to the bright light, what appeared before me was breathtaking. Unlocking the door, I slid it open slowly, stepping out onto the dew covered deck, pulling my arms close into my body to keep warm against the cool breeze.

Just beyond the grassy area near the patio to my room was a beautiful, long sandy beach that stretched far until it met the rolling waves of the water. The wind was blowing enough to cause tiny white caps just beyond the shoreline. A flock of seagulls glided over the top of the water, skimming for small fish to catch for breakfast. Most of the shoreline was tree covered, displaying breathtaking views of golden oranges and fire red leaves. It was at that moment, as the breeze blew softly through my hair, that I realized fall had officially arrived. It was my favorite season and I had been missing all of the wonderful changes that were happening all around me.

It was as if I were seeing fall for the very first time. Taking a deep breath of the brisk air, I suddenly felt my mind clear and the weight that had been holding me down for far too long lift off of my shoulders and float away with the passing breeze. I tried to imagine what this morning would feel like last night before I fell asleep. It was going to go one of two ways: either wake up filled with regret for leaving or wake up filled with relief that I left. What I feel at this very moment, I knew deep in my soul, was relief.

After freshening up and grabbing a quick bite to eat in the lobby, I returned to my room before venturing out for the day. The piece of paper I had written the phone number down on for the vacant building I saw last night was peeking out of the top of my purse. Not far enough to fall out, but far enough for it to catch my attention and call me over there; I could either push it back in or pull it out.

I pulled it out.

Having just left my old life not even twenty-four hours ago, I didn't want to jump into anything too quickly. Not many people get the chance to start their lives over again, to go for their dreams with everything they had, and I was being given this chance. I wanted to do it right this time.

I stared at the paper and tucked it back into my purse, deep enough where it wasn't going to fall out, and swung my purse up over my shoulder. Before committing to this location, I wanted to see what the town looked like in daylight and get a feel for the kind of people that live here. The few I met in the middle of the night seemed wonderful and I couldn't wait to see what the rest of the town was like.

Returning to the lobby, I found an older woman working behind the counter. As I approached her, she greeted me with a friendly smile, swiping her salt and pepper hair across her forehead.

"Good morning, you must be Nancy. I checked in last night and Phil told me I would find you here this morning. I'm Cora." I extended my hand towards her.

Reaching over the counter, she shook mine back, her hand delicate. "I am Nancy. It is so nice to meet you. Phil told me a nice young lady checked in late last night. Were you able to get some good rest?" she asked.

"Yes, I did, thank you. I was actually thinking of staying a couple more nights if the room is still available. I was planning to do a little exploring around town today and check out what your town has to offer. I'd love some suggestions, if you have any?"

Nancy turned to the computer and clicked her mouse, scrolling through the screens. "It looks like that room is available for the rest of the week. I will tentatively put you in there until Friday and if you change your mind and want to check out sooner, just let one of us know." She printed an updated statement and slid it across the counter for me to sign.

"Thank you so much Nancy, I really appreciate your help." I folded my copy into quarters and placed it into the outside pocket of my purse.

"So, do you have anything in mind to do for your first day here in town? There are a lot of shops to check out on Main Street. If you like to read, there is a fantastic used book store called The Book Mark just a few blocks down. There is a little knick knack shop with tons of different home type items. The restaurant on the next block over has a wonderful homemade chicken and dumpling soup. It would be good on a cold day like today." Her face lit up as she was describing all of these places to me. I could tell that her love for this town grew deep.

I stood there for a moment taking in all of her suggestions. "Wow, thank you for all of those wonderful ideas. It was so dark last night when I got into town I wasn't able to read many of the building names. Those are all great ideas, and I love to read so I will be sure to stop by The Book Mark. I think I will just hop in the car and see which places jump out at me. I guess that is kind of how I ended up here, one pit stop at a gas station, a wrong turn, and bam. Now I am staying for the week. I can't wait to get started."

I adjusted my purse back up onto my shoulder and walked towards the exit. Nancy came around from behind the desk to tidy the lobby. Picking up a Styrofoam coffee cup in one hand, wiping the coffee ring off the table with the other.

"What are your plans after the end of the week? Are you just passing through or do you plan to stick around a while longer?" she asked, tossing the empty cup into the garbage can near the front door.

"I'm not really sure just yet. Right now I'm looking for a new place to call home. I guess I will just wait and see what the week brings," I replied, watching the colored leaves blow pass the back window towards the lake.

"Well, then I hope you find what you're looking for, my dear. Please let me know if Phil or I can be of any help to you during your stay with us. There are some cute little houses on the other end of town for sale. Be sure to check out the old town library, too, if you have time. There are a bunch of old articles there that will tell you a little history about Maple Falls. The librarian's name is Maryanne; she'll help you find whatever you need."

Nancy continued to walk the lobby, straightening plants, dusting, and arranging the furniture just right.

"Thank you for everything Nancy," I said, pushing open the front door.

"Oh, and Cora?" she shouted out to me. "Be sure to check out the lake this week, too. I find it to be so calming and peaceful down there. It may be a good place for you to sit and gather your thoughts. Do bundle up; the wind coming off the lake can get pretty chilly this time of year."

I smiled and nodded back at her before walking through the door.

My shoulders sunk as I approached my car. Even if only for a few short hours, I forgot about the giant mound of boxes overtaking my back seat. I waited a few minutes for my car to warm up and for warm air to finally start blowing out of the vents before backing out of my parking spot. After waiting for three cars to pass by, I turned right back onto the main road and headed back into town. No one was behind me so I was able to drive slowly down the block, reading all of the building signs along the way.

The first block had a bank, a small gas station, and a restaurant. That must have been the one that Nancy was telling me that had the chicken soup I could not stop dreaming about. A little further down, I found the fire station, the police station, and the library. Great to know where they all were, but none of them appealed to me at the moment. A couple of blocks later, I came up to a few shops that I wanted to check out.

The first one that caught my eye was Sweet Peas. The large glass display windows were lined with fall leaf garland, surrounded by different types of homemade items, household things, and knick knacks for around the house. I parked in the first parking spot I found on the street and got out of the car. After a car passed by, I jogged across the road, covering my face from the mist that began falling from the sky. The weather had turned quickly and it felt very much like fall. The breeze blew the leaves down the sidewalks, gathering in the recessed areas near the shop entrances.

Pushing the door open, the smell of pumpkin spice rushed to my nose. I took a deep breath as I pushed the door closed tightly behind me. The front of the store was filled with shelves of gifts, set up as a tourist area. A spinning rack of postcards creaked as I spun it around, catching the attention of a lady who appeared from behind a curtain that was hanging in a doorway near the middle of the store; her long coffee brown hair flowing behind her as she walked.

"Good morning, welcome to Sweet Peas. Is there anything in particular that brought you in today?" she asked.

"Good morning. I was just noticing the wonderful smell in here. This candle smells similar; is this the one you're burning?" I asked, holding the lid in one hand and the open candle in the other.

The woman set the box she was carrying down onto the counter and came over to help me. She reached out to look at the label on the candle I was holding.

"Yes, that's the same one, you have a great nose. It happens to be my best seller and I have a hard time keeping it on the shelves this time of year. Right now, I think that's the last one I have in stock until my new shipment arrives later in the week." She straightened some of the candle jars, spreading them out around the table to make it appear more full.

"I can see why they sell out so quickly, it smells wonderful. There is just something about fall and pumpkin spice that go so well together; like you can't have one without the other." I held it back up to my nose for one last sniff before placing the lid back on. "I will definitely be taking this one."

She smiled. "Good choice. If you'd like, I can set it on the counter for you while you continue to look around. It'll be there when you're ready to check out." She grabbed the candle from me and walked back to the counter. "By the way, I'm Carla Chapman if you have any other questions," she said, turning back towards me.

"Thank you Carla, I'm Cora Westerling. I'll definitely come find you if I do."

I continued browsing the store, starting with the outer walls first. The back of the store was set up in a bunch of small cubicle sections, each one belonging to a different artist. One had crochet hats, mittens, and scarves. Another was filled with beautiful stone bracelets and necklaces. I was drawn into the next section, filled with journals and pens. One entire box in the back seat of my car was filled with blank journals. It was one of those things that I could never resist buying, hoping someday to fill them with recipes of my own and rewrite some of my grandmother's.

I reached down and picked one up from the back of a standing stack inside of a long wicker basket. It was sky blue in color, covered with shiny silver stars, catching the lights from the ceiling. In the middle, it read, "Reach for the stars." My grandmother's face flashed in my mind. As the years passed, it was getting harder and harder to remember the little things about her, but that was a phrase she used often that I will never forget.

Immediately deciding that I had to have this journal, I went in search of a matching pen to go along with it. Journals and pens were the same as fall and pumpkin spice: one needed the other. I lifted five pens out of the jar before finding the perfect one. It was clear with floating silver glitter that ran up and down the pen as I turned it from side to side. The glitter matched perfectly with the stars on the front cover.

Knowing how jammed my car already was and having very little space left, I decided not to walk the rest of the shop, fearing I would find something amazing and end up having to strap it to the roof of my car. I walked back to the counter where I found Carla unpacking another box from a shipment she had received.

"Found some more treasures I see," she said, grabbing the candle she had set on the counter behind her.

"One cannot buy a new journal without buying a new pen to write in it," I said, placing the two items onto the counter, both of us laughing at the same time.

"That's very true, and a matching pen is even better." She scanned the items and placed them into a small brown paper bag, folding down the top flap. "If that will do it for you today, your total is thirteen dollars and ninety-three cents."

I reached into my giant purse and ruffled around until I found my wallet, pulling out a twenty. "I think I need to put 'buy a smaller purse' on my to-do list. I love this big one because it holds so much, but I can never seem to find my wallet."

Carla smiled and handed me my change, sliding the bag closer to me. "Are you new to the town or are you just visiting?"

Either everyone in this town knew each other and could spot an outsider, or I had a tattoo on my forehead that said tourist. I had yet to meet someone in this town who didn't know I wasn't from here before even asking me.

"Perhaps both, I suppose." My response came out in more of an unsure question than an actual answer. "It began as just a quick pit stop to sleep for the night, but now I can't seem to bring myself to drive away from here. For now, I'm staying near the end of town in the hotel until I decide what I want to do. There is just something so comfortable about your town and I feel like I need to explore it a little more."

Carla nodded along while I spoke, seeming to agree with what I was saying. "No need to explain it to me. I had the same thing happen to me many years ago. I was passing through here with a few of my girlfriends on a weekend getaway and fell in love with this town. Six months later, I packed up my things and moved here. A year later I met my husband and we have lived here ever since."

"There's almost something magical about it, but I just can't quite put my finger on it. Do you understand what I'm talking about?"

"No need to explain, I completely understand. If you do decide to stick around for a while, a few of the women in town meet up here every Thursday night to work on whatever craft project they have going; you're welcome to stop by and meet some of them and bring your own work. Are you much of a crafter?"

I wanted to laugh out loud, but I didn't want it to come off as rude. "Unless it contains flour and in the form of batter, I can't make a thing."

Carla laughed, tipping her head back; the light catching her glossy lips. "Well I'll tell you what, why don't you stop by this Thursday and meet everyone and you can bring the dessert. That is, of course, if you decide to stay in town that long. I'm sure we can come up with a project for you."

It was only my first day in town and I was already making friends. I thought I had forgotten how to do that after sitting alone in my apartment for the past few years.

"I booked my hotel through the end of the week. I would love to stop by and meet some of your friends," I said, grabbing my bag off of the counter.

"Then I will see you on Thursday night around seven o'clock. You better bundle up out there; the weatherman said possible snow later in the week. The wind off the lake down where you're staying can get pretty chilly."

Carla sounded just like Nancy. I turned back and smiled on my way out the door. "I'll see you on Thursday."

I placed the bag of my new items on the seat next to me and turned the key. I placed my hands near the front vents to warm my fingers, frozen already from walking the short distance across the street. My stomach began to grumble, reminding me it was time for lunch. I hadn't noticed any other places to eat besides the restaurant near the hotel. Checking my mirrors for anyone coming, I pulled out of my parking spot, making a u-turn in the middle of the street and headed back the other way to find a warm meal. Ever since Nancy told me about the chicken and dumpling soup, I couldn't get it out of my mind.

Chapter
Three

When I pulled up to the restaurant, several cars were driving around trying to find a spot to park. Grabbing one of the last spots in the lot, I hurried inside to get a seat, noticing a large group coming towards me. The young hostess was standing near the podium in the lobby, writing down names quickly as more and more people began to pile through the door. Either this was the only place in town serving lunch or the soup really was that good. I squeezed through the crowd of people already waiting, turning my shoulders from side to side until I found the hostess on the other side.

"How many?" she asked without even looking up.

"Just myself," I replied.

"Name?"

"Cora."

"Have a seat and we'll call you when a spot opens up." The hostess looked around the restaurant snapping her gum, taking notice of what tables were being cleared, erasing those sections from her seating chart and replaced her pen back into her messy top bun.

I moved to the side for the next group to come in, getting pushed further and further back in the crowd. Just as I got as far from the podium as I possibly could, my name was called.

"Cora, party of one," the hostess shouted over the crowd.

I didn't think that announcement could sound any more depressing. I waved my hand in the air as I weaved back up to the front. I followed the hostess to a section in the middle of the restaurant, passing numerous booths nestled against the windows that overlooked the parking lot. She sat me at a half moon shaped bar with bright red bar stools, pushing a left behind newspaper to the side. From the looks of it, the area should have come with a neon blinking sign that read "dining alone." Joining three other singles, I pulled out the barstool and opened a menu. Glancing around the room, I noticed a table of truckers wearing plaid shirts and stocking caps, as the waitress placed plates of gravy-laden French fries and bowls of chili in front of them. A few minutes later, my waitress came by.

"Can I start you off with something to drink?" she asked, holding her pen in one hand and a small lined notepad in the other.

"Sure," I said, running my index finger down the beverage section on the laminated tri-fold menu. "I will have a hot tea with lemon and a glass of ice water please. Do you have any lunch specials today?" I wasn't sure if this was the type of place to have daily specials or not, but it was worth asking.

"We have a cup of soup and a sandwich for $5.99."

"That sounds simple, I'll have that. I'll take a turkey sandwich, chicken and dumpling soup, and kettle chips please." It seemed so much easier to order the special than to make another decision and pick something off the menu, unsure of when the waitress would return.

"Okay, I'll put that order in for you and bring your drinks right out. My name is Megan if you need anything else." She tucked her notepad back into her apron and disappeared into the kitchen.

The smell of bacon wafted by me as another waitress balanced a tray of BLTs passed me, nearly losing the pickle off the side of the plate. I pulled back the red paper tab from my napkin, releasing my silverware. Lifting my knife up, I picked a dried up piece of food off the tip with my fingernail, sending it sailing through the air. The dishwasher appeared from behind a wall, pushing a shiny metal cart with two giant dishpans on it. Gathering the old dishes and wiping the table down quickly, a new set of customers were placed there before the water streaks had time to dry.

My food arrived quickly and the soup was every bit as wonderful as Nancy had said, maybe more. I finished my sandwich in record time, not realizing how hungry I really was. Only having gas station snacks for the past day or so, eating a real meal felt amazing. The older I was getting, the more I was learning to appreciate the smaller, simpler things in life. I took the last bite of my soup, tilting the bowl to be sure to get every last drop of broth and pushed my empty dishes forward on the bar. Rinsing it down with a quick sip of water, I stood from my stool, brushing the bread crumbs off of my lap.

The waitress came by with my tab, handing it to me with one hand and delivering a steaming piece of apple pie to the diner beside me with the other. "Have you saved room for dessert?"

"No, thank you," I replied, placing a hand across my stomach.

I lifted my tea mug and placed a ten dollar bill underneath along with my tab and zipped up my sweater. I swung around, throwing my purse over my shoulder, and bumped right into another customer, slamming into their chest.

"I'm so sorry, I wasn't paying attention to where I was going," I said, feeling my cheeks turn hot with embarrassment.

"Don't apologize; I shouldn't have been standing so close behind you. I take it you found the hotel just fine last night? At least I hope so. I didn't see much room left in your car to sleep in there."

I recognized that voice right away. "Officer Harper!" I was completely caught off guard seeing him there. "Yes, I did find it, thanks to your great directions." *Did I really just say that?* "We haven't properly met, I'm Cora Westerling."

"It is nice to put a name with your face. I'm Brad and this is my daughter Lily." He looked down at a little girl gripping his hand and half hiding behind his leg.

"B. Harper, now that makes sense. I saw your name plate on your shirt last night."

"I wondered how you knew my last name," he replied.

I crouched down, getting closer to Lily's height. "It's nice to meet you Lily. You have a beautiful name. How old are you?"

She looked up at Brad and then back to me. She slowly lifted her arm into the air, raising four tiny fingers, letting out a giggle.

"She's a little shy at first, but once you get to know her, she never stops talking," he laughed.

"I understand. I'm a little shy myself at first. Are you two going to have a lunch date together?" I watched as Lily walked circles around his legs, wrapping both of her arms around him as she walked.

"We are; I have the day off and I promised to take her out to lunch and some ice cream after." Lily stopped walking, peering up at me from behind Brad.

"Well, please don't let me keep you. I was just on my way out anyway. I'm sure I'll see you around town again. Enjoy your lunch and nice meeting you, Lily." I waved to her as I walked away, tucking my hands into my pockets.

Brad shouted toward me, "Are you staying in town for a while?"

Turning my head back to him, I shrugged my shoulders. "I'm still not sure, yet, but I'm really starting to like it here."

He smiled at me as I turned around to leave. As I got outside, I peered through the window spotting him and Lily being seated at a corner table, watching him pull out Lily's chair for her and helping her up. I definitely wouldn't mind running into him again very soon.

I parked my car in the parking lot back at the hotel and walked around the front of the building to the walking path that led to the lake. The grass was still damp from the morning dew, not having much opportunity to dry with so little sunlight. Beyond the gravel path was a wooden slat walkway nestled among some tall grass where the sand and grass met. Pine railings ran along both sides of the walkway. I ran my hands along the top as I walked towards the water, the surface rough and uneven. As I looked down, I noticed there were hundreds of carvings in the railing tops along both sides, running from one end to the other.

Some of the carvings dated back twenty to thirty years while others were more recent. Some had full names, some just their initials, some had dates, some just the year. 'CMP was here 1993' 'N+P 1986' 'Ken & Rebecca'. Each one had their own special meaning, left here to preserve for a memory, so they could come back and say, "I was here once."

As I reached the end of the walkway, after reading over thirty different carvings, I noticed the last one along the rail, closest to the water, "B+H 9-8-07." It had a heart carved around the initials and "I do" above the heart. It must have been their wedding date, maybe even their wedding location. The sandy beach stretched all the way down the shore and would make a beautiful setting for a wedding. I could picture chairs lined up along the beach, waves rolling up onto the shore in the background of the ceremony, paddling away in a canoe off into the sunset.

The docks had been pulled from the water for the season and were lined up neatly along the shore. The sand was still damp from the mist that had been coming down all day, making it easier to walk on. Seagulls were walking along the shoreline looking for small fish that had washed up; some looking in nearby trash cans for food left behind. The closer I got to them, the further away they walked. A family of mallard ducks walked along the sand under the docks heading for the tall grass.

The waves along the shore were rolling in one right after the other as the wind began to pick up. I reached down to touch the water, the freezing cold waves washing up over my fingers. As the waves rolled back out from the shore, it washed the sand off the top of a gray heart shaped rock. I picked it up, running my fingers through the ice cold water, rinsing the sand off of the bottom. Using the cuff of my sweater, I dried it off and tucked it into my pocket. Unsure if it was another sign being sent to me, the last thing I was going to do was ignore it. Maybe there was love in this town for me after all.

As the sun began to set on my first official day in Maple Falls, I stood in my hotel room window gazing out at the lake as the last glowing rays of light began to disappear behind the tree lined horizon. A flock of geese flew overhead in a V-formation.

With dinner time approaching, I freshened up my makeup in the bathroom and headed back to the restaurant next door. Tomorrow's agenda would likely consist of finding other places to eat in this town. If I wasn't sticking out as the new girl in town, I was soon to be known as the lonely girl who eats every meal by herself at the singles' bar.

I glanced across the street as I walked outside, catching a gust of wind that sent my hair blowing backwards. I thought about driving to avoid the gusts of cold air coming from the lake, but the car would hardly warm up before having to turn it right back off again. I zipped my sweater up to the very top and tilted my chin down to protect my face from the wind.

The dinner crowd was much different than the lunch crowd had been. For lunch, the restaurant was filled with people dressed in fancy business attire, meeting with clients or co-workers. Tonight it was filled with elderly couples, young couples, and families; kid's heads bobbing up and down in the booths.

Once again, I was seated at the singles' bar in the middle of the restaurant, placed between and elderly man and a woman who looked to be in her fifties. Not having the space I did before, I sat on the stool, placing my purse down on the floor in between my feet. I looked around at everyone's plates near me as I pondered what to order for dinner. I was always curious what the popular items were in restaurants. If a lot of tables had ordered the same thing, I would assume it was a good meal and order the same.

At least one person at every table had a bowl of soup, that I knew was a given having had a bowl for lunch already. I looked to the man on my left, quietly eating a cheeseburger, looking not even remotely interested in starting up a conversation. Peering to my right, the woman had her menu open, also deciding what to order.

"It seems like the soup is pretty popular here, nearly everyone has a bowl on their table. Is there anything else you would recommend?" I asked her, flipping open my menu.

"Everything," she replied with a laugh. "I've never had a bad meal here. I have a hard time deciding every time I come." She was dressed in a business suit with a briefcase resting near her feet.

"You must be from around here then? I just got into town last night and I don't know much about this place, yet," I said, looking to the next page.

"I've lived here my whole life. I usually come in here once a week. The food is amazing and the staff is wonderful. They know me by name and are always so friendly." She closed her menu, having finally decided on a dinner.

The waitress came by and took our orders. I ordered the soup again, still frozen from the short walk over here. We handed our menus back to the waitress as she disappeared behind the counter to enter in our orders.

"It feels so comfortable here. I've been here less than twenty-four hours but I have yet to find anything I don't like. Everyone I've met seems so nice and helpful. I thought places like this were only in the movies," I smiled, taking a sip from my water glass.

"It really is a great little town; I can't imagine ever moving away from here. What brings you to Maple Falls?" she asked, picking up her water and taking a sip, holding the straw gently between two fingers, her long manicured nails standing out.

I looked down at the counter, still unsure of how to answer that question. I ran away from home? I'm starting my life completely over? Just passing through town on my way to who knows where? Why did it seem like every conversation started with that same question? Why are you here and where are you from? This place feels safe to me; it feels like I could really make a life here for myself. I was afraid that if I hopped back in my car and drove out of town, I would never find another place like this, no matter how far I drove. I'm afraid to commit, but even more afraid not to. My grandmother taught me that honesty was always the best policy.

"Up until yesterday, I was living in a city about eight hours north of here. I decided I wasn't happy with the life I was living so I packed up my car and left, landing here to sleep for the night." There, I said it. Plain and simple, and to the point. No point in beating around the bush, making up excuses because I was ashamed of what I did.

To be honest, I was proud of what I'd done as it has made me realize how strong I really am.

"Wow; that is brave. It takes a lot of guts to do something like that."

"I quit my job, left an unhealthy relationship, and just started driving. I had no real destination in mind. I just knew where I didn't want to be anymore." I took another sip of my water. "I pulled off the freeway to use the restroom, missed the freeway entrance, and ended up here in town. I'm staying at the hotel next door for now, unsure of my next move." I sat there trying to read the look on her face, wondering if she thought I was as crazy as I must have sounded.

"What does your gut tell you? Surely you must trust it if you left all of that behind." She sat there, waiting for my response, running her fingers through her shiny honey-colored hair.

I thought about it for a moment, really trying to feel what it was saying. Smiling, I finally answered, "To make Maple Falls my new home." I was a little surprised at my answer, having only been here one day. I was never one to go against a gut feeling, and I truly was beginning to feel happy again, even in such a short amount of time.

She looked a little shocked by my answer, too, pausing for a moment. "Well, then, I guess you do have a destination in mind. I don't even know you, but I'm happy for you," she said, holding her water glass up in the air. "Cheers to you and your new beginning."

I held up my glass, tapping it against hers. "To my new beginning," I said, taking a deep, relieving breath.

The waitress returned ten minutes later with our meals and we ate together, carrying on our conversation as she told me more about Maple Falls. She shared the town's traditions, little secret places to visit, where all of the good deals were, and a little about the upcoming fall festival.

As we finished, the waitress came by to collect our dishes, placing the checks between us. Before I could grab my bill, she picked them both up off the counter.

"Let me buy your dinner for you. I'm sure it isn't easy starting over without a job and having to stay in a hotel. I know it isn't much, but I'd like to help you out a little. Save your money for a down payment." She smiled at me as she stood from her stool, wallet in hand.

"Are you sure? It really isn't necessary."

"I'm happy to do it, and I won't take no for an answer."

I followed her up to the register, still in awe of her generosity. As my eyes welled up, I used my sleeve to wipe away the tear I couldn't stop from escaping.

"I hope you find what you're looking for here. I'm not surprised you fell in love with it so quickly, most people do." She placed her hand on my shoulder. "I'm Jackie Fleming by the way. Our conversations got away from me and I don't think I ever introduced myself."

"It was so nice to meet you tonight. I'm Cora Westerling." I reached up with both hands, wiping them across the tops of my cheeks.

"Well, Cora, I work down at the bank on the next block. Please come in to see me if you need anything. I'd be happy to help you out in any way I can." She collected her change from the cashier and tucked it back into her wallet.

"I'll take you up on that at some point, I'm sure. Thank you again, Jackie. Have a great rest of your night."

"You as well," she replied, zipping her coat and disappearing through the door into the cold night.

The wind from the lake was really blowing now, the light mist turning into tiny flakes, spiraling around like mini tornadoes up and down the sidewalks. Before returning to the hotel, I stopped at my car in search of a box that was stuffed in the back seat, containing my robe, slippers, and favorite flannel pajamas. I didn't think I would need them but made sure to keep that box accessible just in case the nights got cold.

I fished around in the back until I found the box. Luckily, between that box and another, I found the toiletry bag I wasn't able to locate earlier. Containing only my toothbrush, toothpaste, a hair brush, and my mascara, I stuffed it into my huge purse, making it one less thing to awkwardly carry through the hotel lobby. I slung the robe and pajamas over my arm, pulled my purse back up onto my shoulder and tucked my slippers into the curve of my other arm.

The misty sleet began falling harder, making the sidewalks slippery and the parking lot a glazed over ice rink. I slid my way to the door quick enough to not get completely soaked, but slow enough to not fall flat on my butt. No one was in the lobby when I walked through so I speed walked down the hallway to my room before anyone saw me carrying all of my loose things.

One perk of living in a hotel was an endless supply of shampoo, conditioner, soap, and fresh towels. I walked into the bathroom, placing my pajamas on the counter top, and turning the bathtub faucet on as hot as it would go. Finding a small bottle of soap in a basket next to the sink, I poured some under the water spout, creating a growing mound of bubbles that smelled of lavender. The mirror gathered a thin layer of fog as the room filled with steam from the hot water. Dipping my toes in first, I gradually slid the rest of the way in, resting my head against the back edge of the tub closing my eyes, breathing the steam in deep.

I couldn't help but picture my life here: sitting on the beach in the summer, reading a book with my toes in the sand, eating ice cream on a sidewalk bench watching the town walk by, walking from store to store in the winter doing my Christmas shopping, buying decorations for my home. I could picture all of it, except one thing: my actual house. As lovely as the hotel was, it was only temporary. I would miss the continental breakfast and ready made coffee every morning, but the cost would soon be too much and I would have to find a house.

As my mind continued to wander, I couldn't help but go back to that building with the tiny cupcake sticker on the door. My dream has always been to open my own bakery. Maybe this was finally my time; the direction I was being pushed in with my attempt at my new life. I paid close attention to the details in the bakery I worked at for over three years, making mental notes each day, visualizing what I liked and what I didn't, what I would do differently if it were my own place.

Growing up it was just me and my mom, working together in the kitchen every night. She would make dinner and would always put me in charge of the dessert. When I was seven years old, my mom bought me a cookbook for Christmas. She didn't have a lot of money for gifts that year so along with the book, she bought me a sack of flour, a container of sugar, and tiny bottles of other baking ingredients I would need to bake with. She wrapped each one individually so that I had more gifts to open. That cookbook was the best gift I ever received from her, even more special than any past Christmas where I had gotten a bunch of toys. It was something I held so close to my heart for all these years. Twenty-six years later, I still use it to bake desserts.

Before leaving my apartment, I triple checked that I grabbed it off the shelf in the kitchen and packed it safely in a box. The corners of some of the pages had stuck together and a thin layer of flour covered the pages of my favorite recipes that I made over and over again. Probably so many times I didn't even need to look at the recipe, but used it more for the memories than the words on the page.

The water temperature began to cool and my fingers were covered in wrinkles. Beginning to shiver, I climbed out, toweling off quickly, the cold air sending goose bumps up my arms. I put on my flannel pajamas and slid my arms into my fleece robe, pulling the tie around my waist tightly. Having forgotten socks in an unknown box in the car, I placed my feet into my slippers, hung my towels up, and walked into the other room.

The room was quiet but cozy, the lamp glowing in the far corner of the room. Outside the window, the moon reflected brightly off the lake. Leaves continued to fall, blowing through the air with the never ending wind. Small piles of white slush began to gather in the corners of the patio just beyond the sliding door. Opening my purse, I pulled out the phone number for the vacant building again. I really had nothing to lose by calling to inquire. I was just calling to find out a little about the building, it's not like I was committing to buy it. I reached for my cell phone and began dialing the number. At this hour, the realtor was likely to not be in the office to answer the call. I would leave a quick voicemail and call it a good step.

Taking a deep breath in, I pushed the green call button, releasing it slowly. It wasn't like the old days where you could call from a landline and quickly hang up when you changed your mind and no one knew who had called. As the line connected, my number would come up on their phone immediately, so there was no backing out.

The phone rang three times. Just as I was reciting the message I was going to leave on the voicemail in my head, it stopped ringing.

"Hello, this is Alice Coleman," the voice answered on the other end.

My heart stopped at the sound of her voice, catching me completely off guard. I had a plan for the message I would leave, but I hadn't been prepared for if she actually answered.

"Hello?" Alice repeated.

"Hi—my name is Cora. I found your phone number on a for sale sign in a vacant building in town. I hope it isn't too late to be calling." I wasn't sure what else to say so I stopped, giving her a chance to reply.

"Is it the one off of Hearthside Lane or the one on Oak Street?" She sounded preoccupied on the other end.

"Oh—it's the one on main street a few blocks into town. I'm not sure exactly what it used to be but it had a cute little cupcake decal on the window of the front door."

"That would be the old bakery building. What would you like to know about it?" I could hear Alice typing on the computer in the background. "Give me just a minute to pull up the listing so I have it all in front of me." The line was quiet for a moment. "Alright, I have it up, shoot."

The fact that it used to be a bakery made me even more excited. I leapt off of the bed, grabbing my new star notebook and pen, opening it up to the first page. "I guess for starters, is the building for sale or is there an option to rent?" I scribbled a circle in the top corner of the page until the ink came out of the pen.

"Right now, the building is for sale. It is, or I should say was, a bakery on the main level and there is an apartment that could be rented out for extra income on the upper level if you wanted to do so," Alice explained.

I stopped writing my notes. "An apartment? That's perfect! I'm new to the area and I'm currently living in a hotel in town. I would love to take a look at the building if you're available in the next couple of days. I know it's kind of last minute, but something this week would be best," I said, clasping my hands together, knowing I only had my room until the end of the week.

Alice paused. "The only open time I have tomorrow is at ten in the morning, otherwise it would have to wait until the weekend.

Would you be able to make that time work for you?"

"Yes, that time is great." I was pacing the room at an alarming speed, my heart racing out of my chest. I gave her all of my information in case something changed and she needed to reach me. "I will see you tomorrow at ten. Thank you so much for fitting me in on such short notice."

"I have you written on my calendar and I will see you in the morning." The line clicked as she hung up the phone.

Yesssss, I whispered to myself, collapsing onto the bed. I couldn't remember a time in my life when I was this excited. My heart was still racing as I lay there, phone still in hand. I grabbed the notebook that was on the bed next to me and jotted down Alice's name, number, and the time of our appointment, and placed it on the desktop. Eager to get to sleep so the morning would arrive quicker, I climbed under the covers and lay there, excited about my potential future life.

Chapter *Four*

I woke the next morning feeling like a child on Christmas day. Jumping out of bed, I ran into the bathroom for the fastest shower I had ever taken, threw on a little makeup, and blow dried my hair just long enough so it wouldn't freeze outside.

Grabbing my purse off the desk, I stuffed my room key into the outside pocket and darted down to the lobby, hoping to catch a quick cup of coffee and a muffin to eat on the way. The breakfast area was quiet, only two tables with people drinking coffee and reading the morning paper. I reached in the case for a blueberry muffin, peeling the wrapper off as I walked out of the room.

"Good morning, Cora," I heard a woman shout. "Out to do more exploring today?"

I turned around to see Nancy waving from behind the desk. "I am actually. I'm really excited about it, but I'm running late. I'll be sure to tell you all about it when I get back later this afternoon." I flashed a smile and pushed through the door, balancing a muffin in one hand, coffee in the other.

The block that the bakery was on was very busy, causing me to circle around the surrounding blocks three times before I could get a parking space on the next street over. Taking one last sip of coffee, I pushed open the car door, locking it behind me as I hurried across the street towards the bakery.

A woman wearing a pinstripe black dress and black knee high leather boots was sitting on the bench under the front window, making notes on a pad while holding the edges of the paper down with her other hand, fighting against the breeze. Her neatly combed brunette hair was getting tangled in the wind.

"Alice?" I asked the woman as I got closer.

Picking up her papers and stuffing her phone into her pocket, she stood up to greet me. "Yes, you must be Cora. It's nice to meet you," she said holding out her hand.

"Sorry, I hope I didn't keep you waiting too long. I wasn't expecting the parking to be so difficult at this time of the day," I explained, shaking her hand back.

"Parking is busy around here from the time these businesses open until the time they close. It is great if you're a business owner, not so great if you're the customer," she laughed, unlocking the lock box that hung from the door handle. "As you can see, this is the main entrance to the bakery on the lower level and I believe there is a separate private entrance in the back for the apartment upstairs I was telling you about."

I glanced upward, noticing the large windows from the apartment overlooking the main street. "It looks great from the outside; I'm hoping it's the same for the inside."

"You had mentioned that you were staying at the hotel in town? Did you sell your home or are you new around here? The apartment may be an added perk for you if you are interested in living above a business. If you opened your own, it would be the shortest commute in history. You'd save a lot on gas money too." Alice had a bubbly personality and seemed very outgoing, perfect for someone in real estate.

"Yes, I'm staying there until the end of the week as of now. I've only been in town a day or two, but I'm looking for a reason to keep me here. I'm hoping I just found it."

Alice pushed open the front door and I followed close behind her, amazed at the sight inside. All of the cases were covered in white sheets to keep them protected from the dust. The sun shone through the front drapes, reflecting off the bright white walls. The tables were still around the bakery, the chairs flipped upside down, resting on the table tops. A clock made of whisks was hanging on the wall near the cash register. The second hand wasn't moving as the batteries must have died. The wall behind the front counter had beautiful built-in shelves with arches above, framed with a custom carved molding.

Three pendulum lights hung above the counter with glass cups surrounding the bulbs in the shape of upside down cupcake cups. I walked to the back to find an immaculate kitchen, equipped with brand new ovens, bake ware, and large mixers placed on flawless stainless steel counters. The storage closet just off the kitchen was fully stocked with unopened bags of flour, sugar, baking powder, and powdered sugar.

"Was this bakery ever open for business? It is so clean in here, like the kitchen has never been used," I asked, walking through the kitchen, running my hands along the edge of the cold steel counters.

"I was placed as a co-agent on this property by another agent in my office recently and I hadn't even gotten a chance to do a walk through before now. From what I understand, they had a big grand opening celebration here, but a few months after opening, the owner got very sick and they had to close. Sadly, she passed away and the place was put up for sale shortly there after."

Alice pulled down four white chairs from the top of one of the tables, placing them on the floor. She placed her briefcase on the floor and sat down in one of them, opening her folder and pulled out a stack of paperwork.

"It looks like it was put on the market several years ago but hasn't had much activity. The family knew the listing agent so they let him handle most of it over the past couple of years. I am new to the area so I haven't met the owner. The other agent had a few big projects come up out of town and asked if I would help him cover this listing while he was gone in case there were any showings. To be honest, you are the first one I have had call me about it since he left six months ago."

I pulled out one of the other chairs, joining her at the table. Alice slid a bunch of papers toward me. What she told me about the building so far was not at all what I expected to hear. I pulled the papers closer, spreading them out across the table to take a look over them.

"Here are the papers with a little more information about the property. As I stated before, the building sale includes the bakery down here and also the apartment above. I'm not sure if it is finished up there or not, we can go take a look there next." She flipped through her papers once more, making sure she didn't miss any.

"So the price listed here is for the entire building?" I asked.

"Yes, that's for everything. It seems a bit low to me for this building given its location, but like I said before, I am not sure how complete the apartment is." She stacked her papers back up, leaving them in a pile on the table. "Shall we head upstairs and see what the apartment is like?"

"Yes, that would be great," I said, standing from the table.

The entrance to the upstairs was in the back of the building, just outside of the kitchen located in a small back foyer. Unlocking the door, it led to a tall dark stairway lit by a single bulb mid way up the stairs. A small window at the top gave some extra light on the top landing.

Alice found another key on the ring for the apartment door. As she slid the key in, I held my breath, hoping to find at least a semi-livable space. She turned the key and slowly pushed the door open. What was on the other side was nothing like I expected.

Alice stepped through the doorway, moving aside to allow me to follow. Coming up the tall and dark stairwell, the sight upstairs was nothing in comparison. Bright rays of sunlight beamed through the windows, shining on the light colored carpeting throughout the apartment. It was full of natural light, the woodwork golden and gleaming. A couch and a coffee table sat near the middle of the living room, positioned parallel to the stack stone fireplace on the far wall.

Next to the living room was a small dining room overlooking Hearthside Lane at the front of the building, the windows I peered up to from the street. A small pass through countertop separated the dining room from the kitchen. The appliances were all there and seemed to be fairly new, hardly used like the ones downstairs.

"This place is beautiful; so much natural light shining in through the windows. After the dark stairwell, I wasn't sure what to expect." I walked over to the mantel, glancing around the main living areas of the apartment. "It's so clean, too, similar to downstairs. Does the couch and coffee table stay with the place?" I walked over and sat, testing out how comfortable the couch was. I sunk in just enough: not too firm, not too soft.

Alice checked the listing sheet she brought up with her. "I would assume they do; it says sold as-is with all its contents." She folded the paper back in half, placing it under her arm. "I think the bedrooms are down the hall."

I walked down the hall, pausing at the first doorway. I turned the handle slowly, pushing the door open to another brightly lit room. Walking inside, my chest got tight as I looked around. The walls were painted a light bubble gum pink with a lemon accent wall. Along the yellow wall, slid into the corner, was a tiny toddler bed covered in a white eyelet comforter. In the other corner rest a lone glider rocking chair, still and somber. Inside the closet hung two tiny pink empty hangers.

"She had a daughter," was all I could get out. I could not hold back my tears and one rolled down my cheek. "Are you sure you got the right story about the owner of this place? Maybe it was rented out to another person. Maybe she wasn't the one who lived up here."

Alice cleared her throat. "Maybe we should check out the rest of the apartment." She walked through the doorway and disappeared down the hall.

Turning around, I followed her out. The next door down was a nice sized bathroom followed by the bedroom door that rest at the end of the hall. I walked to the windows to get a look at the view. One window faced the front of the building, looking out over the main entrance. The window on the opposite side of the apartment looked down the street showing the lake in the distance.

"There is a beautiful view of the lake and the hotel. I could get used to looking at this every day."

"The walk-in closet over here is pretty big," Alice called from across the room.

"Pretty big; it's huge. I think the bathroom in my old apartment was smaller than this," I said, pulling the drawers open. "I've always wanted a nice closet with drawers and shelving in it."

"Well, that is the apartment. Are there any other questions you had about it? If not, we can head back downstairs and look over the rest of the paperwork." Alice turned and started walking back down to the living room before I could answer.

"No, not that I can think of." Taking one last look at the lake, I followed her back downstairs, closing the door behind me.

Sitting back at the table, she opened her files again, pulling out a large stack.

"I will give you a few things to look over while you decide if you're interested in the building. Here is a copy of the property disclosures and also a copy of the listing. It will tell you a little more about the building; room dimensions, price, taxes, what is included with the sale. The disclosures will tell you if there have been any problems with the building, be sure that everything is in working order."

She handed me more information than I could possibly process at that moment, making my head spin a bit. When she was finished stacking what seemed like endless paperwork in front of me, she gathered it back up and neatly placed it all in a company folder and slid it across the table back to me.

"My business card is attached to the front so please feel free to call me with any questions that may come up or if you decide you would like to make an offer. My cell and my office number should be on there. Do you have any questions for me before we go?" She sat waiting for me to answer.

I had so many questions running through my head but was unable to form a full sentence containing any one of them. More of them pertained to the lady who owned the bakery than questions about the actual building. Was it her child's room? Did she rent it to someone else? Was she married? My brain was spinning around in circles and I was trying to make sense of the past thirty minutes of a whirlwind of information since I walked through the door.

"Cora, are you alright?" Alice asked, waving her hand slowly in the air in front of my face, trying to get my attention.

"Sorry," I said, shaking my head back and forth. "I'm fine; thank you for taking time out of your day to show me this building. I will take all of this information with me and look it over. You will definitely be hearing from me in the next couple of days when I've made a decision."

"I'm happy to help, and like I said, please don't hesitate to call me if any questions come up. If you do decide to stay in town, be sure to check out the fall festival this weekend in the park near the lake. There is good food and a lot of craft vendors to buy some handmade items from. A lot of locals have booths so it might be a nice place to check out and do some people watching if nothing else."

Alice stood from the table, walked around the bakery, and turned off the lights, her boots tapping along the wooden floors, and met me back at the front door.

"Thanks, I will be sure to check it out. I'm pretty sure I'll be sticking around for a while, I really like it here." Taking one more look around the room, I pulled open the front door, walking back outside. "I will call you once I've made a decision."

Alice locked the door behind her, placing the keys back into the lock box. Sliding the folder of paperwork under my arm, I walked the two blocks back to my car. I climbed into the front seat, placing the folder on the seat next to me. Sitting there for a few minutes, I just stared at it, wondering what my next move should be, praying for another sign to show me the way. Knowing it was such a huge decision, I didn't want to jump into it too quickly. Not only would I be starting over in a brand new town, I would be buying a building, not just renting, like I had always done in the past. Then, on top of all of that, I would have the pressure of starting up my own business from scratch and having no choice but to make it successful.

Part of it was more exciting than anything I'd ever done before; the other part scared me more than anything I'd ever done before. You can't live your dreams without putting yourself out there to make them come true. I knew what my heart was telling me to do, but for some reason, my brain just wasn't on the same page. It was being cautious for once and I couldn't ignore that part. I was always taught, for as far back as I can remember, to make a pro and con list when I was faced with a tough decision. Tonight I would make that my mission, my first official assignment for my new journal.

I looked up from the folder, and there it was, my next sign.

Chapter
Five

I pulled into the bank parking lot, finding a spot near the front door. I walked inside and went right up to the receptionist's desk. The receptionist was on the phone with a customer; she looked up at me and smiled, holding one finger up in the air.

I glanced around the quiet lobby as one person was being helped by a teller at the small enclosed window and another waited patiently behind them in a roped off area. A pen dangled on a thin chain, hanging off of the small counter near the ropes, deposit slips spread out across the top. An older man in a security guard uniform glanced up from his newspaper briefly, giving me a half smile before returning to his article. Most of the office doors were closed and many of the employees were nowhere in sight. Checking my watch, I assumed most of them had gone out to lunch. I was hoping Jackie was still here, but if not, I knew where she liked to eat and would be able to find her easily. The receptionist hung up with the caller and immediately placed another call on hold.

"Did you have an appointment?" she asked, pulling up her calendar.

I walked back over to her desk. "No, I was just wondering if Jackie was available."

"I know she's in today, let me call back to her office and see if she's at her desk. Please have a seat and I will let you know if I'm able to reach her."

I walked over to the waiting area and sat down while she answered the call that had been holding. The chairs were leather covered, letting out a slow puff of air as I sat, sinking slightly. Crossing one leg over the other, I let out a loud sigh that almost seemed to echo throughout the large lobby. It felt as though I was in the middle of a whirlwind, not quite sure which direction to go. A few moments later, Jackie appeared in front of me.

"Cora? It is so nice to see you again," she said, holding out her hand. "Come on back to my office and let me know what I can help you with today."

I followed her to the back corner office looking out to the main street. Jackie motioned towards the chairs on the other side of her desk. Pulling one out, I sat slowly.

"So, what brings you in today?" Jackie pulled a lined yellow notepad out from her top drawer and grabbed the pen sitting next to her keyboard, clicking it.

"Thank you so much for meeting with me. I would have made an appointment, but I just had a few quick questions and was hoping to not take up too much of your time. I'm not even sure if you can help me, but thought you could possibly point me in the direction of someone who can."

I pulled the folder out that was tucked under my arm and placed it on the desk. Pulling the paperwork out that Alice had given me; I slid them across the desk to her to look at.

"I was wondering what it would take for me to be able to purchase this building, or if I would even qualify, for that matter. Maybe we could start there?" I sat up very straight in my chair, gently biting on the corner of my fingernail.

"I see; and have you taken a look at the property yet?"

I could feel my face light up. "Yes, I just came from there and the realtor took me through the entire building. It was so beautiful and I just know this is what I'm supposed to do. It even has an apartment on the upper floor of the building so it would also solve my problem of where to live. I've dreamed of owning my own bakery since I was a little girl and there is an amazing one for sale right down the street; it seems too good to be true."

Jackie's face was serious, with a slightly wrinkled brow, as she looked through the paperwork. She scribbled a few notes down onto her paper and grabbed her mouse, entering those same numbers into her computer.

"To start with, I'll have to run a credit check on you and see what type of loan you qualify for and for what amount. I had one of my afternoon appointments cancel so I can probably run some numbers for you later today." She pulled open the bottom drawer of her desk, pulling out a file. "I will need you to fill out a few papers to get me started. Once I have all of the numbers and it looks good to go ahead with the loan, I will have you come back in and fill out the loan paperwork."

She handed me a pen and I got to work. Ten minutes later Jackie had everything she needed from me and I was once again nervous and excited. I was trying not to get too excited though as I currently had no job and no residence. I'm no banker, but I can't imagine that would look very appealing on the loan application.

"Thank you again, Jackie. I look forward to hearing from you soon." I shook her hand once more, showing myself out.

Grabbing some lunch to go from the restaurant, I headed back to my hotel room to process everything that had happened in the last few hours and begin writing out my pro and con list. I pulled out the chair at the corner desk in my room, placing my lunch on one side of me and my new journal and pen on the other. Flipping to the front page, I wrote *Pros* on the top of one side, and *Cons* on the other, drawing a line down the middle. I set the pen back down to think for a moment before writing anything down.

The first thought that flashed into my mind was the little girl's room in the upstairs apartment. A million questions were fluttering around and it was driving me crazy not knowing any of the answers. I wasn't sure if it was appropriate to ask anyone around town having not been here that long and I didn't want to appear nosy.

Pushing it out of my thoughts as best as I could, I grabbed my pen and began on the pro side. First, and probably the most important pro, was that it would be fulfilling my lifelong dream of owning my own bakery. The next few were pretty easy, too: settling in a friendly town, an apartment was included so I wouldn't also have to buy a house, they left behind a few pieces of furniture so that would save me some money, living where I work would mean no commute and less gas money. I was starting to get on a roll as the list continued. When I couldn't think of any more pros, I flipped over to the con page. Staring at the blank page, I slumped back into my chair.

Most of my life I've been a very positive person, never wanting to see things in a negative light, but a decision this big really needed to be looked at from all angles. I tapped my pen against the page. The first thing I wrote down was the large investment and the huge commitment, two things I have never really been big on thus far. I have never owned a home and have always been satisfied renting. That way, there was no real commitment and I could change my mind at a moment's notice. The most expensive thing I have ever purchased was my car and even that wasn't a lot of money, because I bought it when it was a few years old.

I felt my chest begin to tighten slightly as I continued on with the con list and it was getting longer than I thought it would be. Not wanting to get too discouraged, I turned back to the pro page and began to read them over again and there it was, clear as day at the top of the page staring me right in the face: *fulfilling a lifelong dream.* What could possibly go on the con list that would make me not want to do this? Most people in their lives would never get to see their real dreams come true, and here I was doubting myself. For once in my life I was in complete control and all I had to do was take a leap of faith and believe that everything was going to work out the way it was supposed to. If my loan was denied, then that would be my sign that this wasn't for me. But if I didn't at least try, I would always wonder what if, and even worse, live with the regret of never having given myself a chance to succeed.

Seeing all I needed to see on the pro list, I closed my journal, placed my pen on the top, and slid it to the back corner of the desk. I grabbed my to-go box containing my Cobb salad and climbed into bed, turning on the TV. Surfing through the channels, I settled on a sappy romantic movie that had already started. I pushed the lettuce around in the box with my fork, eating all of the hardboiled egg slices and avocados first.

As I finished picking apart my salad, I closed the flap on the box and tucked it into the garbage bin near the side of the dresser. I lay back on the bed, listening to the wind howling off the lake as the leaves rustled across the patio. The sun was quickly making its decent, resting just above the tree lined horizon across the lake. The days were getting shorter and shorter and it would be dark out soon.

Not wanting to go stir crazy waiting for the phone to potentially ring, I got up, got my shoes on, and headed out for a walk. The air was brisk and the temperature continued to drop as the sun sunk lower in the sky. I stopped by my car first, hoping to find my jacket that I had stupidly buried in a box. Popping open the trunk, I found it in the third box, only after getting a glimpse of the sleeve poking out of the top flaps. I slid on my coat, zipping it to the top and stuffing my hands directly into the pockets. Inside them I was pleasantly surprised to find an old pair of mittens I must have left in there from the year before. Grabbing my cable knit beanie out of the same box, I pulled it down over my already frozen ears.

With the sun nearly set and the cold air blowing against my face, I made a quick stop at the restaurant to grab a coffee to keep me awake. The early dark skies were tricking my brain into thinking it was later than it really was.

The restaurant was slow when I walked in. The lunch rush was over and the dinner rush had yet to begin. The singles bar was completely empty; only a few booths were filled. The hostess came to the front right away to take my order, filling a large to-go cup to the top with coffee. I walked over to the bar area, pouring one creamer and two sugars inside, stirring it with a flimsy straw I pulled from a dispenser. I slid my thumbs around the edge of the lid ensuring it was on securely, having learned my lesson the hard way more than once. Waving goodbye to the staff I already knew by first name, I pushed open the front door and began my walk further into town.

The streets were lined with cars from end to end and the street lights were beginning to flicker on as the sky darkened. Leaves rustled in the breeze with the passing wind. I wrapped both of my hands around my coffee as I walked, trying to keep them warm even through my mittens. The single lane traffic began to back up at the red light. Several pedestrians rushed through the crosswalks before the light changed, stopping on the other side to talk to a familiar face. Many of the businesses were getting ready to close for the night, and

I watched as they straightened up their offices through the large front windows and turned out the lights. The bookstore I drove passed earlier was across the street. Sneaking out between two parked cars, I checked both ways and ran across the street, trying not to spill my coffee.

The warm air almost burned against my cold face as I pulled open the front door. The smell of used books brought me back to my childhood. I was greeted by a young woman working behind the counter, pricing a box of books and loading them onto a cart to be shelved.

"Welcome to The Book Mark. Is there a certain author I can help you find?" she asked, tucking a strawberry blonde curl behind her ear.

"Not really, I just happened to drive by earlier today on my way to an appointment and wanted to come back and check it out." I slipped my mittens off, placing them back into my pockets, walking over to the wall of colorful book spines to browse.

"Is there a certain author you prefer to read? Most of the sections are pretty clearly marked and should be in alphabetical order, but if you can't find something you are looking for, please just ask." She continued placing stickers on the upper right hand corner of the covers, lining them up alphabetically on the cart.

"I'm open to reading anything really. A good mystery, a sappy romance, whatever happens to catch my eye. I know they say not to judge a book by its cover, but I am totally guilty of doing it." I placed my finger on the top of the spine, pulling a book out from the shelf. The picture was a lake with a small canoe floating in the middle. I flipped it over to read the back.

"Well, my name is Katie; let me know if you have any questions." She finished filling the top shelf of the cart and began placing them on the bottom, moving to the floor to work.

"Thank you," I replied. I made my way down the side wall, finding a clearance area in the back of the store. Used books were already a steal, but clearance used books were almost too tempting to look at. I did have to remind my self that I was still living out of my car so I didn't have a ton of extra room to buy a lot of things just yet.

After spinning all three of the round racks and another rounded table, I decided to skip the other side wall, having already picked up four books. Not having had a ton of time to read before, it was something I was definitely looking forward to now that I was unemployed and homeless. I walked back to the counter to find Katie, following the clicking sound of the price gun with each dispensed label.

"Oh good, you found a few you liked," Katie said, setting her marking gun down onto the counter. "I just finished reading this one; I think you'll like it. I really enjoyed it."

"I hope so, have you read any of these other ones?" I glanced up at her, a name tag that read K. Hoffman pinned to the upper corner of her shirt.

Katie looked through the other titles, stacking them up as she rang them up on the register. "No, I've only read the one, but one of my friends read this one and said it was really good," she replied, holding one up. "She doesn't tend to read much, so for her to actually finish it, it must have been good."

We both started laughing at the same time. She picked up the four books and placed them into a small brown paper bag. I placed my money onto the counter and held out my hand for the change. Katie folded over the top of the bag and slid it across the counter to me. I folded the flap over another time, making it smaller and placed it into my purse.

"It was nice meeting you, Katie. I'm Cora. I hope you have a great rest of your night."

"Thank you, enjoy your new books. If you get a chance, come back in and let me know if you liked the one that I read. I would love to hear your point of view on it. I'm here every day." Katie sat back down on the floor and continued marking the remaining books.

"I'll do that." I took one last sip of my coffee and tossed the empty cup into the metal trash can outside of the bookstore, the same one that was placed outside of the bakery. My mind flashed to Brad, back to the night I arrived in town. My cell phone began to ring, pulling me out of my thoughts. It had played through almost the entire song before I managed to find it in the very bottom of my purse. It was a local number calling, one I didn't recognize.

"Hello?" I answered, hoping I could catch it before it went to voicemail.

"Hi Cora, it's Jackie. I ran some numbers for the purchase of the bakery. Is there any way you can come down to the bank so we can go over them? I'll be here for another hour or so if you can make it today."

I pulled my jacket sleeve up, checking the time on my watch. "Yes; definitely. I am out on a walk in town now, but I could be there in about ten minutes if that is alright? I'm only a few blocks away."

"That works for me, I'll see you then." Jackie hung up the phone.

The butterflies were really fluttering around in my stomach now. Was this like a doctor's appointment where they couldn't give you the bad news over the phone and made you come in to hear it in person? I thought about walking back to get my car, but figured it would be quicker to continue walking after looking at the backed up traffic. It was only three blocks down and it would take a lot longer to go back in the other direction.

As I approached the bank, I paused to take a deep breath before pulling open the door. My life was about to go one of two ways. Either I would get approved and move forward on the purchase, or I would not qualify and would have to start over again. One would keep me in this town permanently, and the other would probably force me to move on with my journey, driving once again to find the right place for me. I grasped the handle and pulled hard against the wind, finding Jackie waiting inside the lobby for me.

Here goes nothing, I thought, making my way towards her.

An hour later and with what seemed like a half of a ream of paper, I walked out of the bank with a smile fixed to my face. My cheeks were seriously beginning to hurt from smiling so long. Jackie had run all of the numbers and I had been approved for the business loan, qualifying for a larger amount than the price of the bakery. Now the big question; do I make an offer on it?

Alice suggested that there had been little to no interest in the building lately so my hope was to write an offer for less than the asking price if possible. Luckily, if they wouldn't want to budge on the price, the building needed no work and there was even a fair amount of supplies in the closet to get me started. The investment would be large as a whole, but the start up costs would hardly amount to anything. A few cleaning supplies and that would be about it.

The sun had completely set by the time I left the bank, a faint glow on the very bottom of the horizon remaining. The wind was still strong, sending my hair sailing back behind me as I walked into it. Walking against the wind was going to be a much colder walk back to the hotel than I anticipated.

Since I had to pass it on my way, I decided to stop by the restaurant for a quick dinner, hoping to beat the dinner crowd. Not too many people were out and about, yet; most were still leaving their offices, heading for home.

Home. I was so close to having one of those, too.

I reached into my purse and pulled out my phone. Sliding my mitten off, I dialed Alice's number, hoping to catch her at the office. The ringing paused shortly and then continued again, rolling from her desk over to her cell phone.

"Hello, this is Alice," I heard on the other end of the line.

"Hi Alice, it's Cora. Do you have a quick minute to talk?" I asked, quickly crossing the street.

"Sure, I'm in my car just leaving a showing I had with a client. Have you made a decision about the bakery?" Alice's phone was cutting in and out making it hard to catch all that she was saying.

I squeezed my way through a crowd that was gathered on the sidewalk. "Yes, I just left the bank and I've been pre-approved for a loan to purchase the building. I was wondering if you have time to meet up soon to go over the paperwork again and possibly write up an offer." Simply saying those words out loud made me even more excited about it.

"I'm free the rest of the evening, my other client cancelled. Would tonight work for you?"

"I'm headed to the restaurant near the hotel now to grab a quick dinner, would you want to meet me there? I could go in and get us a table and we can go over everything." I could see the brightly lit sign for the restaurant on the next block. Most of the wind was being blocked by the buildings now so I slowed my pace a little.

"I'll tell you what; why don't I swing by the office on the way and grab a buyer's packet and meet you there in about fifteen minutes."

"Perfect. I'm about a block away now so I'll get us a booth and see you shortly." I hung up the phone, dropping it back into my purse and slid my mitten back onto my frozen hand.

Chapter
Six

When I walked through the door, there were still only a few tables full of people. The wait staff was bobbing in and out of the kitchen while the hostess sat patiently at her front podium.

"Good evening, Cora. One for dinner tonight?" she asked, grabbing a menu from the shelf next to her.

"Actually, I'm meeting someone here in a few minutes. Is there a booth available?"

"Of course, would you like to be seated now or wait here for your guest?"

"If I could get seated now that would be wonderful. Then I can order some hot tea and warm up a bit from the walk over here. It sure is getting cold in the evenings," I said.

Grabbing a second menu, the hostess nodded as she led me towards the middle of the restaurant, passing by the singles bar.

"Is this booth alright for you?" she asked, gesturing me into the seat.

"This is perfect. I've never sat anywhere but at the counter so it will be nice to have a different view of the place." I placed my purse on the seat and slid into the booth, choosing the seat that faced the front door.

"Your waitress will be with you shortly," she said, placing the menus on the table, and returned to her position near the front entrance.

A few minutes later the waitress came by, taking my drink order. As my hot tea arrived, I picked through a small container of flavored tea bags, choosing a chamomile blend. Placing one hand on the handle, and the other on the lid, I poured the steaming hot water into my mug, the hot steam rising up warm against my face. I opened a packet of honey and poured a few drips in, leaving the rest for another glass. I picked up the lemon wedge next and squeezed it into the water, returning it to the small plate that rest under my mug. Grabbing my tea bag, I began dipping it in and out of the water, turning it a light brown color.

Resting the string on the outside of the mug, I grabbed the glass with both hands, wrapping them around it to warm them. The honey coated my throat nicely as I took a cautious sip, blowing on it until it met my lips.

The cold wind over that last few days had dried out my lips and the hot tea made me notice it more. Reaching for my giant purse, I began riffling once again into the bottom, using both hands to break apart the piles of stuff that had taken up residency inside. As I continued to dig, I saw a shadow cover the table out of the corner of my eye.

"Hi, Alice. I'm just trying to find my chap stick in this bottomless purse of mine," I said, not looking up. "I really need to invest in a smaller one, I think." When Alice didn't sit down, I paused, looking up.

"Oh, I'm sorry! I thought you were somebody else. How are you tonight, Officer Harper?" I was surprised to see him standing there, a little caught off guard.

"I didn't mean to startle you. And please, call me Brad." He was dressed in full uniform, tilting his ear to his radio that rest on his shoulder, listening to the dispatcher on the other end.

"Well, Brad, is there something I can help you with?" I wasn't sure what to say to him. I still had one hand resting in my purse, having forgotten what I was even looking for in the first place.

He smiled. "No, I just noticed you sitting here alone and thought I would stop back here and say hello. I was wondering if you were still in town or not. Have you decided what you are going to do yet?"

I pulled my hand out of my purse and took another sip of my tea before answering. "As a matter of fact, I have. I'm meeting a realtor here in a few minutes to write up an offer on a cute place I found."

Brad leaned his ear back down to his radio.

"158," the dispatcher called out, pausing for a response.

"158," he repeated back to her. He held up his finger, backing up slightly from the table. The dispatcher relayed a call to him, but I wasn't able to hear much from where I was sitting. "I'm really sorry, but I have to run. Good luck with your offer. If it all goes through and you stay, maybe we can grab a coffee together soon."

"I'd like that," I said, and he smiled, walking to the front and out the door. I watched him walk to his squad car parked outside the windows, turn on his lights, and speed away.

Several groups of people walked in together, all waiting in line at the front to be seated. Peeking around the booth, I spotted Alice near the back and motioned her over, briefcase in hand.

"I'm sorry it took me so long to get here. I was trying to print the paperwork and the copier kept jamming. I rarely use the thing and I'm convinced it hates me. Luckily I found a buyer's packet on another agent's desk so I borrowed it and will just replace it later. Hopefully they don't need it tonight," she grinned, sliding into the booth across from me.

"That's okay, I've just been trying to warm up with a cup of hot tea; I think it may finally be taking effect," I said, still griping both hands around the porcelain mug.

"If you want to get started right away, we can go over all of the information, get some numbers down, and see if we can tie up all the loose ends and get this offer on the table." Alice reached into her briefcase and proceeded to pull out several folders thick with paperwork inside.

Two salads, a cup of soup, and two pieces of pie later, we both had full stomachs and an offer written.

"How long will it take until we hear something back do you think?"

Alice placed all of the papers back into their correct folders, sliding them safely back into her briefcase. "I'll talk with the other agent in the morning and see how he would like me to present the offer to the seller. If the seller is available to meet tomorrow, we could hear back as soon as tomorrow night depending on whether they decide to accept our terms or counter."

I could feel my eyes widen with excitement, followed fairly quickly with familiar butterflies in my stomach. "Wow, that's really fast."

Alice stopped organizing her things and turned to face me, looking me right in the eyes. "I know this is a lot of change in a very short amount of time. Are you sure you're ready for all of this?" She sat silent, waiting for me to give her my answer.

"It is a ton of change, but change is good right? It was my decision to leave everything I had and start over from scratch. I have to stick by my decision and know that it was the right one for me. I know that if I didn't move forward and went back to where I was again, I would be living a complete lie, not truly living my own life the way I wanted to live it." I scraped my fork along my plate, getting each leftover crumb from the piece of pie I devoured. "It's time to stand up for myself and do what I have always wanted to do—and this is it."

Alice stared at me; really trying to read me, see if I was telling her the truth. She smiled. "It takes a brave person to do what you did. You should be very proud of yourself."

I looked back at her, needing the words of encouragement she had just given me. I was so thankful for meeting Alice and having that support from a nearly complete stranger, in a town that was truly beginning to feel like home.

"Thank you, I think I will feel better when I know if this deal goes through or not. I'm just a little nervous putting all of my eggs into the bakery's basket. Say a prayer for me tonight, because if this doesn't work out, I don't really have a plan B."

Alice reached across the table, touching my arm. "I will do everything I can to make this happen for you. We've written a really good offer; even if they counter, we still have some wiggle room. We'll both say a little prayer and you go home and get a good night's sleep. I will call you tomorrow as soon as I hear something."

She zipped up her briefcase and stood from the table, sliding her arms into her jacket. Grabbing her scarf off of the seat, she wrapped it twice around her neck, tucking the ends into the top opening of her jacket.

"You're right; everything will work out the way it is supposed to. If this is where I'm supposed to start my new life, then everything will work out." Taking one last sip of my now lukewarm tea, I slid out of the booth.

"Hang in there; everything will turn out just fine. Did you say you walked here? Can I offer you a ride back to the hotel?"

"I have a good feeling about it. I did walk here, but I'm fine, it's just down the block."

As we walked out of the restaurant, we said goodbye again. I lifted my hood up to cover my ears from the whistling wind. I thought for a moment I saw a few tiny flecks of white blow past me. It seemed a little too early in the year for snow, but it definitely wasn't far off.

When I walked into the lobby of the hotel, I found both Nancy and Phil standing behind the counter and a warm fire crackling in the corner. Nancy waved me over as she pulled on her jacket.

"Are you switching shifts for the night?" I asked.

"Yes, he's taking over for the night and I'm headed out to craft night with the ladies. Would you care to join me?"

"Carla actually invited me a few days ago when I stopped by her shop. I would love to join you; can I have five minutes to run to my room and freshen up?" Nancy agreed to meet me in the lobby in a few minutes, giving her time to run back to her room and grab the project she had forgotten.

When I returned to the lobby, I found Nancy rearranging the chairs again, making sure they were perfectly lined up with the fireplace.

"I'm all set to go, just one problem; I've never crafted before, so I have nothing to work on."

"That's no problem at all. You can check out the different projects the other ladies are working on and see if something piques your interest. Between us all, there are many talents and we can probably teach you anything you want to learn."

"What about life? I could really use some teaching in that area." We both let out a loud laugh. "I told Carla I would bring a dessert if I came by, can we stop by a grocery store on the way to pick something up?"

"I've got you covered; I baked cookies this afternoon while Phil covered the desk."

Nancy waved goodbye to Phil and pushed the front door open. Her car was parked in the first spot near the door in an assigned spot. I climbed into the front seat, pulling the collar of my coat up closer to my frozen chin. She started the car, turned the heat on high, and pulled out onto the street, making our way to Sweet Peas.

The day crowds had gone home and the nightlife was just getting started. Grabbing the last parking spot in front of the shop, she grabbed her bags from the backseat and we walked up to the front door.

Inside still smelled of the pumpkin spice candle; the store front lights were off, having closed for business to the public. Three long tables were set up near the back of the store, surrounded by folding chairs. Two tables to craft on and one for holding all of the wonderful looking treats everyone brought to share with the group.

Four ladies had gathered by the tables, laying out their latest projects. The overhead bell rang behind them as another person walked in. I recognized her right away, so nice to see a familiar face.

"Cora, you made it," Katie said as she walked closer.

"Yes, Nancy reminded me so I decided to ride with her."

"I'm so glad. How is everything going? Have you started any of the books you bought, yet?" she asked, setting a bowl of spinach dip and some Hawaiian bread on the snack table.

"I did; I started the one that you recommended last night. I couldn't put it down, but finally got too tired and was forced to stop," I laughed.

Two more ladies came in after Katie and we all picked a spot around both of the tables. There were scrapbooks being made, crocheting, knitting, painting, you name it. There were more craft skills in this room than I could ever learn in my lifetime. Nancy grabbed the last spot on an end so I followed Katie around to the other side. She reached into her bag, pulling out a ball of yarn and a shiny metal hook.

"What are you making? Is that knitting or crocheting? I've never been able to tell the difference." I could feel my cheeks begin to flush with embarrassment as all of the ladies paused what they were doing to look up at me, the room silent.

Katie burst out laughing and the other ladies followed. "Knitting is usually done with two pointy needles, crochet is done with one hook," she explained, placing her items on the table and hanging the bag across the back of her chair.

"So, then you're crocheting something," I said, trying to sound knowledgeable.

"Yes, very good. Have you ever crocheted before? I could teach you if you'd like. I didn't really have a specific project in mind to work on tonight so you can practice with my yarn if you want." She pulled out her chair and sat down.

"I suppose I could give it a try, I can't get any worse than I am right now."

Once the women had all arrived, we went around the table introducing ourselves and telling everyone what our current project was that we were working on. When it was my turn, I laid it all out there: a current nomad, residing in a hotel with no crafting skills. If nothing else, I got a few laughs and met some nice people. Nancy had also brought yarn and began making a scarf.

I learned a little bit about everyone and I was glad that I came. When it was Katie's turn, she dove on the sword.

"I'm Katie, I work down the street a The Book Mark, I am currently planning my wedding, and I will be teaching Cora her first craft." She looked over at me to confirm. With a smile, I nodded.

"I didn't know you were getting married; how exciting! Are you getting married here in town?" I set the yarn down, now only able to concentrate on the wedding details.

"I am actually; we're having the ceremony down at the lake and the reception in the hotel banquet room." She smiled across the table at Nancy.

"It's kind of a town tradition," Nancy added. Several of the women nodded in agreement.

"I had no idea; that sounds so wonderful. Is that what all of the initials on the walkway are from? I saw a bunch carved into the railing when I was there the other day and there were so many."

"Some of them are from the couples who were married there, some are from visitors to the town, young couples in love. The first spring after we purchased the hotel, Phil built that walkway and we were the first ones to carve our initials into it. We had no idea it would turn into something so big."

I turned back to Katie. "So, when is the big day?"

"Its next month so I hope the weather holds out that long. I could have sworn that I saw a few snowflakes on my way over here. I don't really want to get married in a blizzard."

"I thought I saw some, too," I said.

As the night continued, I walked around to each of the ladies, checking out their projects and getting to know them a little better. There wasn't much to know about me, other than the fact that I was living in the hotel and was single. I wasn't sure if everything would go through with my offer on the bakery so I decided it would be best to keep that information to myself for the time being. I just told everyone that I would continue to stay at the hotel until I found a place of my own, which wasn't a lie. I was just choosing not to elaborate on my situation just yet.

As great of a teacher as Katie was, crocheting was not coming naturally to me so I stopped trying and mingled the rest of the night instead. My attention was drawn to a lady hand stitching a quilt down at the other end of the table. I walked over to her to get a closer look.

"What are you working on?" I asked, pulling up an empty seat next to her.

"I'm finishing up a quilt I'm tucking away for when one of my daughters get married," Linda said, pushing the needle up and down through the layers of lavender floral fabric.

"That is exciting, when are they getting married?" I asked.

"After they get engaged," she laughed, shooting a glare down the row to one of her daughters.

"Ha, ha, mom, very funny." Mary, her middle daughter, was sitting on the other side of the room. "I'm sure Alex will propose soon, he's just busy with some out of town business right now. You do have another unwed daughter, you know. Maybe you can bother Ali for a while."

Linda smiled back at her daughter. "I know, but your older sister is already married so you should be next." She continued to stitch along the edges where the different colors of fabric met, not looking up for a reaction.

Two hours and a few too many snacks later, the ladies began wrapping up their projects for the night. Linda had finished half of the quilt she was working on, and Nancy was cutting the end of the yarn, finishing the black scarf she started when we got here. Weaving in the ends of the yarn, she got up from her chair and walked over to me as I stood at the snack table taking yet another cookie.

"I happened to notice the last few nights you have gone out in this cold without a scarf on. So, I found some extra yarn I had sitting around and made this one for you," she said, holding it out towards me.

"You made this for me?" I asked, rubbing my hand along the soft wool. "Nobody has ever made me anything like this before. I can't believe you just whipped this up like nothing in the past two hours." I flipped it over the back of my neck, letting the ends dangle on either side of my body. Stepping towards her, I embraced her.

"We can't have you being cold out there, you know. This should help to keep you warm," she said, grabbing my hands, and stepping back to admire her work.

"Thank you so much, it was very thoughtful of you." I turned, facing the rest of the room. "Thank you all so much for inviting me tonight and making me feel so welcome. I really hope to someday call this place my home."

"We would love to have you, Cora," Nancy said, gripping my hand a bit tighter.

"We meet here every Thursday night so feel free to stop by whenever you're free. We'll get you crafting, yet," Carla laughed.

"I haven't given up on teaching you how to crochet," Katie added.

"Be careful what you say, Katie, I may hold you to that." I grabbed my purse from the table and waited for Nancy to finish packing up her things. Walking to the door, I turned to wave to them all again, smiling not only on the outside, but also on the inside.

Chapter
Seven

I woke the next morning to find the towel still wrapped around my now damp hair. Sitting up, I ran my hands over it, trying to calm the craziness the towel had created overnight. Rubbing my eyes, I squint to read the time on the clock. Blinking quickly, I did a double take; nine o'clock. I could not remember the last time I slept this late.

I walked to the bathroom to hang the damp towel to dry, attempting to calm the craziness that was my hair. I wet one side to attempt to get it to stand down while fluffing the other to try to make the two sides match. Slipping on my shoes, I made my way down the hall, following the smell of bacon and waffles coming from the breakfast room.

Walking into the room, I found Nancy there, bright eyed and cheery, wiping down the tables and pushing chairs back in.

"Am I too late for breakfast? I slept longer than I planned to."

"Good morning, Cora, I was wondering if I had missed you this morning. Please feel free to take anything that's left. I was just starting to clean up from the large crowd this morning. You look like you got a good night's sleep." Nancy smiled, walking over to the next table.

I wasn't sure what she meant by that comment. Either I looked fresh and rested, or I looked like a complete mess that slept like a rock. After my quick glance in the mirror this morning, I would probably vote for the latter.

"I can certainly run over to the restaurant to grab something; I don't want to mess anything up that you've already cleaned." Looking over at the counter, there were only a few donuts, one muffin, and some dry cereal left.

"I don't have a lot left, but if you would like some cereal and a donut or two, please go ahead."

I walked to the cooler, grabbing a small carton of milk and a bottle of apple juice, tucking them under one arm. Adding a container of cereal, I finished it off with a chocolate covered donut sprinkled with chopped nuts. Balancing it all, I grabbed the closest table to the counter.

"Thank you, this should get me sugared up and going for the day. Paired with a shower and a cup of coffee, I should be good to go. Is there any coffee left?"

Nancy walked over to the tall standing chrome pots. "I believe so; I try to keep the pots fresh throughout the day."

I walked over to the coffee pots, grabbing a Styrofoam cup, and filled it almost to the rim. Adding a packet of sugar and a hazelnut creamer, I stirred it carefully and returned to the table.

"There is no hurry so feel free to take your time and enjoy your breakfast. Plus, it's nice to have a friendly face down here to talk to." Nancy walked to the sink to rinse her rag and continued to walk around wiping the remaining tables.

"Thank you, I would hate to try to balance all of this down the hallway to my room. I doubt that it would all make it down there without me wearing some of it." I opened my milk and poured it into my plastic cereal container.

Nancy chuckled. "So what do you have on your agenda today? Planning to stay another night?"

"If my room is still available, I would love to stay another night. I do have some exciting news; I found a place I fell in love with and wrote up an offer last night with a realtor. I think she is submitting it this morning so I'm waiting to hear from her." I took a bite of cereal.

"That's wonderful, Cora. Did you meet with them before we went to craft night? I'm so excited for you, even though I'll miss seeing your face around here every day."

"Yes, I met her before I came back here last night. I didn't want to say anything at craft night in case it doesn't go through, but I wanted to at least tell you about it." Before I could tell her any more, a little blonde ball of energy came bursting into the room, wrapping her arms around Nancy's leg, Phil following close behind.

"Good morning, Grandma," she said, still griping her leg.

"Hi sweetie, have you been keeping grandpa busy this morning?" Nancy looked over at Phil who was trying to catch his breath after chasing her down here.

"Are there any donuts left?" she asked in a tiny voice.

Phil laughed from the doorway. "I told her that if she ate all of her breakfast and got dressed, we could come down and see if there were any small donuts left in the cabinet. I don't think she needs much sugar."

Nancy grabbed her hand and walked her over to the case where the donuts were, spotting the perfect one. "I think this one has your name on it." She opened the cabinet, placing the donut onto a napkin.

"It does?" she asked, wide eyed.

"It sure does," Nancy told her. "Would you like to meet one of grandma's new friends?"

The little girl nodded her head, following Nancy over to the table where I was sitting. I reached for my napkin, wiping any food that may have been on my face.

"Cora, I would like you to meet my granddaughter."

"Lily, right?"

Nancy gave me a puzzled look. "Have you two met already?"

I smiled at Lily. "It is so nice to see you again. Would you like to join me?" I asked, motioning to the chair across the table from me.

Nancy helped her pull out the chair and placed her donut on the table. Lily picked up the donut, looking at the top, bottom, and around the sides.

"Grandma, I don't see my name on here anywhere. I thought you said this donut had my name on it."

Nancy and I burst into laughter. "It's just an expression sweetheart. It just means that this donut was meant for you." She took one last look around it and took a bite.

"I actually have met Lily before. I ran into her and Brad at the restaurant a couple of days ago. I had no idea they belonged to you, though. She is so adorable." I watched her tiny hands pick the donut back up again for another bite, leaving a ring of white powder around her lips.

"They belong to us alright. We watch Lily overnight sometimes when Brad's working. I think her favorite part about it is going to the swimming pool and the donuts in the morning." Nancy walked over to the cooler and grabbed a small bottle of juice for Lily.

I couldn't take my eyes off of her sweet little face, now completely covered with white powder. Realizing I left my phone back in my room, I checked my watch, wondering if Alice had submitted my offer yet. Taking the last bite of cereal, I picked up my bowl and empty milk carton and walked them over to the trash bin.

"I better get going. I have a few phone calls to make and my realtor is supposed to be calling me." I walked back over to the table where Lily was still sitting, licking powder off of each finger one by one. "It was nice to see you again. I hope I get to see you again really soon." I brushed my hand over the top of her head.

"Her daddy will be here to pick her up in about a half an hour, but she will probably be back later tonight if the babysitter isn't available. I will be sure to let you know if she comes by again." Nancy picked up the powder covered napkin, wiped the rest of the table off, and tossed it into the trash bin on her way back up to the front desk to find Phil.

"I think it will take me more than half an hour to get ready so I will definitely come and look for you later tonight. Maybe we can play a game together if your grandma has one. Would that be okay?" I asked her, crouching down to her height. Lily looked up at Nancy, nodding in approval. She smiled back at me and ran down the hall to catch up to Phil.

"Good luck on your offer. Let us know if you hear anything about it," Nancy said, returning behind the counter.

"I definitely will, see you later," I yelled as I made my way back down to my room.

I opened the door and went directly to my phone to find one missed call, a new voicemail, and two text messages. Alice left a message saying that she was on her way to the office to meet the other agent and submit the offer. The first text read that she had given him the offer to look over. The second text read that he was meeting with his client at ten thirty to go over the offer with him. Typing her back, I let her know that I got her messages and to let me know when she heard something.

After a quick shower to fix my out of control hair, I checked my phone again: nothing. I got dressed, dried my hair to avoid another incident, and paced around the room. Spotting my book on the nightstand, I picked it up, curling up in the oversized chair near the patio door and opened it up to where I left off.

Nearly two hours later, I had gotten completely sucked into my book and lost track of time. My phone was lying on the bed still on vibrate. Picking it up, I see a text I missed from Alice thirty minutes ago. I open the text to read the entire message. *Offer was submitted and accepted! No counters! When can you meet to finalize everything?*

My heart skipped a beat as my knees gave out, forcing me to sit down on the bed. From a skipped heart beat to now a racing heart. Was this really happening? I was about to commit to a new life, in a new town, and a new business venture. My future was a blank journal just begging to be written in.

After my hands stopped shaking, I picked my phone back up to call Alice. She asked me to meet her at the office in twenty minutes to sign all of the paperwork. They were eager to sell and I had already been pre-approved so there was really no reason to wait. I raced around the room unable to stand still, suddenly only able to find one shoe. I grabbed my purse off of the desk and searched frantically for my phone, soon realizing it was already in my hand. Finding my other shoe underneath the chair, I slipped it on, trying to walk towards the door at the same time, almost falling twice as I hopped along.

I walked at a faster pace than usual down the hall to the lobby. I spotted Lily running around the lobby in her swimming suit and an inner tube around her waist.

"Cora," she yelled as she whizzed by me.

"I thought you weren't going to be here still," I asked as she passed by me again.

"I get to go swimming. Do you want to come swimming, too?"

Nancy was checking someone out at the front desk. She peered over in my direction, checking that Lily was still nearby and hadn't gone into the pool area alone. Her tight blonde curls bounced up and down and she skipped around the table, her bright blue eyes matching the color of her bathing suit.

"That sounds like a lot of fun, but I have a meeting I have to go to right now. I think it's the perfect day for an indoor swim though. I love the mermaid on your bathing suit." Lily looked down, also showing me the fish across the back. "Is grandma taking you swimming or is grandpa?"

Nancy finished up with the guest and walked over to Lily and me. "Her daddy had a special work meeting this morning and is going to be late picking her up. I think grandpa could use a little break so I was going to take her swimming for a bit to see if it will burn off some of her energy."

"Well, I'm sure he'll be here just as soon as he's finished." I stood back up, picking my purse up off of the ground. "I also have a meeting to get to. I will be back later to tell you all about it." I zipped my jacket, wrapped my new scarf around my neck, and walked out the front door.

The drive over to the real estate office was a bit of a blur. It still hadn't sunk in yet and seemed so surreal. A week ago I was working at a job I wasn't happy at, living in a place I didn't like, with a man who didn't seem to care about me. That was all about to change. I was making my own choices for my life; no one was making them for me any more. I was about to get the life I had always dreamed of. Nothing could go wrong.

I pulled up to the office and immediately went inside to find Alice. The receptionist at the front desk called her in her office and she came right down to meet me.

"Thank you for coming down on such short notice. The seller is ready to go and is waiting in the closing room with his agent. The agent flew home last night for a week so it couldn't have been any better timing. I think this may go down as the quickest closing in real estate history."

I slipped off my coat, draping it over my arm as I followed Alice's lead towards the closing room. "I'm still in a bit of shock too that everything is happening so quickly. I thought it would be a few days until we heard back and another month at least until any sort of closing."

"I think the seller just wants to move on from it and with his agent in town for only a few days, there is really no reason to wait as long as you are okay with everything. And after this, you can move in as soon as you want and won't have to live out of your car and a hotel anymore." Alice laughed.

"That sounds wonderful, although I will miss the free breakfasts every morning."

"Well, the good news is that you will be living above a bakery; I'm sure you will have plenty of fresh baked goods down there to choose from."

Alice pushed open the wooden door to the closing room, holding it open for me to come inside. I exhaled a deep breath as I entered the room.

"Are you ready?" Alice asked.

"For a new start at life—definitely!"

I walked passed Alice, entering the room and found a seat at the oversized rectangle table. The seller and his realtor were having a conversation near the window, overlooking the main street of town.

"Good morning, gentlemen," Alice said, joining me at the table. "We are all set to go if you are."

"We're all set," he replied, both of them turning around to sit across from us at the table.

When I looked up, my heart stopped. Standing in front of me was the agent and the seller, who also happened to be Brad Harper.

Chapter
Eight

My posture immediately changed at the sight of him, feeling as
though I began to sink down into my chair a little lower. Seeing the
look on his face, I sensed that the feeling was mutual as he looked
very uncomfortable. My mind began to fill with a million different
questions and I could not focus on anything Alice was saying. Did he
used to run the bakery? Was the apartment his old home? Did that
bedroom upstairs used to belong to Lily? What happened to his wife?

I gripped the edge of the table with both of my hands, catching
my breath and attempting to slow my heart rate down while trying
to wrap my head around it. My emotions were on a rollercoaster and
I wanted nothing more than to get off of the ride. The closer came
into the room, slamming a huge file of papers onto the table,
snapping me out of where my mind had wandered.

Alice opened her folder, each paper having multiple tags marking
the places we needed to sign on them. I reached for the cup resting
in the middle of the table and grabbed a pen, nervously clicking the
end over and over again. Both Alice and the other agent got up from
the table and walked to the copy machine to make copies for

everyone. Clearly they were both very comfortable in the closing department, watching them make piles of papers up and down the countertops like it was no big deal. I, on the other hand, could not have been more uncomfortable. I wasn't sure if I should talk to Brad or not. He was making a pretty obvious effort to not make eye contact with me from across the table. The last time I saw him he was so friendly and outgoing and now he was completely closed off.

Part of me wanted to start rattling off questions to him, but the other part of me was still trying to sort them out in my brain and couldn't manage to get one out if I tried. The copy machine stopped running as the room filled with the scent of hot paper as both agents returned, joining us at the table.

"I'm Alex and this is my client, Bradley Harper. It's nice to meet you," his agent said.

I looked over at Alice, hoping for her to reply for the both of us. She reached her hand across the table. "It's nice to finally meet you, Bradley, I'm Alice and this is my client, Cora. I have been looking after your listing while Alex has been out of town."

We both gave a half smile and an awkward hand shake. The closer came to the table, more paperwork in hand.

"All of the papers from both parties are here and ready to go. I just need signatures from both of you on the correct lines and you will be all set to go." She spread the papers out on the table, making two piles: one for the buyer, and the other for the seller.

Brad leaned in and grabbed a pen from the cup. His agent watched him sign, making sure he didn't miss any of the lines and slid the papers across the table for me to sign afterward. When he got to the last paper, we both looked up, making eye contact for the first time since we sat down. The butterflies in my stomach were doing back flips now, making it even harder to concentrate. His shoulders drooped and he blinked slowly as he slid the last paper across the table to me, quickly turning his gaze away from me.

Thirty minutes later, the deal was complete. Brad reached into his jacket pocket and pulled out a key ring containing all of the keys to the building. He set them on the table and reluctantly pushed them towards me. Our gaze met again as my hand met his halfway to take the keys. His hand rested on the keys, while mine rested on the sparkling cupcake keychain that was attached to them. He didn't want to let go and I felt bad taking them.

The agents both stood from the table as he released the keys to me. They shook hands with each other and then with both of us. Alice had another appointment to get to and excused herself from the room. Alex walked over to the closer, asking her questions about another client they were closing with later in the day.

I grabbed my jacket off the back of my chair and slid my arms in, placing the keys into my pocket, running my thumb along the cupcake keychain before dropping them in. Brad made his way around the table towards me. I cleared my throat three times before he got there.

"I certainly wasn't expecting to see you here this morning." I wasn't sure what else to say, still in shock he was here.

Brad let out a deep breath, half smiling. "I would have to say the same. When you said you were staying in town and writing up an offer on a place, I never put two and two together that you were buying our place, I mean, my place." His look was somber, a very hard expression to read.

The nervous feeling returned to my stomach. "I was going to tell you about the place I found, but you got called away and I never got the chance. I would have told you about it sooner, but I had no idea you were the owner." I came off a little bit defensive.

"How would you have known? You aren't from around here and don't know anything about me really." He zipped up his jacket, looking ready to get out of the room as quickly as he could.

I was taken aback by the tone of his response and could feel the walls he had just put up. "I guess you're right, I don't know anything about you or this town, but I hope to change that. That's why I've decided to stay."

He seemed to be having a hard time continuing the conversation and I wasn't in the mood to force it. This was supposed to be an exciting day for me, a fresh new start for myself and he was making me feel guilty about it and I wasn't sure why. I have been dealing with people around me for years who tried to bring me down and I was not going to let him do it, too. I just signed the papers and signed my new future.

Brad walked over to his agent, shook his hand, and left the room without another word. I could feel the cold air coming off of him as he walked past me. Taking a deep breath, I grabbed my purse off of the table and headed to my new home to take a closer look around.

The drive to the bakery was quick as it was only a few blocks away. I turned left on the street just before the building, heading down the back alley to find the assigned parking space Alice told me about. I placed my car into park and walked up to the back door. I hadn't noticed it from the inside the last time I was here so I was unsure of where it would lead on the other side.

After trying four different keys, I finally got the door open, turning on the light switch just inside the door. The room I entered was a tiny foyer with two doorways off of it and a mailbox slot. The door to the right was locked so I tried the other. Not wanting to fumble around with the keys again, I was pleased to find it unlocked. I pushed it open, leading into the back entrance of the kitchen.

The room looked much bigger to me than before, feeling very

intimidating and full of white space. Feeling as though the walls were closing in around me, I picked up my pace towards the front lobby. Everything was still draped in white sheets and no natural light was able to come through the windows. It felt so dark and lonely. My heart began to speed up as I stood there, looking around at this dimly lit room where the silence was almost deafening. I ran to the front door, turned the lock, and pushed it open, almost falling forwards from pushing it so hard.

Taking a deep breath, I pulled in as much air as my lungs could hold. The air was crisp and I could feel its coldness all the way down to my lungs. With each breath I took I could feel the panicked feeling fade, breathing in calm and exhaling the fear. Getting in one last breath of fresh air, I turned back inside, locking the door behind me. Upon returning, the room seemed a bit lighter. I pulled on the edge of the sheet that covered the main counter, revealing a cash register and a beautiful glass display case with three long shelves inside. Picturing my own creations inside of that case, I began to feel the excitement return again.

I walked around the rest of the lobby, pulling off the remaining sheets one by one, transforming the look and feel of the room completely. I draped the sheets over my arm, gathering as many as I could hold and carried them back to the kitchen. After placing them in the laundry bin, I walked into the office. The fluorescent lighting took a moment to adjust to as I flipped the light switch up. The desk was placed near the side wall, a cushy gray chair resting behind it. In one corner was a tall black metal filing cabinet. Pulling open the top drawer, it was still lined with empty green hanging files.

I pulled out the chair and scooted closer to the desk. The chair was comfortable and felt brand new. A thin layer of dust lay across the top of the desk, leaving behind a faint square outline of where a computer monitor used to be. To my right was a small closet with empty hangers dangling from the bar. The round black clock hanging near the doorway had stopped and a few paintings still remained on the walls. Peering down at the floor, I noticed a pink string peeking out from underneath the door.

Standing from my chair, I walked over to the door and pushed it shut, exposing a bubblegum pink apron hanging on a silver hook affixed to the door. I grabbed the edges of it, holding them out. The name "Hope" was embroidered in black on the upper left side near the top. Dropping the sides, I left it hanging there, turned off the light, and walked back out to the lobby.

I feel as though I'm aimlessly wandering around, making new discoveries at every turn. Wanting to make the place my own, I had to know everything there was to know about the building, what was left behind, and what I needed to buy.

The register looked new as well. Pulling open the cabinet doors underneath, I found the cord for it and plugged it in to the outlet on the wall. It lit up right away, making a loud noise at first as the receipt paper loaded on the top. I ran my hands along the hand carved designs that bordered the arched display shelves behind the counter. The place was so tidy other than a faint layer of dust on some of the shelving; no crumbs on the floor or messes to be found. Not wanting to reveal the bakery quite yet, I decided to leave the window coverings on, only uncovering the small side windows that appeared near the top by the ceiling for some natural light to shine through.

Off the kitchen through yet another door, I discovered a washer and dryer for all of the bakery linens. A side cabinet was filled to the top with fresh white linens, towels, and rags. A line of hooks bordered the adjacent wall, containing one white apron per hook.

I pulled my new journal out of my purse and walked the entire main floor once more; making notes along the way of things I needed to buy and other decorating and organizing ideas that came to mind.

At the top of my list—figure out which key worked for each lock.

I finished the main floor fairly quickly, not having much on my "to buy" list, which was a relief. Standing again in the back entrance, I took another stab at the keys, trying to figure out which one unlocked the next door, realizing that it was the door to the apartment upstairs. Only having been here a day or so ago, I was having a hard time remembering things about the place.

As I opened the door to the dark stairwell, I paused to add "paint stairwell white and buy more lighting" to my list. It was about as creepy and uninviting as stairwells came. Knowing that on the other side of this door would be my new home, I tried to remember the good feelings I had about the place when I was here last, pushing all of the questions that filled my head again with each step up I took.

The sun shined bright on the other side of the door, creating a ray of dust-filled light through the living room. I walked over to the windows, peering down at the street below. The shops seemed busy with people popping in and out, walking up and down the sidewalk carrying shopping bags and talking on their cell phones. The temps were still cool, noticing the rising clouds of steam above everyone's heads, their breath trailing behind them as the walked.

I placed my journal on the kitchen counter that separated it from the dining room and walked inside. The refrigerator door was propped open with a large white towel. Pulling out the towel, I pressed the door closed, finding the plug behind it, barely able to fit my arm in the small space to plug it in. The cabinets were fully stocked with black glass dishes: two different sized plates, coffee mugs, and cereal bowls. One less thing to add to the list, knowing I had left all of those items behind.

Grabbing my phone, I programmed the clock on the microwave just as it began to ring.

"Hello?" I answered.

"Hi Cora, it's Alice. I wanted to make sure you got into the building okay and see if you needed anything. I just finished up with my client and have some time before my next appointment if you do." Her phone signal was cutting in and out as she drove.

"Hi Alice, thanks for checking in on me. Everything is going good, just walking around and checking it out a little closer, plugging in all of the appliances. I walked the main floor already and just came upstairs. When I finish up here, I am going to head back to the hotel and gather up my things and finally check out," I replied, pacing up and down the hallway.

"Perfect, I'm glad everything is going well. Please don't hesitate to call if anything comes up with the building. I'll check in with you again in a week or so if that's okay."

I smiled. "That sounds great, thank you so much. I'll talk to you soon." I hung up the phone, placing it on top of my journal on the counter.

Before heading back to the hotel, I carried all of the boxes that were still in the car upstairs, stacking them along the wall in the empty dining room. Opening the flap of the first one, I discovered the new candle I bought from Sweet Peas. I un-wrapped it and placed the glass jar on the stovetop, adding a lighter to my list to buy so I could light it for my first night in my new place.

An hour later I returned to the hotel to find the lobby empty. I made my way down the hall for the last time to pack up the small amount of items I had brought in from my car over the last week. Trying to save a little money, I took all of the travel sized items from the bathroom to get me by for a few days. Placing the last of my clothes and my toiletry bag into my small suitcase, I zipped it up and wheeled it to the door. Taking one last look around the room, I stopped near the patio door, getting one last look of this beautiful view. A few couples were walking down by the beach and two young kids were skipping rocks off the shore.

I grabbed my room key off the top of the dresser and left the room, wheeling my suitcase behind me. While passing the breakfast room, I spotted Nancy inside, brewing a fresh pot of coffee.

"You're back," Nancy said, closing the top lid of the coffee dispenser. "I take it you're ready to check out?" Something was different about her; her tone of voice towards me and her mannerisms had completely changed since I saw her this morning.

"I am; it will be so weird not coming back here every day. I really liked staying here." Nancy turned and walked towards the front desk. I followed behind her, pulling my room key out of my pocket, sliding it across the counter.

"So everything went well with your closing I take it?" she asked without looking up.

The way she said it made me assume she already knew. I sat there trying to read her, but wasn't sure I was reading her right.

"Yes, everything went great actually." I looked around the lobby and noticed Lily wasn't running around anymore, assuming she had already been picked up and she had spoken to Brad. "Brad must have been by to tell you about it already."

Nancy stopped what she was doing on her computer and looked up at me, stone expression on her face. "I'm just surprised you didn't tell me earlier that you were buying the bakery." She turned back to her computer and continued typing.

"I had no idea the bakery belonged to Brad. I just learned that you were Lily's grandparents this morning. It wasn't something I was trying to hide, but we haven't had a lot of time to chat and everything happened so quickly." I could feel myself getting defensive and tried to dial it back a bit.

"I'm sorry, I know you are still new around town and are still trying to figure things out. I know how hard it was for Brad to sell that building and I just wish you had given me a heads up so that I would have been more prepared when he told me about it. He is pretty upset and I hate to see him like this." She printed out my receipt and grabbed it off of the printer. "I think the sale of the building is bringing up feelings he had buried and didn't want to deal with. Now that he can no longer hold onto that material item, he will have to find a way to move passed it."

"I understand, trust me, I was completely caught off guard when I walked into that closing room and saw him standing there. I really don't know much about his situation. I do know that I will miss seeing you every day; I hope you will come by once I have the place up and running. You have been so wonderful to me since I arrived in town and can't thank you enough." I tucked my receipt into the side pocket of my purse.

"I'm sure you will find out more over time if not from him, probably from me. He just needs some time to process it all I think." She filed her paper away and leaned her elbows up onto the counter. "I would love to come by and visit you. Do you have big plans for the place, yet?" I could see her face begin to soften.

"Please, come by any time. I plan to keep it similar to what it is right now, just a few tweaks to make it my own. I have dreamed of having a bakery since I was young and I feel like this is finally my time to give it a try. I hope it won't upset him seeing the bakery reopen. It was never my intention to hurt anybody by all of this."

Nancy slid her hand across the counter, placing it on top of mine. "You go for your dreams. He knew when he placed the building up for sale that it wouldn't stay vacant forever and that someone would open it up again someday. He just needs time to deal with that and he will in his own way."

I smiled. "I appreciate you more than you know. I will let you know when I start baking; I would love for you to be one of my taste testers."

"You let me know when and I will be there. I can even bring a couple of the ladies from craft night along too if you'd like a few more opinions."

I laughed. "That sounds perfect; I will let you know when I get things up and running. I'm hoping to settle into the apartment over the next couple of days and get to baking soon after that. I would love to be open for business before the holidays if I can pull it all together." I pulled up the handle on my suitcase. "Thank you again for giving me a place to stay and for your hospitality. You took me in when I was completely lost and I will forever be thankful."

"You will do well, Cora. I can see your determination in your eyes. If it is alright, I would like to check in on you in a few days."

"That sounds wonderful," I replied. Tilting my luggage, I pulled it behind me and walked out the door.

Chapter
Nine

An hour and a half later, after a stop by the grocery store, I arrived back at my apartment. If I keep making large shopping trips like I did, I would have the strongest legs in town after climbing up and down this stairwell over and over. Making a mental note to pack my bags a lot more full next time to avoid the six trips I had to take tonight, I loaded the last of them on my arms so I could get them all in one last trip up.

My refrigerator felt fairly cold after having plugged it in earlier so I began stocking the shelves and the drawers with all that I bought, stacking the boxed items on the counter to put in the pantry down the hall afterward. After putting everything away, I either had a lot more storage than I thought, or I really didn't buy as much as it seemed.

I walked back to the dining room and stood in front of the stack of boxes along the wall. Knowing I had to start somewhere, I opened the flaps of the first box on the top of the stack nearest to me. Bracing myself for the mess of random items I may find inside, I was relieved to find it full of clothes. I carried it back to my bedroom and placed it along the wall in the closet and went back to try my luck at another. After five boxes in a row of clothes and realizing I may have a shopping problem, I finally got to a box with helpful things inside.

I filled the medicine cabinet and all of the drawers with my bathroom items, finding out I owned four different sized curling irons, not remembering the last time I used any of them. I found my towels and placed them neatly on the towel racks, along with my soap dispenser and toothbrush holder. The color of the walls was cream so it was neutral enough to match the plain blue towels I hung. I wasn't sure of the theme I was going for just yet, but organized seemed to suffice.

Back in my closet, I pulled my clothes out of the boxes, hanging them on hangers and placing them on the rod in order of color and sleeve length. Some people may call it OCD; others would call it a time saver in the morning. If there was a certain shirt I had my mind set on wearing, I knew right away if it was clean without having to rummage around. There was a tall standing dresser along the wall on the other side of the room. After stacking my jeans in a pile as I unpacked them, I carried them over, placing them in the drawers, leaving the top for my underwear, bras, and socks. Continuing on with my OCD, I folded each pair, lining them up in perfect lines from the front to the back of the drawer, also pairing colors and like items together. It was never something I found myself doing before I met Chris, but having lived with him for so long, I must have picked it up. Feeling a bit rebellious, I picked up one pair of socks, unfolded them, and placed them the opposite direction in the drawer, slammed it, and walked away.

I hung my robe on the hook on the back of the bathroom door on my way down the hall and walked back to the dining room, stacking the empty boxes back where they were before. I grabbed my purse and plopped down on the couch, digging through it aimlessly to find the book of matches I tossed in there when I stopped by the gas station earlier. After nearly dumping the box into the bottom of my purse, I refastened the flap. I pulled the lid off of my new candle and scratched the match along the side of the box, creating a large flame at the end of the stick, lighting the wick. The smell was so amazing; I could smell it before the wax had even begun to melt. I had been saving this for the first night in my new home. Never did I think that I would be lighting it so soon.

I wrote down a few more things on my list that I was out of or missing around the apartment. The few pieces of furniture that were left had been covered in sheets so the dust around here was minimal. Noticing a decent layer of dust on the top of the ceiling fan blades, I made sure not to turn them on before cleaning them. Having decorated most of my old apartment, I took two sets of bed sheets, my pillow, and the quilt my grandmother had made me. I made the bed before relaxing for the night, so exhausted that I feared I may not get up again.

The candle scent had now filled the living room and partially down the hallway. The sun was just beginning to set on another day, my first official day as a new resident of Maple Falls. I walked to the window, catching the bright rays of light shining down, reflecting over the lake down the street near the hotel. The view was perfect from up here. The street lights below began to flicker on, people were leaving work, and cars filled the streets.

The wind howled passed the window, leaking through the side cracks, sending a shiver down my spine, and causing the hair on my arms to stand up. Rubbing my hands up and down my arms, I turned to the fireplace, noticing a light switch near the mantle. Praying that it would turn on the fire, I flipped it up and the flames lit with a loud whoosh. Crouching in front of it, I warmed my hands and legs, turning around to warm my backside.

When the shivering finally stopped, I grabbed the blanket on the back of the couch and curled in, tucking my legs underneath. I peered at the coffee table, noticing the top looked a little crooked. Checking under the base to be sure there was nothing raising it up, I placed my hands on the top and pushed down, lowering it with a loud bang. Startling me, I realized that it was one of those tables that lifted up towards where you were sitting.

Placing my hands underneath, I slowly lifted it towards me. As the lid was lifted, I gasped. Inside were a single notebook, a recipe box, and a pale pink photo album stacked to one side. I lowered it back down quickly on instinct, knowing those were not mine and not wanting to go through someone else's things. After a few deep breaths, I pulled the lid back up, reaching for the photo album. If anything was going to tell me who these items belonged to, this would be my first guess.

I opened the cover and immediately knew who this belonged to. The photo was of Brad, a newborn baby, and the most beautiful woman I have ever seen who could only be one person: Brad's wife.

I continued flipping the pages of the book, looking fully through it twice. The album was filled with pictures from holidays, vacations, their wedding, and a ton of Lily as a baby. They looked so happy in every photo, so full of life and what appeared to be the perfect little family. I couldn't help but wonder what had happened to her. She looked so young and fit, not sick by any means. It was something I would have to ask Nancy about later on.

After the second flip through the album, I placed it back into the coffee table, picking up the notebook. Opening up to the first page, I discovered beautiful hand written notes. Some pages were recipes; some were notes about the bakery, business plans, and new ideas of baked items to add to the bakery's menu. It was the bakery's bible and was full of great information. She had such a vision for where she wanted to take her business. Clearly an organized person, she spelled all of her dreams out onto the pages. A wave of sadness fell over me, knowing that she never got the chance to live out all of her dreams. She had plans in there about classes to teach children how to bake, plans for Lily and her to work there together and teach her everything she knew. It broke my heart knowing that Lily would never know of the plans her mother had for her; things they would never get to experience together.

When I reached the end of the notebook, I moved on to the recipe box. The box looked vintage and copper in color. I pulled open the lid, revealing a box full of handwritten recipe cards. Reaching near the middle, I placed my fingers on one, tugging carefully as it was stuck to the card behind it. The one I had chosen was clearly a well used recipe, stained in several places and a thin layer of what appeared to be flour still covered the front.

Across the top of the card read 'Grandma's Ice Box Cookies' written in fancy cursive lettering in black ink. I could tell it was an old one, not seeing this kind of beautiful script these days, very old fashioned and classy. I scraped my fingernail against a crumb stuck to the card, sending it sailing across the room.

I read through the ingredients listed and knew I had most of them in the supply closet I had checked out earlier. I set the card aside on top of the table, deciding this would be the recipe I would start with. Flipping through a few more cards, there were recipes for more cookies, cakes, muffins, and pies. Stumbling across a chocolate fudge brownie recipe and a red velvet cupcake, I placed them up on top of the table as well.

Near the back of the box, there was a handwritten letter folded and tucked inside behind all of the recipe cards. It read:

My dearest Hope,

You are such a special young woman who has inherited my love for baking. Please keep these recipes safe for me and use them one day when you finally open your own bakery. Think of me while you are baking; know that I will always be watching over you. I know you will be very successful in your life and I hope these recipes will help to get you started.

Love, Gram

Hope. That must have been his wife's name. Her apron was the one hanging in the office. That explained the look of the vintage box and the handwritten cards. No one wrote like this anymore, or wrote at all. Everything was typed or in a text; there was something so special and meaningful in a handwritten letter. So much more personal to remember them by, remember how they wrote in their own words. Typed letters or emails lacked that piece of emotion, at least in my eyes.

I refolded the letter and tucked it back inside of the box, closing the lid. Replacing the box inside, I closed the top of the coffee table back down, grabbing the three recipes I pulled out and held them in my hands. As if my head wasn't already filled with questions, these findings seemed to create even more. After seeing photos of her and reading all about her plans for her future, what could have possibly gone wrong? I carried the recipe cards into the kitchen and placed them on the counter to remember to bring them downstairs in the morning. I turned around to the stove and picked up my candle and blew it out for the night.

Walking down the hallway to the bedroom, I paused at the door to the child's room, placing my hand on the handle. Slowly pushing the door open, I stood frozen in the doorway. Some pieces of furniture were left behind, just like the rest of the apartment. A small toddler bed was placed along the wall and a rocking chair sat still in the corner. White sheer curtains still hung in the window, and a few tiny hangers still hung on the bar in the closet. Pulling back the curtains, I peered down to the street, now completely dark with only a small glow from the street lamps. The cars had cleared off of the street and the shops were all closed for the night. A police car drove by slowly below, catching only a silhouette of their face in the darkness, wondering if it was Brad.

When I could no longer see the car, I pulled the curtains back closed and switched off the light, closing the door slightly behind me. I didn't feel as sad in there as I had the first time, knowing that the little girl who used to be in here was Lily was comforting.

I quickly washed my face and brushed my teeth, suddenly exhausted. I have felt more emotions today than I probably have in the past year. My brain felt like it could not possibly hold one more thing, consumed by all of the information I discovered tonight as well as the questions that were already in there. Closing my eyes, I tried to let it all go, let it drift to a place where I could forget about it all until the morning. And within minutes, I was fast asleep.

I woke the next morning to the bright warm sunlight shining on my face through the window. The curtains that hung were sheer and I hadn't realized there were wooden blinds pulled up that I could have closed. Waking up in a freshly lit room didn't bother me, though. I always feel more alert in the morning waking up to a sun lit room instead of a darkened one. I sat up in bed, stretching my arms up in the air, looking around my bedroom. The first of many mornings waking up here and I could not be happier.

Strolling down the hall, I slid my arms through my robe, tying it around my waist as I walked. Since I no longer had the perk of fresh brewed coffee at the hotel, the coffee pot was my first stop. I scooped out the grounds, placing them into the liner, breathing in the strong aroma of the beans. Having stayed up a little too late last night, my eyes were filled with a mild burning sensation. As the pot began to growl awake and coffee slowly streamed into the glass pot, I walked over to the counter and picked up the recipe cards I found last night. I placed them on top of my cell phone to remind me to bring them down with me later.

As the caffeine began running through my veins and a nice hot shower, I began to perk up and was ready to start my day. I grabbed my phone and the recipe cards and headed downstairs to the supply closet. Pulling each out one by one, I placed the flour, baking soda, salt, and vanilla on the table located in the middle of the kitchen. I purchased fresh eggs and butter at the store yesterday, relieved that those ingredients hadn't been left behind, too.

Opening all of the cupboards, I pulled out a few different mixing bowls, measuring cups and spoons, and carried the large mixer that rest at the back of the counter over to the prep table. Setting two of the recipes aside, I decided to focus on the ice box cookies first. After measuring everything out, I began mixing the dough, memories of my grandmother rushing to my mind. The smell of the dough was exactly the same as the cookies we used to make together.

I could picture my grandmother standing behind me in the kitchen, placing her hands over mine as we mixed the dough together with a whisk. She helped me roll the dough out, placing it onto sheets of wax paper and putting them in the refrigerator to chill. Once they were chilled, she guided the knife with me, cutting them into small circle slices. It was her job to place the sheets into the oven because she never wanted me to get burned. In exchange, it was my job to turn the dial and set the timer. It was way back then that I learned to measure and tell time.

I placed the rolls of dough on the counter as I searched the drawers for wax paper. After the third try, I located it near the refrigerator. Tearing off a medium sized sheet, I placed the dough on top, wrapping it up tightly. I continued wrapping four more rolls and carried the tray to the refrigerator to chill them inside. I was thankful I remembered to plug in all of the appliances the night before so it was nice and cool today. As they were chilling, I washed all of the dishes I used to get them ready for the next round of baking later today.

Knowing I had three hours before I could cut the cookie dough, I ran upstairs to get my jacket and purse and headed out to the car. My list of things I needed had begun to grow so I wanted to buy a few of them before it got any longer. Another thing on my list for the day was to check in to the fall festival, wondering if there was still time to get a table and sell some of my baked goods and get the word out that the bakery would be open again soon.

I still wasn't too familiar with the town so I headed right to the place that would be able to me: the hotel. Nancy knew everything and everyone in this town and would be able to tell me exactly where I needed to go.

The parking lot was still fairly full as check-out time hadn't passed, yet. I found a spot on the street, walking up the sidewalk passed the fountain to the front door. The front desk was empty so I made my way to the breakfast room, assuming Nancy was in tidying up from the breakfast rush. Empty. I tried the pool next, thinking maybe she had Lily in there swimming; not there either. Knowing she would turn up eventually, I walked to the breakfast room, poured a fresh cup of coffee, and sat patiently in an oversized chair by the fireplace that overlooked the lake.

"Cora!" I heard from behind me, accompanied with loud footsteps.

I turned around to see Lily sprinting towards me. Seeing that she wasn't slowing down, I quickly placed my coffee cup on the table as she got closer.

"Well good morning, sunshine. You must have had another little donut this morning to have this much energy." I watched as her eyes glimmered. She was dressed in her pink and white polka dot bathing suit with a lime green inner tube wrapped around her waist. "Let me guess, you're going to school?"

Lily laughed. "No, silly; I'm going swimming," she said, twirling around to show off her new bathing suit. "Do you want to come with me?"

I smiled. "I would love to sweetie, but I have a lot of work to do today. Can I go swimming with you another time? It sounds like it would be a lot of fun."

"You're welcome any time," Nancy said, coming down the hall to find Lily.

I picked up my coffee and stood up, placing my hand on the back of Lily's head as we walked over to meet Nancy.

"Thank you, I would love to come swimming another day. I stopped by because I have a couple of questions and thought you would be able to answer them for me. Do you have a few moments to talk?" I asked, taking another sip of coffee.

"As long as you don't mind coming into the pool area with me, this little one is ready to jump in," Nancy said as Lily jumped up and down outside of the pool entrance.

"Not a problem, I'd love to."

The three of us walked into the pool area and I pulled up a chair at one of the tables as Nancy helped Lily down the stairs in the shallow end. Realizing how much Lily demanded her attention, I decided to only ask a few of the questions I had for her. She gave me the contact name and address for the fall festival registration and I left it at that. Anything about Brad and Hope would clearly take longer than the short time we had today and I didn't know that I should ask while Lily was present. I watched her splash around the pool with such a joyous and free spirit, assuming she got it from her mother, seeing very few of Brad's more reserved characteristics coming through.

A second cup of coffee and a great conversation later, I left the hotel and headed to city hall to register for the fall festival the following week. The leaves were falling off the trees in a consistent pattern as the wind blew them across the street. Town was busy again, most people either carrying a shopping bag or a briefcase. Checking out the restaurant parking lot as I passed by, I noticed the lot was almost completely full.

I recognized the old style brick building right away from the description Nancy had given me as I pulled into the parking lot. An oversized clock rest near the top peak of the building, so large I could clearly read the time from down on the street. As I walked through the door, I found a large reception desk with four employees, one at each window station. An older blonde lady with a large bow in her hair motioned me over.

"How can I help you today?" she asked in a monotone voice.

"Good morning. I was wondering if I was in the right place to get information about the upcoming fall festival. I wasn't sure if it was filled already or if it was perhaps too late to enter." I stood there watching her type on her keyboard.

"You can register up until the day before as long as there are still available tables. Let me check to see if there are any left." She typed some more and proceeded to click her mouse around the screen. "What category are you trying to get into?"

"I'm planning to sell my baked goods. I just purchased the old bakery in town yesterday and would like to get my name out there and let everyone know that it will be opening up again soon."

After what seemed like one hundred more clicks on her mouse, she finally got to the screen she was looking for. "You are in luck, I have three tables left. Would you like to go ahead and register for one? The cost is thirty-five dollars." The woman looked up at me over the top of her glasses.

I lifted my purse on to the counter. "I would love to; I'm so excited that you have spaces left. Can I pay cash for the table? If not, I will have to run to the bank to get a cashier's check," I asked, reaching into the bottom of my purse to find my wallet.

"Cash is fine, I just need you to fill out a couple of papers with your information and you will be all set. Do you have a license to sell baked goods to the public?"

I stood there for a moment, not knowing exactly what that was. "Um, I really don't know the answer to that. I just purchased the building yesterday and haven't gotten into the legal part of the business just yet."

"Was the building previously a bakery before the sale? If so, I can pull up the records and see if there is still a valid one in place."

"Yes, it was!" I shouted, praying there was still one there. I gave her the address and she pulled up the records.

"It looks like the license is still good for another six months. You may or may not get something in the mail when it is time to renew it. I would recommend you coming in here to register your business once it is up and running and you can take care of the paperwork then." She handed me a clipboard and a pen with a giant artificial white daisy taped to the end. "If you would like to fill these out while you are here, there are some chairs you can sit in around the corner. There is also a table with coffee so please help yourself to some if you want," she said, pointing around to the right side of the desk.

"Yes, I would like to get everything completed today. Thank you, I will be back shortly." I grabbed my purse off the counter and made my way around the corner.

Five pages of paperwork later, I returned to the desk to hand it all in. The same lady helped me as before, still no more of a personality. Upon returning the papers, I was handed a receipt and a map of my location for my table along with all of the details of the event, and I was on my way. Still having another thirty minutes before my cookie dough was ready I made one more stop on my way home.

Chapter
Ten

I park in front of the coffee shop that Linda and her family owned, right along side a large brown delivery truck. I only met Linda the one night while crafting, but if I was going to meet new people, I needed to continually put myself out there. The front of the building was top to bottom brick with a large display window lined with tables on the other side. The aroma of fresh ground coffee beans filled my nose as I pulled open the door, breathing it in deep. The air was warm and the scent was amazing. The back counter along the wall was chrome and lined with espresso machines, grinders, and metal tins. A small wooden shelf hung just above the counter filled with bottles of flavoring, and chocolate and caramel drizzles. Linda peered around the wall from the back as I walked in, a brass bell jingling overhead as the door pushed open.

"Good morning, Cora, it's nice to see you this morning. What brings you in today?" She greeted me with a warm welcome.

"You remember my name," I said, a little surprised. "I was wondering if you had a few moments to talk. If you're busy I can certainly come back later; I was in the neighborhood."

She walked out from behind the counter, wiping her hands on a white cotton towel, tucking it in to her apron ties. "I always have time for my customers. Can I offer you a cup of coffee? It's on the house."

I mentally tallied how many cups I had already drank today while out running errands. Starting with the one I had at home before I left, my count seemed to be in the area of four cups. "I better not; I've had a lot already today and fear I'll already be awake until next week," I said, both of us laughing together.

"So what can I help you with today?" She stood next to the counter, straightening the baskets of treats that lay perfectly spaced across the top, filled with frosted rice crispy treats and tiny bags of chocolate covered coffee beans.

"I was wondering if you had a current contract for the baked goods that you sell. I don't see many pastries in the display cases so I wanted to check and offer some I could make for you." As I peered in the cases, there were a few rows of mammoth muffins but beyond that, there wasn't much to choose from.

"Roger and I were just having this conversation the other day, actually. I had mentioned to him that you bought the old bakery after talking to Nancy and asked him if I should come to you and ask the same question." A smile spread across my face. "Are you able to make up a few samples for us to try? I would love to see what kinds of things you make. Nothing goes better with hot coffee than a fresh baked pastry."

"Absolutely; let me know what kind of desserts you're interested in and I will whip up some samples for you." I clapped my hands together in excitement.

"Nothing particular in mind; something that looks good and tastes good would be a great start." She walked towards me. "I'm looking forward to seeing what you come up with." And with that, she gave me a hug. I was starting to get the feeling that hugging is what you did before you leave somewhere. Nothing I was accustomed to, but something I was beginning to enjoy.

I hugged her back, thankful for another wonderful person I was lucky enough to add into my life. "I'm excited to get started on some things for you. I have a couple of new recipes I stumbled upon that I was going to try later today, so if those go well, I will bring some by."

"I can't wait to taste them," she replied.

"Taste what?" a man's voice asked as the front door flew open, bell ringing overhead.

"Good morning, Will, I was just talking to Cora about her baking some new pastries to sell here at the shop."

Dressed from head to toe in brown, he pulled a two-wheel cart behind him stacked to the top with boxes.

"I see; if you need a taste tester, I'm about the best in town." He laughed as he tilted his cart upright.

"Will, I'd like you to meet Cora. She just moved to town and purchased the old bakery."

"Well that is perfect because I just so happen to be looking for bakery goods just about every day. Some refer to me as a sweet tooth with legs."

I looked him up and down, not believing a word he said based on his appearance.

"Lifting all of these boxes every day at work definitely helps keep me in shape. If I had a desk job, I would most likely look like a completely different person." He laughed as he stretched out his arms in front of his stomach. "Is Roger in back? I can run these back there for you if you'd like."

Linda nodded and motioned him to the back office. He pushed his foot on the bottom bar of his cart, tilting it towards him and pushing it towards Roger who was waiting in the office doorway.

"I'm sure you will get to know Will pretty well once you start ordering supplies for the bakery. He has been delivering to us for years. He's always in a good mood and never has a shortage of funny stories."

"Is this place for real? I have yet to meet a person from here that isn't wonderful. Aren't there any unpleasant people that live here?"

The bell chimed once again above the door, three women rushing in from the brisk air.

"Well—ask and you shall receive," Linda said, peering at each one of them as they came in.

Without even saying a word to Linda, they stared us both up and down as they walked passed, seating themselves at a table near the back corner of the room. After a countless number of hair flips, lipstick checks, and adjustments in their chairs, they motioned Linda over to take their orders.

"Hoity-toity, party of three is calling. I'll let you get on with your day and I look forward to tasting what you create soon."

I gave Linda a quick hug and made my way to the door, holding it open for Will as he followed behind me.

"It was nice to meet you, Will, I'm sure I'll see you again very soon once I place some supply orders later in the week. I'll be sure to have some samples laying around on delivery day."

His face lit up as he lifted his cart into the back of his truck, securing it to the side with two black bungee cords.

"I look forward to it. It was nice meeting you, too." He waved as he climbed into the front seat.

I climbed into my car, turning up the heat dial a few more notches as I watched him pull his delivery truck ahead and around the corner to his next stop.

∞

The breeze was blowing as I arrived back at the bakery, sending shivers down my spine. Rubbing my arms up and down, I searched for the thermostat, locating it near the office door and turned it up three degrees. Trying to speed up the process, I turned on the oven to preheat and warm the kitchen.

Opening the refrigerator door, I grabbed the tray of dough and pushed on it with my finger, making sure it was cold enough to cut. Grabbing a clean knife from the drawer, I unwrapped the rolls of dough from the wax paper and laid them out across the cutting board, being careful to slice them all the same width.

The cookies filled five metal cookie sheets by the time I was finished. Just as the oven beeped that it was preheated, I carried each one over and slid them onto the metal oven racks. Still unsure of how to use the oven, I looked around and found an old wind up timer on the counter near the stove. It was just like the one my grandmother had in her kitchen. I wound it around to fifteen minutes and placed it on the center counter.

The dishes were still stacked near the sink from making the dough earlier this morning. I loaded what I could into the dishwasher and hand washed the rest, pausing to check on the cookies twice. I wasn't familiar with how this oven baked yet and the last thing I wanted to do was burn my first batch of cookies and read too much into it as a bad sign.

I could smell the cookies before the timer rung, filling the kitchen with an appetizing aroma that made my stomach growl. I slid on a red oven mitt and pulled out the trays one by one, carrying them to the tall free-standing chrome cooling rack. They were golden brown on top and formed in perfect circles. I had to resist the temptation to pull one off and stuff it into my mouth.

Giving them a few minutes to cool, I pulled out one of the trays and placed a couple cookies onto a plate on the center counter. The smell was so familiar, bringing me right back to my childhood in my grandmother's kitchen. Closing my eyes, I took my first bite, savoring every moment, going back to that place that made me so happy when I was younger.

As I took my second bite, there was a knock at the front door. Peeking around the corner from the kitchen, I wasn't able to see who it was as the curtains were still draped in the windows. I pulled back the lace covering on the front door window and smiled. It was Nancy.

I unlocked the deadbolt and the chain above it, letting Nancy inside.

"Come in, it's freezing outside," I said, motioning her inside.

Nancy took a deep breath. "Something smells wonderful in here; are you baking?"

"I'm trying out an old recipe in my new kitchen. The cookies are still warm if you would like a couple of them. Have a seat and I'll bring some out."

Nancy pulled up a chair at one of the front tables as I went back to the kitchen. I loaded a tray of cookies onto a plate while brewing a fresh pot of coffee. It had been a few hours now since my last cup so I figured it would be okay to have one more. A few minutes later, I joined Nancy back at the table, cookies and coffee in hand. I placed them on the table, setting the serving tray on the table next to me.

"I figured you can't have cookies without a nice hot cup of coffee." I scooped a tiny spoonful of sugar from a small dish I found in the cupboard, along with a container with creamer. Stirring my coffee with my spoon, I tapped it on the edge of my cup and placed it on the table.

"They do go well together, especially on a cold day like today. Thank you so much." Nancy took a bite out of her first cookie. "Well it appears that you are very comfortable in the kitchen; these are wonderful," she said, pouring herself a cup of coffee. She set the pot back down on the table, picking up her cookie for another bite.

"Thank you; it has always been my favorite room in my house. I used to bake with my grandmother in her kitchen when I was a little girl. My greatest memories growing up were with her."

Nancy noticed how my face lit up when I talked about it. Glancing around the bakery, she took notes on everything I had done so far; nothing terribly noticeable having not been there in over a year.

"Are you settling in alright? This area looks fantastic; looks ready to open any day now."

I joined her gaze around the room. "All I really did was un-cover everything. It was so clean and immaculate that there really wasn't much to do. It's hard to believe that this place was ever open for business. Everything is so new." I grabbed another cookie off of the plate, not being able to resist.

"Well, most of it is. She was only open for about six months before she closed. I guess there really wasn't much time for it to get dirty. Hope put a lot into this bakery; she had a lot of big dreams for it, and for Lily." Nancy glanced down at the table.

"Hope; was that Brad's wife's name?" I asked casually, having already known from my findings upstairs. I wasn't sure I wanted to tell Nancy just yet of what I found. I didn't want to upset her seeing how hard it was for her to even bring up her name now.

"Yes, her name was Hope and she was a wonderful woman. She and Brad had been together since high school and were married for quite some time before settling down to have children. She wanted a lot of kids, but unfortunately, she would only get the chance to have one." Nancy got up from the table and slowly walked through the bakery, running her fingers along the counter as she went.

A part of me wanted to know more about Hope, but I didn't want to pry. I was just getting to know Nancy and her family and I didn't want to come off as too nosy. I watched her as she walked around, feeling her reflecting back to when the bakery was open once before. She paused near the front counter, turning back towards me.

"After Lily was born," Nancy continued, "she knew it was time to make her dreams of opening her own bakery come true. She had always wanted to do it for herself before she had Lily, but after having her, she knew she wanted it for her, too. She too baked with her grandmother when she was young." She began to wander again. "She planned on passing those recipes down to Lily and to make so many more memories with her. She was planning to have a parent and child baking class once a month, something simple that she could teach them together, having Lily by her side, of course."

I remembered reading some of those plans in Hope's journal. There were a lot more that I hadn't gotten the chance to read, yet, but knew she had big plans for their future.

"That sounds like a wonderful idea. Maybe that's something that I will be able to do here; something to carry on Hope's plans for the bakery."

Nancy stopped walking again, looking over at me. "I think that's a great idea, she would have loved that. Being that you didn't know her name, I will assume that Brad hasn't mentioned her to you?"

I looked back at her and shook my head. "I was going to ask, but wasn't sure it was my place."

Nancy came back and joined me at the table. She released a deep breath as she sat down, taking another cookie from the plate. "Hope was the best daughter-in-law a mother could ask for. She was kind and loving, always helping others before helping herself. She opened the bakery right about the time Lily turned one year old. I remember because she had her birthday party here in the bakery. It was decorated in a pink princess theme; balloons and crepe paper everywhere," she said, pointing around the room.

I could picture what it must have looked like in my mind. "I bet it was beautiful."

"It was; she baked a huge pink cake that was probably the size of Lily at the time," she laughed. "I remember a few months after that, she wasn't feeling well. She went to see the doctor, but they brushed it off as a virus and told her to go home and get some rest for a couple of days and she would start to feel better. A few days later, she felt worse so Brad took her to the ER. After running some tests, they discovered she had a very aggressive form of ovarian cancer." Nancy paused, her voice cracking, catching in her throat.

I reached across the table, placing my hand on top of hers and handed her a napkin from the tray I brought out. She dabbed her eyes, took a sip of her coffee, continuing.

"She was no longer able to run the bakery so they thought it would be best to close it temporarily. The staff she had working with her at the time were amazing, offering several times to run it for her so she wouldn't have to close. In the end, she thought it was best to close the doors permanently as she wasn't getting better. A month later, she passed. They made her as comfortable as they could, but by the time they discovered it, there was nothing they could do for her." She picked up another cookie from the plate. "Brad took leave from work and gave her as much time with Lily as he could. It was so sudden and unexpected that it took him a while to process it all, to really believe what had happened. I still wonder if he has taken time to fully grieve, even now."

"I'm so sorry, that is awful. I understand if it is too difficult for you to be here with me." I lifted the plate, offering her another cookie, but she declined.

"It was definitely difficult coming down here and knocking on that door. Like I said, I hadn't been here since he closed it up, so I wasn't really sure what to expect. I don't think Brad has been back inside either. The apartment wasn't their main home, it was just a place to go during work hours to relax and give Lily a place to play and nap; sometimes Brad would come by for breakfast in the morning after working the night shift and go upstairs to sleep for a few hours. He always wanted to be close to Hope and Lily; if they were here, he was here."

Part of me was relieved to hear that they didn't actually live upstairs for some reason. I was already afraid that Brad would never come into the bakery, but praying someday he would be able to.

"Where are Hope's parents? Were they able to help out with Lily at all?"

"When Hope got sick, they were angry that it wasn't discovered earlier. They thought that somehow Brad should have known something was wrong and he should have taken her in sooner. After the funeral, they left town the next day and we haven't heard from them since."

I sat across from her trying not to make it too obvious how shocked I was, picking my jaw up from what felt like the basement floor.

"A few months later, Brad hired a company to come here and cover everything and take any personal belongings they found and return them to him. He thinks they did a pretty good job, but he never actually came back in to check. He waited a couple more months before deciding to place the building up for sale. A large part of him wanted to keep it open for her, many offering to help him do so, but the other part of him knew he couldn't continue it without her."

I suddenly realized why those items were left upstairs. Brad never actually cleaned out their things, someone who was unaware that the table pulled open, like me, hadn't seen them inside. I looked up at Nancy as she dabbed the corners of her eyes again.

"Would you mind coming with me for a minute? I think I have something you may want."

She nodded and followed me up the dark stairwell to the apartment. I pushed open the door and motioned for her to sit down on the couch.

"I found something the night I moved in and I thought you may want to have it." I reached for the top of the coffee table, lifting it up towards us, revealing the album, journal, and recipe box. "I noticed the table was a little crooked when I walked by it and after pushing down on the one side, I noticed it was a lift-top and I found these inside."

I reached for the photo album first, placing it on the couch cushion in between us. Nancy reached over, picking it up slowly and opened it to the first page.

"Towards the middle of the album, there are some photos of you and Phil. I wasn't sure what I should do with them or if I should even say anything, but I knew that you would know what to do with them. I assume the company that came in here wasn't aware that these were inside and missed them."

I watch Nancy as she turned page after page, memories soaring through her mind. I reached for the recipe box, pulling open the lid. "The cookies you just ate were from a recipe I found in this box."

"I knew those cookies tasted familiar. This box of recipes belonged to Hope's grandmother and it was where she got most of her recipes she used for the bakery. When we received the boxes after they finished cleaning out the building, we noticed they were missing. Brad didn't want to come back inside to look for it and insisted that no one else come in either." She flipped through a few of the cards, pulling them up and smiling. "After a couple of days, I think he did come back to look, although he would never admit it to me. He wasn't sure where it could have been and gave up trying. I'm not sure he was convinced it was even here, assuming he would find it later somewhere in their home."

Nancy pulled another card out of the box. "This is the frosting recipe she used to make the frosting for Lily's birthday cake," she said, rubbing her fingers along the layer of flour that lay across it.

"It was never my intention to throw it out; I stayed up all night looking through it. I wasn't sure if it would be okay to use any of them, but something was telling me to, so I baked the Ice Box Cookies. It was like they were left behind for me to find or something."

I waited for Nancy to reply, certain she would think I was completely insane.

"Like a sign. Hope was always a believer in signs. Brad never followed her visions when it came to signs; he was more of a realist when it came to life. He only went along with them to humor her I think. I, on the other hand, have always believed in signs; that there is some stronger force telling us where to go in life and all we have to do is read them along the way."

I smiled, being able to relate to Nancy at that moment. I was afraid that she would think I was being too nosy or stealing Hope's ideas, but it wasn't that way at all. I was beginning to feel a motherly connection with Nancy, something that I haven't felt in a really long time.

"It was signs that led me here, to your town, to this building, possibly to Brad and your family. I had no idea that when I picked up and left my life that I would be here, having coffee with such a wonderful woman in a bakery that I bought. I'm finally living my dreams and something definitely brought me here to you."

Nancy straightened the recipes, closing the lid, and placed it back inside the coffee table. She flipped through a couple more pages in the album before returning it as well.

"I believe that, and if that is what you feel, then go with it and find out why you were sent to us." Nancy glanced into the table once more. "What is that other book in there?"

"It is a journal that Hope must have kept. Most of it contains plans she had for the bakery and future plans for Lily. I would imagine she hoped to run the bakery with her as she got older?"

"Yes, she wanted nothing more than to share her love of baking with her daughter."

I reached for the journal offering it to her. "Would you like to take a look?"

She thought about it for a moment. "No, I think this was enough for me for one day; maybe next time."

I nodded, returning the journal to the table, pushing the top back down.

"Can I ask you a favor?" Nancy asked, turning to face me on the couch.

"Of course."

"Leave these here for now and don't tell Brad about them, not just yet anyway. I think the sale of the building has been hard enough for him to process right now; let's take it in steps. I'm so thankful you shared this with me. I feel so relieved knowing that these items have been found and are in good hands."

We stood from the couch and made our way back downstairs, walking her to the door. I told her to stay put while I ran to the kitchen, returning with a baggie filled with extra cookies I baked.

"Take these with you and share them with Phil and Lily. If Brad would like some, please share them with him, too. If I have them sitting around here, I am sure to eat them all. That is one thing I have always struggled with as a baker: not eating all of my creations."

She hugged me tight, thanking me for the cookies before leaving. I locked the door behind her, going back to the kitchen to put away the rest of the cookies for the festival.

Chapter
Eleven

The next morning, I woke to a gray gloomy sky: low hanging clouds and a light mist falling down. Having planned to walk up and down the street passing out fliers to the local businesses, I was now rethinking my plan. I fished around in a few boxes I stuffed in the bottom of my closet, finding an old backpack, placing my flyers inside to keep them dry.

With a quick shower and a coffee to go, I climbed in my car and headed to the far end of town. Being fairly early in the morning, street parking shouldn't be too hard to come by. I pulled into the parking lot of the hotel, deciding to start there and work my way down that side of the street to the other end of town.

I walked inside to find Nancy behind the front desk helping two guests, motioning for me to have a seat. I walked over to the coffee and poured a cup, adding a packet of sugar and a small hazelnut creamer. Finding a seat near the fire, I set my backpack along side the chair and leaned back, crossing one leg over the other. Blowing on it gently, I took a small sip, sending warm steam up against my face.

"Good morning, Cora. What brings you in today?" Nancy asked, pulling up a seat next to me. "Not that you ever need a reason to come by."

"I know that, but today I actually have a reason for stopping." I picked up my backpack off the floor, unzipped it and pulled out a flyer. "I was wondering if you would be so kind as to hang up one of my flyers. It has all of the information about my grand opening and I would love to get as many people as I can to come."

I handed the flyer over to Nancy and she looked it over. "I would be happy to hang it up for you and I have the perfect place to put it." She walked over to the desk and taped it to the top of the counter. "There, now every guest who checks in or out will see it. If you have another you can spare, I can hang one up in the breakfast room also. Have you been baking anymore sweets since I was there yesterday?"

I reached into my bag and handed her another flyer. "After you left, I spent the next three hours going through recipes and experimenting with a few of them. I filled most of the refrigerator with things to bring to the festival. I also created a few samples for Linda to try for the coffee shop. My plan is to deliver the rest of these flyers around town this morning, and go back to the bakery to package everything up this afternoon."

"Well that sounds like an awful lot of work for one person; can I offer you a partner to help move things along quicker?" Nancy asked, pointing to herself.

"I would love that. Please know that you don't have to, only if you want to. I don't want to interfere with any plans you have here."

Nancy walked back behind the desk. "I do have one small thing that may come along with it, though, if it's not a problem."

I walked over to the desk to see what she meant. As I approached the counter, Lily jumped up from behind it.

"Boo!" Lily shouted, catching me by surprise.

"Well good morning, Miss Lily. Were you hiding back there to scare me?"

Lily came out from behind the counter to talk to me without having to jump up and down to see over the counter. "No, grandma put down a blanket for me on the floor and I was coloring. But you didn't know I was there so I tried to scare you. Did it work?"

"Yes, it did, I definitely didn't know you were back there. What are you coloring?" I asked, kneeling down in front of her.

"Do you want to see?" Lily grabbed my hand and walked me back behind the desk to her coloring spot. Picking up her crayon, she colored the last empty spot on her page. "Can you tear this out for me?" she asked, holding the book up in the air.

"Sure," I replied, placing it on the counter top to make it easier. "Here you go."

Lily took the picture from me and placed the book back down onto the floor. She closed her crayon case and stacked it on top of her coloring book. Picking the picture back up again, she handed it back to me. "I colored this for you."

I knelt down next to her, accepting the picture. "It is the most beautiful picture I have ever seen. I just so happen to have a giant refrigerator in my kitchen with nothing on it. I have been looking for a great piece of art to hang there and I think I have finally found the perfect one. Thank you so much." I reached to her for a hug, stroking her fine blonde curls that fell down her back.

"I'm glad you like it; I can make you another one later if you would like. Grandpa will be up to get me soon so I won't have time today."

"I would love that; it will be worth the wait. For now, this one will work perfectly." I released Lily and stood back up slowly. "I better get going; I still have a lot of flyers to deliver and then have to get back to the bakery to get ready for the festival."

"What time would you like me to come by? If Brad gets held up at work for some reason and needs to sleep late, will it be alright if I bring her with?" Lily looked up at me with the sweetest blue eyes, a face I could never say no to.

"Let's plan on two o'clock and I think the only way we will ever finish on time is if Lily is there to help us." Lily looked up at me, jumping with excitement.

Lily gathered up her coloring supplies and ran down the hall towards Phil who was waiting at the other end. "See you later, Cora," she yelled, waving behind her as she ran.

As soon as Lily was out of sight, my smile faded as worry took its place. "Does Lily have any memories of being at the bakery? Will it upset her being there?"

"She was only a year old the last time she was there. I'm certain she has no memory of being there or that it used to belong to her mother. Brad may have court before his shift later tonight so we will likely have her until tomorrow morning if I had to guess."

"What about Brad, will he be upset if you bring her there? I really don't want to cause any problems." My mind was fluttering in and out with a million questions like it had the other day.

Nancy assured me that there was nothing to worry about and if Brad had a problem with it, she would handle it. I took a deep breath, trying to let it go and focus on all that I had still ahead of me today. I said goodbye to Nancy and made my way back to the car to my next stop.

I stopped by a dentist office, the grocery store, and several others I hadn't been in before. The receptionist at the clinic took my flyer reluctantly, setting it on her desk and off to the side. She told me that she needed permission before hanging anything up and would ask the doctor if she remembered later in the day. For all of the nice people I had met, there were only a few unfriendly ones, but every town had to have at least a few. As I walked passed the front window, I peered back inside, seeing her toss it into the garbage under her desk. I guess I wouldn't want to invite someone like that to my grand opening anyway.

Finishing up the side of the street I started on, I headed back to the bakery to pick up the samples to bring over to Linda. Tossing them into a plastic container, I sealed the lid shut and jumped back into the car and went to meet her at the coffee shop.

When I arrived at the coffee shop, there were three people waiting in line and all but two tables were full. Apparently this was the caffeine crash hour and everyone needed to replenish. Linda waved to me and let me know she would be with me when she could. Mary was working with her behind the counter along with another woman I had never seen, grinding beans and steaming foam for cappuccinos. They passed each other weaving across to different ends of the counter seamlessly, like they had been doing it for years. Mary looked up at me and waved hello, too.

When Linda finished ringing up the last customer, Mary made their order while Linda joined me at a high top table near the front window. "Are these the samples you were working on already? How do you work so quickly?"

I opened the lid of the container, revealing the samples I had made. "I had a little extra time while baking for the festival tomorrow and I also threw in some of the things I was making to bring there."

She peered into the container, taking note of all of the different flavors inside. "Let me call the girls over to taste a few too since Roger is busy back in the office. I trust their judgment and we're always looking for an excuse to eat sweets."

She waved them over to join us, four coffees in hand. "I guessed that you probably had sweets in that container so I grabbed us something to go with it. What do we have here?"

"Cora, I don't think you have met my other daughter, Ali. She's our youngest and also helps out around here throughout the week."

I extended my hand out across the table. "It's nice to meet you, Ali. I met your mom and sister at craft night over at Sweet Peas. Do you craft, too?"

She laughed under her breath. "I would like to think I can, but I usually pass. No offense, but I feel like I'm too young to be sitting in a room of old—er women crafting on a Thursday night."

Linda shot her a look along with Mary. "Just because you are younger than me doesn't make me that old. It's only a few years and those ladies are fun," Mary said, defending herself.

I pointed out all of the things I made: red velvet cupcakes, fudge brownies, three kinds of cookies, and a slice of apple pie. Each grabbing a fork, they took a bite of each one, deciding which would be best in their coffee shop.

"I don't think any of these will last long in the case. If the customers don't order them, I'll eat them all myself." Mary laughed, taking another bite of the brownie. Ali nodded as well.

"I second that; I would like to have any of these available for sale. When the festival's over, let's sit down and write up a purchase order for your first trial run and see how it goes from there."

"That sounds wonderful. I'm so excited to get started baking for you and move forward with my grand opening." I reached around inside of my bag, pulling out another flyer. "Would you mind hanging one of these up? I'm trying to get the word out about the bakery and I would really appreciate it."

Linda grabbed the paper from me. "I would be happy to. If you would like to make something up about where the goodies are coming from that we are selling, I would love to advertise that as well."

"I would love to do that. Thank you so much." I stayed for

another half an hour, jotting down ideas they had and getting to know them a little bit better.

Returning to the bakery, I had just enough time to hang up my bag before there was a knock at the front door. I opened the door to Nancy and an overly excited Lily who was ready to get started. She ran passed me and headed right for the kitchen.

When we walked into the kitchen, Lily was practically bouncing off the walls with excitement, letting out loud shrieks, so loud I was amazed that they were coming from her tiny body.

"Grandma, look! That is the picture I made for Cora!" Lily ran over to the stainless steel refrigerator to admire her work a little closer.

"I had to dig around a little bit to find some tape, but I wasn't going to give up. I think it's perfect for my new kitchen. Are you ready to start packaging? We have a lot of work to do."

I walked to the front and grabbed one of the chairs sitting at a round table and carried it back to the kitchen for Lily to stand on. Before they arrived, I laid everything out across the long counter in an assembly line fashion.

"The first station is for the baked goods, and then the next is to place them in the wrappers. After they're wrapped, they will need to be tied with a ribbon. Then the last step is to place one of my business card stickers to the bottom of each package. Which job would you like?" I walked Lily to each station so she could see what each one entailed, running her tiny hands along the counter as she went. Looking at them very closely, walking up and down twice, she had made her decision.

"Hmmm—I think I'll do the stickers, because I love stickers. Well that, and I don't know how to tie, yet." She wrapped her hands around the back of the chair and dragged it to the end of the counter and climbed up.

I walked to the beginning of the stations. "I will do one set all of the way through, so that you both know what they should look like." I grabbed the first plate of ice box cookies out of the refrigerator and placed them onto the empty space left on the counter. "I think I will sell these in sets of three, because one cookie is never enough."

Sliding on a pair of plastic gloves, I picked up three cookies, stacking them one on top of the other, and wrapped them tightly in the clear cellophane wrapping. Grabbing a precut piece of silk ribbon, I wrapped it around one way, twisted it, and turned it the other direction, finishing it off with a small bow on top.

"Next will be your job. You will peel one sticker off of the paper and place it right on the bottom. Would you like to try this one to make sure you know how to do it?"

I flipped the stack of cookies upside down in front of her. Lily picked up one of the stickers, bending the edge to release the corner. Using her tiny fingers, she peeled it back off of the paper. She looked up at me before placing it, making sure she was putting it in the right spot, pointing to the middle of the cookie, waiting for an approving nod. Once I gave it, she carefully placed the sticker on, rubbing it carefully around the edges to be sure it stuck and wasn't going to fall off.

"How is that?" she asked, holding it proudly in the air.

"I think you definitely picked the right job, that sticker looks amazing." She looked over at Nancy, showing her as well. "What job are you going to do, grandma?"

"I think I will stand in the middle and tie all of the ribbons." Nancy walked over to the center of the counter next to Lily.

While the three of them stood there wrapping, tying, and labeling, Lily entertained them with one of her silly stories. She was a great story teller and very animated, filled with faces and hand gestures as she spoke. When the story came to a hand gesture part, she would have to set down what she was doing to get it just right. I learned a lot about her through those stories. Most of them were about what she liked to do, places she'd been, and people in her family.

I learned that she loved swimming in her grandma's hotel pool, coloring was her favorite activity, her favorite color was pink, and that her favorite thing to bake was cutout cookies with mounds of frosting and sprinkles on top. She told me all about her cookie cutter collection she had at her grandma's house and that she loved baking with her. Nancy had never mentioned it before so it caught me a little by surprise.

When all of the items had been wrapped, tied, and labeled, I placed them back into the refrigerator. As I loaded the last tray, Lily jumped down from her chair eager to start another task.

"I want to keep helping; can I put stickers on anything else? Maybe you need to bake more things for the festival," she said, wandering around the kitchen.

"I think we're all finished for the day. You were the best little helper."

"Well..." she said, her voice trailing off.

"What is it?"

"Well—you didn't make any fun cookies. Where are all of the fun shapes and colors? People love those kinds of cookies, or at least I do. Can we make some for the festival?" She held her hands together, resting them under her chin, begging Nancy or I to say yes. Even at a young age, she already knew how to use those beautiful blue eyes of hers.

"I'm free the rest of the day, but you'll have to ask your grandma." Both of us turned to Nancy, waiting for her to answer.

"I have to get back to the hotel and give grandpa a break for an hour or two, but if it is alright with Cora, then it is fine with me. I can pick you up when I'm finished." Nancy leaned down to Lily, giving her instructions to behave and listen to Cora. She was jumping up and down so quickly with excitement that I wasn't even sure she was listening.

We walked her to the front door, locking it behind her. Returning to the kitchen, we each started at an end of the kitchen, opening drawers along the way until we find the one that contained the cookie cutters. After her third attempt, Lily found the right one.

"I found them!" she shouted, scooping her tiny arms into the drawer, pulling out as many as she could hold. I grabbed the remaining ones and laid them out on the counter. We found a Christmas tree, a pumpkin, a bunny, a dog bone, a heart, and a shamrock; there appeared to be one for each holiday season.

"Which one should we start with? Its fall so we should maybe do some leaves with yellow, orange, and red frosting on them," I said, finding a maple leaf in the pile.

Lily walked around the counter, taking a close look at all of the cutters. Nearing the end of the line, she paused, grabbing one off the counter and quickly hid it behind her back. "I think I have a good one," she said. "Pick a hand."

I hadn't played that game in years. I thought about it for a moment, and then chose her left hand. I guessed wrong, and then touched her right arm for my next guess. Slowly pulling her arm out from behind her body, she revealed the cutter she had chosen.

"Ta-da!" she yelled, holding it up in the air. "It's the pumpkin."

"Pumpkins are everywhere this time of year. Great choice," I said, giving her a high five.

We gathered up all of the remaining cookie cutters we chose not to use and placed them back into the drawer. Needing fresh ingredients, I walked Lily over to the supply closet to grab what we needed, handing her small containers of flour, sugar, vanilla, and baking power. She grabbed each one, carrying them over to the counter, returning quickly for the next.

I carefully handed her a carton containing a dozen eggs, watching her carry them gently on her tip toes all the way to the counter. She whispered *Shhhhh* as she walked to be sure she didn't get distracted and break any of them.

"The last thing we'll need is butter. I have some in the top drawer of the refrigerator; can you reach it by yourself?"

She ran back over to try, stretching her arms up as long as she could. Pulling out the drawer, she reached inside, pulling out a box of stick butter and pushed it back closed, shutting the large door behind her.

"I did it, Cora," she said proudly. She placed them on the counter with the other ingredients and climbed back onto her chair. "Now what?"

"Well, now we take all of the ingredients we pulled out and put them all together to make the dough." Reaching for the flour, I measure out two cups in a large measuring cup. "Would you like to pour it into the bowl?"

I handed Lily the measuring cup, waiting for her to wrap her little hands around it before letting go.

"Go ahead and carefully pour it all into the bowl," I instructed, holding the bowl steady for her.

She moved her hands over the mixing bowl and tipped the measuring cup on its side, pouring the flour in. She then added the sugar, and baking powder. I set the bowl aside and grabbed a second one.

"Why are you getting another one?"

"That was all of the dry ingredients; now we will mix all of our wet ingredients in another bowl. Then, when all of those are mixed, we will dump the dry ingredients a little at a time in with the wet and together they will make the dough."

I grabbed an egg out of the carton, positioned myself behind Lily, and handed her the egg, placing my hands around hers.

"Do I get to crack the egg?" she asked, eyes wide. "Daddy never lets me crack the eggs. He said that I make too big of a mess and that he doesn't like to eat shells, whatever that means."

"Of course you get to, that is the best part of baking. I'm just going to help you a little." I placed the egg into her right hand and gently tapped it on the side of the bowl, cracking it through on one side. "Now put your other hand right here," I said, helping her place her hand on the other end of the egg. "Now carefully push your thumbs into the crack of the egg and pull the shell apart." As she did that, the yolk slipped into the bowl.

"I did it!" she said, shrieking again, jumping up and down on the chair. I kept my arms around her so she didn't fall off the chair.

I leaned over the bowl. "And look, no shells." Lily grinned from ear to ear. Something so small and simple gave her such joy. Seeing the thrill in her eyes amazed me. Never having children of my own, I realized how much I needed this, how much I wanted this in my life.

Lily reached up and gave me another high five. We cracked the other egg into the bowl and mixed all of the ingredients together. As she stirred the whisk around the bowl a few extra times, I walked to the closet, coming out with another container of flour.

"What is that for? I thought we mixed everything already?"

"This is the best part of making cookie cutouts." I reached my hand into the container, pulling out a fist full of flour and placed it directly in front of Lily. "Take your hands and spread this all over the table." She looked up at me, wondering if I was joking or not. "Go ahead."

She slammed both of her hands on the pile of flour, causing the white dust to fill the air. Giggling loudly, she pushed the flour around the table making a huge mess, but she was having so much fun doing it.

At that moment, I couldn't help but wonder what it would have been like if Lily had been doing this with her mother instead of with me. A wave of guilt rushed over me as I watched her. These were the things that she was supposed to be doing with her mother. She was the one who was supposed to teach her how to crack an egg, not me. She was the one who was supposed to be picking out which cookie cutter to use, which color of frosting to make. She was never going to get those things from her, never learn her love of baking from her, and never know the secret ingredients that she used.

I stood there and watched her, flour dust souring through the air with each pass of her hands. Then it hit me: a sense of responsibility and pride that I was the one who was brought here to do those things for her, to teach her how to crack an egg, to use *my* secret ingredients, to love baking. She may never get those things from anyone else. I have her mother's recipes, secret ingredients, plans for her future. I was determined to make those happen; to be sure that Lily is present in this building, present in this kitchen, and learns all about what her mother built for her.

When she was finished spreading the flour, I reached my hand into the bowl and pulled out a large chunk of dough. Grabbing the rolling pin, she placed her hands on the sides, placing my own over the top. Rolling the dough thin, we were finally ready to cut.

"Can I do the first one?" she asked, holding the pumpkin one in her hand. She placed it on top of the dough, pushing it down with all of her might. Lifting it back up, she beamed at the perfect pumpkin shape that lay before her. "Daddy said that mommy's favorite season was fall and that she loved pumpkins. So I think this cookie should be for her." She smiled up at me and grabbed another cutter and continued on.

"I think that is very sweet of you," I said, not sure what else to say. I wasn't sure that Brad had told her much about her mother, but I guess she did come up in conversation here and there.

We filled six trays of cookies before all of the dough had been used. I turned on the oven light, illuminating the inside.

"Pull your chair over here and you can watch them bake."

Lily hopped down and pushed her chair over, placing it directly in front of the oven door. I pulled it back about five feet, not wanting her to get too hot.

"Have a seat, you can watch them as they melt down a bit and then turn a golden brown when they're finished." Lily stood there for a second looking around. "Did you lose something?" I asked, wondering what she was looking for.

"There's only one chair; where are you going to sit?"

I smiled. "I think I'll just stand next to you and start cleaning up the kitchen while they bake."

Lily turned towards me, placing her hands on her hips. "But if you stand, you will be too tall to see into the oven."

"You have a good point; I'll just go out into the other room and grab another chair."

"But you'll miss it," she shouted. "Just sit in this one."

I looked back at her confused. "But if I sit there, where will you sit?"

"On your lap silly."

My heart melted along with the dough in the oven. I walked over to the chair and sat, helping Lily up onto my lap. She reached behind her, grabbing my arms and wrapped them around the front of her, holding her in place. She placed her hands over mine, making sure to keep a tight grip. Leaning back, she rested her head against my chest and peered through the oven window as the cookies began to turn a light golden brown.

"Thank you for teaching me to bake today," she said, followed by a long yawn.

I squeezed my arms around her tighter, placing my chin on top of her blonde curls, unable to reply in actual words. "Mmm hmm," was all I could get out. Lily let out another yawn, her head feeling heavy against me, slowly leaning to one side. Carefully peeking around the side of her, her eyes were closed.

Checking the timer on the oven, I knew I couldn't hold her much longer before the first batch of cookies were finished, although I would have loved to have sat there for hours. I leaned her to one side, resting her head in the bend of my arm, placing my other arm under her knees. Slowly moving to a standing position, I walked her to the back stairwell and up the stairs to the apartment.

Pushing the door open with my elbow, I carried her into her old bedroom and placed her in her tiny bed. Pulling the blanket I had draped over the back of the couch, I returned to her room and covered her carefully as not to wake her. As I backed out of the room, I heard the timer ding from the kitchen for the cookies. I hurried back downstairs, leaving the apartment door open behind me in case she were to wake up.

I slid the oven mitt on quickly and pulled the two cookie sheets from the oven and placed them on the cooling rack, disappointed that Lily hadn't gotten to see all of her hard work completed. After placing the next two trays into the oven, my cell phone began ringing on the counter.

"Hello?"

"Hi, Cora, it's Nancy. Is Lily doing okay?" she asked.

"She's doing great; we were having so much fun baking that she fell asleep. We were watching the cookies bake through the oven door together and she fell asleep on my lap. I hope you don't mind, but I carried her upstairs and laid her down so she could sleep." There was a pause on the other end. "Nancy? Are you still there?"

"Yes, I'm still here. I'm glad she had fun; you must have worn her out. I have to cover the front desk for a while longer before I can come and get Lily. There was a flood in one of the hotel rooms and Phil needs to clean up the mess and move the guests into another room. Will that be a problem?"

I set the timer for the next batch. "No, that's not a problem. I'm sorry to hear about the flood, take as much time as you need. Lily is asleep and I was just planning on cleaning up the kitchen from our cookie mess. It shouldn't take me long and I'll head back upstairs in case she wakes up. You can just call me when you're on your way." I hung up the phone and got to work on the pile of dishes gathered in the sink.

Chapter Twelve

When the cookies were all baked, cooled, and frosted, I turned off the lights in the bakery and walked upstairs to check on Lily. I stuck my head into her bedroom, seeing that she was still snuggled up under the blanket tucked up to her chin.

In the kitchen, I brewed a fresh pot of coffee, not knowing how long Nancy would be and not wanting to fall asleep and miss her call. Tossing a bag of popcorn into the microwave, I carried my cup of coffee into the living room, placing it on a cork coaster. I reached for the remote to fill the silence in the room. The cable was supposed to be turned on sometime today. As I pushed the power button, the sound came on before the picture, and I clapped my hands with excitement that it was up and running. Unable to find the guide, I flipped through the channels one by one, trying to find something that I recognized on TV. I came to a movie I used to watch all of the time with my grandmother, leaving it set on that channel while I went to get my popcorn.

I pulled the microwave door open as the scent of burnt kernels started to fill the air. Finding a bowl in the cupboard and the salt shaker, I poured it into the bowl, got comfortable back on the couch, and covered up with the quilt my grandmother made for me. The commercial break ended as I sat down, tucking my legs under the quilt.

An hour and a half later as the credits began running across the television, my phone began to vibrate across the coffee table.

"Hi Nancy," I whispered so I didn't wake Lily.

"Hi, sorry it is so late. We had a few things come up after the flooded room that Phil had to take care of and I was the only one available to watch the front desk. Is she still asleep?"

I crept down the hall and peered into her room. "Yes, she's out cold. All of the baking must have worn her out."

"I bet it did. Would it be okay if I came to pick her up in a few minutes? She should stay asleep for the ride home. She's used to it with her dad's strange hours coming and going."

I pulled her door back closed. "You're certainly welcome to leave her here to sleep for the night and get her in the morning." The thought of waking such a peaceful little girl worried me.

"That is sweet of you to offer, but she'll be fine. I wouldn't want to put you out; I will leave here in the next five minutes." With that, the conversation was over.

I walked back downstairs to turn on the smaller light above the register and unlock the front door, instructing her to come upstairs when she arrived.

Ten minutes later, Nancy arrived, following the smell of popcorn up the stairs and gently knocking before entering the apartment.

"Come on in, have a seat on the couch. I was just going to dump the rest of the coffee unless you would like a cup. I made it fresh an hour or so ago."

"No, thank you, but I'd better not. I need to be awake bright and early in the morning for my shift and I don't want to be up any longer than I need to be tonight."

I rinsed the coffee pot under cool water and placed it into the dish drainer in the other side of the sink. "Is everything alright at the hotel? You said there was a flood; how bad was it?" I sat back down next to her on the couch, covering my legs back up with my quilt.

"Yes, everything is under control now. One of our guests was running a hot bath and while they were waiting for the tub to fill, they decided to come down to the lobby to grab a fresh cup of coffee. Well, we got to talking and she forgot the bathtub was running. Needless to say, instead of running a bath, she ran and entire bathroom and part of the hallway." Nancy leaned her back against the couch, looking completely exhausted.

"Oh no, I wish I could have helped you guys in some way. Was Phil able to get it all cleaned up? Is there anything that still needs to be done that I can help with?" I grabbed another handful of popcorn, offering some to Nancy.

She reached her hand into the bowl and tossed a few pieces into her mouth. "You already helped us a ton by keeping Lily. I'm not sure how things would have gotten done if she would have been there."

"Well, she was no trouble at all here, we had a lot of fun baking and I was happy to have her. It gets lonely around here and it was nice to have the company. She must take after her mother because that girl loves to bake and sure knows her way around the kitchen. Are you sure I can't get you something to drink?"

Nancy finished the last few kernels in her hand. "I suppose a little water would be nice if it isn't too much trouble."

"Not at all, I have bottles in the refrigerator so you can take it with you when you go." I lifted the blanket off of my lap and walked into the kitchen to get her a bottle. "Lily is in the bedroom if you want to get her. I could carry her downstairs for you if you'd like."

"You know what? I will take you up on that. I'm not that old, yet, but carrying her down all of those stairs in the dark and being so tired makes me a little nervous."

I handed Nancy her water as we walked down the hall to where Lily was sleeping. I slid the dimmer light switch up just enough to see how she was lying, making it easier to pick her up. I lifted her carefully, resting her tired head against my shoulder as she wrapped her arms around my neck. Back down in the lobby, Nancy slowly slipped each of Lily's arms into her jacket so she wouldn't get too cold on her drive back to the hotel.

I pointed into the kitchen. "I packaged a small bag of cookies for Lily to take home since she didn't get a chance to eat one of her creations tonight. Would you mind grabbing it for her, then she can have some tomorrow when she wakes up, with your permission of course."

Nancy walked into the kitchen and grabbed the cookies off the counter, placing them into her purse. "That was very sweet of you, I'm sure she'll appreciate that."

I walked towards the door as Nancy propped it open. "Are you coming to the festival tomorrow? I would love for you to stop by my booth if you can."

"I have to work the desk in the morning for a bit, but I think I can get Phil to cover it so I can sneak away. He owes me for tonight anyways." She laughed as she opened the back door of her car.

I leaned over, carefully placing Lily into her car seat. She didn't move a muscle as I pulled her arms through the straps, buckling her in. After checking to be sure it was secure, I quietly closed the car door, pressing up against it with my hip to be sure it was shut tight.

"You were right about moving her while she's asleep. I don't think she even flinched." I walked back around to the sidewalk. "Well you know where to find me tomorrow if you're able to come by."

"I will certainly try my best. If Lily doesn't sleep too late, I'll bring her with me. Brad will be by in the morning to pick her up, but one only knows what time, depending on the calls from the night."

Nancy waved over the car at me before climbing in. I stood on the sidewalk as they drove away, watching the car until the tail lights were too far away to see anymore. The wind gusted, sending a shiver up my spine as I walked back inside. Locking the door behind me, I turned the lights back off and went up to bed. I wasn't sure what to expect with the festival tomorrow and I needed all the rest I could get.

The sun shone on my face through the bedroom window, waking me up. I glanced over at my alarm clock and saw I still had ten more minutes until it was going to go off. I rolled onto my back, rubbing the sleep out of my eyes. I was pleasantly surprised to see the sun shining bright after the dark and dreary day yesterday. I was afraid of today being the same, not wanting to stand outside all day at the festival in the cold rain.

I pulled the covers back and swung my legs slowly off the bed, slipping my feet into my slippers I left on the floor the night before. I started a pot of coffee in the kitchen before heading into the shower, hoping the aroma would wake me up when I was finished. I had slept well all night, but still felt extra groggy this morning. I turned the shower faucet on all of the way until steam began to fill the room. I stood under the stream of water for the first five minutes to warm up. Reaching for the shampoo, I lathered my hair up, knowing I needed to look good for my interview later today. Just as I leaned back into the water to rinse, it shut off. Not even a trickle fell from the spout.

My hands were covered in suds and more were beginning to fall down my forehead straight for my eyes. Whipping the curtain open, I grabbed my towel and began patting my face and wiping my hands dry. Of all days for the water to stop working, it had to be today. I wrapped the towel around myself and walked to the sink—nothing. Walking down the hall, leaving a trail of wet footprints along the floor, I checked the water in the kitchen—nothing. If nothing else, at least I filled the coffee pot with water before my shower.

Reaching into the refrigerator, I pulled out four bottles of water and placed them next to the kitchen sink. Bending my head over the sink, I rinsed the shampoo out of my hair with them, thankful I had purchased a case of water the other day. When the suds were out, I went back to the bathroom to grab my conditioner, returning to the kitchen for more water bottles. After the longest hair washing in history and two trips back and forth to the bathroom, I finally finished my make-shift shower.

I finished getting ready, praying the entire time that I didn't lose power, too. The wet hair look was not at all what I had in mind for today. Pouring the largest cup of coffee I could find in the cupboard, I carried it downstairs and began wrapping all of the cookies Lily and I made together. I found a small cooler in the supply room and loaded as much as I could fit inside, grabbing an empty moving box for the remainder. The air outside was still pretty cool so I wasn't too worried about anything going bad. Hopefully it would sell quickly; I was being optimistic that it wouldn't be an issue.

I piled the cooler and box up near the back door and ran upstairs to turn off the coffee pot and refill my mug one more time. Sliding on my coat, hat, and scarf Nancy made me, I carried the boxes out to my car and placed them in the trunk.

When I arrived at the park, I found a parking spot near the side of the lake near most of the other vendors. People were carrying tables and chairs, two-wheeled carts full of their merchandise, craft items, and storage totes. Before unloading any of my things, I wanted to find where my booth was located, not wanting to be the idiot wandering around the park completely lost.

The information booth was located in the center of the park under a pavilion. With only three people in line, I made my way over there feeling it would be faster than walking up and down the countless number of rows of tables. When I got to the booth, it was refreshing to see a familiar face sitting behind the table.

"Good morning, Katie, how are you doing?"

"Hi Cora, I'm great, just helping out at the info booth this year. They didn't have anyone to work it so I volunteered. Do you have a booth here?"

I looked around wearily. "Yes—somewhere. I baked a bunch of cookies, cupcakes, and pies to sell here to help get my name out there and draw up a little business. I haven't opened, yet, but I made a bunch of flyers to hand out for my grand opening next month."

She ran her finger down the list, stopping at my name. "It looks like you are booth number fifty-six. Here is a map to help you find where that is located. The lake is right here so just hold the map this way and you should be able to find it fairly easy."

I grabbed the map and tucked it into my coat pocket. "Thank you for your help. I figured I better ask instead of wandering around like a crazy person."

"I don't blame you; it is a bit overwhelming if you've never been here before. Everyone in town comes out for it; either they have a booth or they're shopping. You should be able to meet most of the town today."

The thought of meeting so many people was overwhelming, but exciting. I wanted to let everyone know I was opening the old bakery and this seemed like an easy way to do so. I waved goodbye to Katie and headed back to my car for my cooler. Had I thought it through,

I would have brought a cart like everyone else. Not wanting to make two trips, I stacked the open box on top of the cooler, balancing them as I slammed the trunk shut.

The booths were set up in rows of ten. Counting them as I went along, I turned at row five and walked down towards the lake. The cold breeze was blowing a little harder down here, making it hard to cover the tables with the linens I brought. After three failed attempts at covering them all, I started over again, doing one at a time and placed the items on top before moving on to the next. If nothing else, it was sure to be an amusing sight for the surrounding vendors to watch.

I placed the pies together on the first table, grouping them together by flavor. I had more cookies than any other dessert so I filled those along the middle table, finishing with the brownies and cupcakes on the last. I grabbed a couple of large rocks that rest under the oak tree behind me to use as paper weights for my flyers.

Pushing the cooler underneath the table, I pulled up my chair and took a seat, already seeing customers roaming the area. There was a little bit of everything here: Christmas decorations, food, locally made maple syrup, mittens made of old sweaters, blankets. I wished I had brought a friend along to watch my booth so I could shop around a little.

As a crowd neared, I finally got my first customer. His name was Henry and he was walking around killing time while his wife did a little early Christmas shopping.

"Good morning, young lady. I spotted your goodies from across the park and my sweet tooth brought me right over to you."

"Good morning, what's your favorite dessert? I hope I have something that you like."

He browsed the tables, checking out each flavor of pie and cookie I had. "I'm a sucker for brownies and cookies," he said, walking back and forth between the two tables. "You know what I always say? When in doubt, buy both!" He held them in the air and laughed.

"I like the way you think." I placed two kinds of cookies and a large brownie into a bag, handing it over the table to him. "I am new to town and wanted to let everyone know that I'm opening up a bakery here in town. I have some flyers here on the table with the date and location if you would like to come by. There will be some free samples to try and it'll be a lot of fun."

He reached down to grab a flyer, placing the rock back down quickly so the others didn't blow away. "How could I say no to free samples? I will be there with bells on and I'll bring my wife along. She has a bunch of lady friends around town so I'll have her spread the word." He tucked the flyer into his bag, tipped his hat, and went on to find his wife.

Over the next hour, I had a lot of curious people stop by: some who wanted to check out an unfamiliar face, and others who were hungry for something sweet. Out of the corner of my eye, I saw a curly haired blonde with bright blue eyes running towards my booth. Lily was eagerly pulling Nancy's arm, trying to get her legs to move faster than they were able. As she got closer, she gave up dragging and let go, sprinting towards me and nearly knocking me down.

"Have you sold out of our cookies, yet?" she shouted, walking around the tables.

"Not all of them, but I have sold a lot. I think people like the shapes you picked out."

Nancy finally caught up, joining us behind the table. "Grandma let me have one of our cookies for breakfast," she said, jumping up and down.

"I can hardly tell," I laughed, looking at a worn out looking Nancy.

Nancy stood for a moment, admiring the tables. "Your booth

looks great. Have you had many people stop by, yet? This is one of the biggest events of the year in town, at least the biggest fall event."

"Yes, I've met a lot of nice people, and a few skeptics. But there is always a mix of both wherever you go." Nancy nodded, agreeing with me.

We chatted for a while, letting Lily eat another cookie. A few more customers stopped by and Lily persuaded them to buy some of her awesome homemade pumpkin shaped cookies. She was definitely a sales girl and made sure each person who stopped by took a flyer. Between customers, she ran around the tables, burning off the sugar she had just devoured.

"Look grandma, there's daddy!" she shouted, racing off into the crowd of people.

"Just a minute, Lily, grandma can't move as quickly as you can." She waved goodbye to me and made her way over to the police station's booth with Brad and Lily. They were handing out pencils, water bottles, and gold police badge stickers. Brad was in uniform and had taken the morning shift at the booth. Once Nancy caught up with them, she left Lily with Brad and came back to see me.

"He had volunteered for the first shift at the booth since we had Lily this morning. This way he can leave right after his shift and be done for the rest of the day. She wanted him to take her shopping around to some of the booths, but I'm sure they'll stop back after a while." She checked her watch on her wrist. "I'd love to stay longer, but I have to go relieve Phil at the desk. Let me know how the sales go later."

I watched Nancy as she disappeared into the crowd. The next couple of hours flew by, and I had to restock the cookie table three times. I had been given a lot of ideas for things to do at the bakery and a few special requests for some favorite items from the locals. Just when I assumed Brad and Lily had left the festival, I spotted her in the crowd, pulling her dad's arm just as she had Nancy's earlier. My stomach instantly filled with butterflies, getting worse each step he took closer. Part of me wanted to crouch under the table like a child and hide, but I knew that Lily would find me.

I walked to one of the side table facing away from them, straightening the brownies, acting like I had no idea they were coming over. Lily jumped up in front of me, trying to scare me like she does best.

"Well, hello again Miss Lily, have you come back for another cookie?" I hadn't made eye contact with Brad yet, focusing solely on her.

"If my daddy will let me have another," she said, using those powerful blue eyes of hers. "Please, daddy?" she begged, pulling down on his arm.

"I suppose, but you can only eat one. You can save the others for after dinner tonight." He reached into his back pocket, pulling out his wallet. "How much do I owe you?"

"No charge, she can just have them." I smiled at him, feeling like it must be the most awkward smile I had ever given.

"Are you sure? I'm happy to pay you for them."

"Its okay, daddy, she told me last night that I could have some today since I helped her bake them." Lily unwrapped one of the cookies and took a bite, jumping around in circles waving her hands through the air.

"Oh really, grandma didn't tell me you guys baked last night. Where did you do that?" He was looking down at Lily, knowing she would spill the beans if asked.

"Grandma took me to the bakery to make cookies with Cora. She even let me put all of the stickers on the bottom of the wrappers. Didn't I do a good job?" she asked, holding a package of cookies in the air.

He checked out the package and patted her on the head. I could tell he was upset and I wanted to disappear, wishing for a secret portal underneath my table. I knew he wasn't going to be happy having Lily there, but Nancy assured me that it wouldn't be an issue.

"I hope that's okay. Nancy offered to help me package everything last night and since she was watching Lily, she came along." The butterflies in my stomach had turned into giant pterodactyls. I swallowed hard, my mouth suddenly dry as a desert, trying not to vomit all over my booth from my nerves. I wasn't sure if it was the uniform, but he seemed more intimidating than before.

"I'll have to talk to Nancy about this later." With that, he was ready to move on to another booth.

I stood there completely frozen, unsure of what had just happened. I wasn't sure what to say and I didn't want to upset him anymore than he already was. He reached down and grabbed Lily's hand and told her it was time to go.

"Wait," she yelled at him. "I have to say goodbye to Cora first." She pulled her tiny hand out of his and ran behind the booth, grabbing around my leg and hugging it tight. "Thank you for letting me bake cookies with you last night. Can we do it again soon?" She stood there staring up at me, waiting for me to say yes.

I looked over at Brad, anger still across his face, maybe even more so now than a minute ago. His eyebrows pulled down, causing a wrinkle in between them.

"I'm so glad you had a fun time; I hope we can do it again soon, too. Have fun at the rest of the festival with your dad." I gave her one more hug and sent her over to Brad who was waiting on the other side of the table.

Just as he was turning to leave, a tall, slender brunette in a slicked back ponytail came walking towards us, notepad in hand. As she made eye contact with Brad, she picked up her pace, trying not to stumble in her heels.

"This is perfect, I was hoping to run into you here," she shouted as she closed in on him. "I'm doing an interview with Cora about the new bakery and I thought I would get a few words from you since you used to own it." She stood very close to him, touching his bicep.

He glared down at her hand before looking up at her, backing away. "No, thank you." Simply stated, but as reporters tend to be, she wasn't going to take no for an answer.

"Well tell me this: are you happy about seeing the bakery reopen? Do you think your wife would have wanted this? Are you seeing anybody?" She smoothed her hair and ran her hand down her pantsuit, staring at him intensely as her pen tip pushed against her notepad.

"If you don't mind, my daughter would like to go and look around the festival. Have a nice day." With that, he grabbed Lily's hand and walked off into the crowd, never looking back.

As soon as they were out of sight, I dropped my shoulders and released the huge breath I was holding. I grabbed for my chair for support, suddenly dizzy and needing to sit down. Unscrewing the top of my water bottle, I drank half of it without even a breath. Breathing in a few nice slow breaths through my nose, I started to come back around again.

The reporter stood there staring at me, taking notes on her notepad. "Do you know Brad Harper? There seemed to be a bit of tension between you both, did something happen that I missed?"

She had no filter and dug her nose as deep as she could into my business. "I thought you wanted to ask questions about the bakery? When you are ready, please ask me any questions you have prepared." I stood back up, not wanting to be looked down upon.

"Tell me a little bit about yourself. Where you're from, why you came to town, your reason for opening up the bakery, you know those types of things." She pulled up a chair and sat, crossing her legs to fashion a table to rest her notepad on.

For the next thirty minutes, I told her as much as I was comfortable sharing, leaving Chris out of it completely. Knowing she would take my answers and word them any way she wanted, I tried to sensor all of what I told her. I kept my answers short and a little vague when it came to my past and what brought me here, focusing more on the bakery and wanting to generate a business there. She took a couple photos of me at my booth and several close ups of what I had baked on the table. I gave her a flyer with all of the information about the grand opening on it and she promised she would add that to the bottom of the article.

"I think I have all that I need so I will let you get back to doing whatever it is you do at these types of things. I will get started on this right away and it should be in tomorrow's paper." She stood from her chair, stumbling a bit on a giant tree root coming out of the ground, catching herself on the edge of the table.

"I didn't realize it would be out so soon. I look forward to seeing it." I shook her hand and sent her on her way. The last hour of the festival was slow; I only sold a couple more things from the table. I walked around straightening what I had left, moving most of it to the front table. I wandered over to a few of the neighboring booths to see what they were selling; purchasing a pair of knit mittens from one, and a bottle of maple syrup from another. The lady who was selling the mittens handed me a business card and told me where to find her yarn shop located down the street from the bakery and invited me to come by and check out the classes she offered. After Katie tried to teach me how to crochet at craft night, I told her that it would probably be a good idea for me to learn the basics.

I began packing up my booth as the festival came to an end. A few customers walked the area, most just passing through on their way down to the lake. A couple of officers walked by, heading to their booth to pack it up. My mind immediately went back to Brad. I couldn't get his face out of my mind; it was a face of anger and disappointment. Shaking my head, I packed the remaining cookies back into the cooler and folded my linens, placing them inside of the empty box.

I was bringing home far less than I came with, making it a lot easier to carry back to the car. Overall, the day went well and almost all of my flyers had been taken. I tucked the rest along side the linens in the box, hoping they wouldn't blow away. The wind had died down a bit since this morning, but it still blew through the trees, catching several leaves in the box I was carrying as they fell from above.

I placed the box and cooler into my trunk and hopped inside the car, turning up the heat. The parking lot was very busy with people loading up to leave. I sat in my car nearly five minutes before attempting to back up. When it finally looked clear, I backed out quickly and made my way back home.

Chapter Thirteen

A construction crew was working along the sidewalk down from the bakery with the water company as I drove by. After removing a section of concrete, they repaired the water pipe after a leak that caused my water to be shut off earlier this morning. Slowing down as I passed I saw the water company packing up their truck while the construction workers scooped shovels full of dirt back into the hole, their breath making small clouds above their heads.

The outside light hanging above the back door gave off a golden glow as I pulled into the alley. The sun was beginning to set and the streetlights in the area began to flicker on. I parked in my assigned spot and popped the trunk, once again grabbing the box and cooler. I placed them on the center counter in the kitchen, emptying out all of the cookies that didn't sell. The silence was deafening and my mind was in overdrive, thinking again how Brad left earlier. I walked over to the radio and turned it on, praying that it already had presets.

I sat down in the chair left behind from last night, resting my face into my palms. I knew he would be upset about Lily being here. Out of all the times, why did I choose then to doubt my gut? I knew it was usually right, but I trusted Nancy instead.

As the commercial break ended, a familiar voice filled the air in the kitchen. "Good evening and thank you for joining us. You are listening to Starting Over with Faith. I am Faith, let's take our next caller."

I sat up straight in my chair, remembering her show from my first night in town. She was a big part of the signs that got me here, making me want to stick around and see what would happen. Truly reaching for another sign, I ran over to the radio and turned up the volume.

"Our next caller is Rita. Please tell us your story." Faith paused, letting Rita take over the air.

"Well, I'm having some trouble starting over. I have always lived my life very safe. I've stuck to the same daily routine, never straying too far from it unless absolutely necessary. Some people call it boring, but for me it's comfortable."

"There is nothing wrong with having routines," Faith chimed in.

"Recently, my company downsized and I was laid off. Now, I have nothing to wake up for in the morning and my routine is gone. I'm completely thrown off by this and don't know how to get passed it. Looking for a new job wasn't part of my day and I am way out of my comfort zone in applying for new ones that I know won't be the same as what I had."

Silence filled the air as Rita waited for the wise words of Faith to fill it. "It sounds like you need to take a step out of your comfort zone, even just a half of a step to start with. Take your first risk and to see where it takes you. Have you followed your routine your whole life?"

"For as long as I can remember. I have been at this job for so many years, I can't even remember what I did before I had it; so long that I can't turn it off overnight."

"Here is what I want you to do. Tomorrow when you wake up, I want you to take a chance and apply for two jobs that you qualify for, but maybe wouldn't normally apply for. You may end up getting one of those jobs and loving it. Without having taken the risk to apply, you would never know or see where it can take you. And then the next day, find another small risk to take, even if it is going to a new place you have never been to before. Life is all about taking risks and in doing so; it could lead you to places you could have never imagined."

The last line Faith spoke hit me hard and it was all I could remember her saying. "Life is about taking risks." I was terrible at taking risks normally, but ever since I came to town, that's all I've been doing. If I didn't take the risk in calling Alice, I would have never known this place was for sale and purchased it. If I would never have brought Lily to the bakery last night, she may not have found her love for baking. Something suddenly sparked inside of me.

I walked back over to the radio and turned it off. I found a paper bag that was in the supply closet and filled it with the leftover cookies. Sliding my coat back on, I grabbed my keys off of the counter and was out the door. Faith's voice kept repeating in my head and it was time to take another risk and see where it took me.

Ten minutes later, I arrived in front of the police station. The front parking lot was practically empty as most of the squad cars were parked in the back. I wasn't sure what vehicle Brad drove outside of work so I couldn't tell if he was on duty or not. All I was certain of was that he worked nights and it was now getting dark. I grabbed the bag of cookies off the passenger seat and walked up the sidewalk to the main entrance.

The lights were dim in the lobby, only a few were on behind the desk where an officer was working at a computer. He sat up high in his chair behind a thick pained window. It seemed a bit much for this small of a town, but I suppose it was better to be safe than sorry. As I approached him, I saw that he was on the phone so I stood back and waited patiently for him to finish, praying it didn't take too long or I was afraid I would lose my nerve and walk right back out the front door.

After five minutes and several paces around the room, he hung up with the caller. "Good evening, ma'am. What can I help you with this evening?" His name badge read P. Sheppard and he was very polite.

"Hello officer, I don't mean to bother you, but I was wondering if Brad Harper was on duty tonight." I stood there waiting as he checked his sheet of paper.

"It looks like he is working tonight, but is out on the street. Would you like me to radio him and have him come back here?"

"NO!" I blurted out. I took a deep breath. "I'm sorry, no," I said again more calmly. "It's nothing important. I just bought the bakery here in town and I had some leftover cookies from the fall festival today and thought you guys would like to have them." I held the bag up over the counter so he could see them through the window.

Officer Sheppard smiled. "We never turn down free food around here, especially if it is homemade. There are some nights that we get so busy we don't get to stop and eat so it's nice when there are goodies lying around in the kitchen. Let me call him in quick so he knows who brought them by."

"That really isn't necessary—." Before I could finish my sentence, he already had his thumb on his radio calling Brad. I felt my cheeks begin to get warm. The nerve and determination I had when I arrived was quickly fading into a million butterflies again.

"He wasn't busy with any calls so he said he would be here in a few minutes. I think he's just down the street. You can have a seat over there if you want while you wait."

I smiled and nodded, not able to get a word out. I walked over and sat in one of the chairs near a small table that faced the front window, hoping to be able to see him pull up and prepare myself before he came inside. My nerves were taking over my body, shifting my weight from one side to the other, not able to control my movements.

A television airing the local news station was on across the lobby. I sat back in my chair as still as I could, reading the closed captions that ran along the bottom of the screen.

After checking my watch three times in less than four minutes, I saw a squad car pull up along side my car and a silhouette of a man climb out of the front seat. I took several deep breaths to try and control my nerves, sitting up straight and trying to keep still. It took all that I had not to leave the bag of cookies on the chair and run right out of the door.

He reached for the door handle, pulling it open and paused once he saw me sitting there. He cleared his throat twice as he walked over to me, and I realized his nerves may have kicked in as well.

"What are you doing here?" he asked bluntly.

I wiped the sweat from my palms across the tops of my legs before standing up. "I just wanted to bring by some of the cookies that didn't sell at the festival today and see if I could talk to you for a moment. I thought you guys could use a treat to help get you through your shift tonight." There, I had gotten out my reason for coming without stuttering or passing out.

Brad stood there for a moment looking at me, saying nothing. It felt like an eternity waiting for his response, wondering if I had something on my face that he was staring at.

"Thanks," he finally said, plain and simple.

"I was hoping to talk to you for a minute if you have a few to spare." My voice was a little shakier than it was before, trying my best to hold it together.

"I guess so. Follow me and I'll show you where you can put the cookies."

I followed him through two secure doors and up a flight of stairs to their break room. No one else was in sight so we wouldn't be interrupted.

I stood in front of him, taking a long deep breath before speaking. "I wanted to apologize again for last night. I had second thoughts about bringing Lily to the bakery. I thought you might get upset about it, but Nancy kept assuring me that it was fine and not to worry." I blurted it out in nearly one long sentence, barely pausing in between.

Again, Brad stood there looking at me, face expressionless. He was definitely in the top five on my list of people that I couldn't read. After no reaction, I continued.

"I want to assure you that it will never happen again. I promise I won't ask Nancy to come by when she's watching her. I know it must have been hard hearing that your daughter was in your wife's old bakery. She didn't say she remembered ever being there so I didn't think it was that big of a deal. She had so much fun baking." He still had no expression on his face. "I'm so sorry." I stood there with my head down, staring at my feet.

After more silence, I raised my head back up to see if he was going to say anything before I ran out of the room. When I looked up at him, he had a half smile on his face; I was confused.

"It's alright; I should be the one apologizing for the way I acted today. I'll admit, at first I was furious that my mom would allow Lily to go there knowing I had never been able to go back inside, even how hard it was for me to simply drive by the building. After confronting her about it, she explained to me how much fun Lily had there baking with you. She filled me in on the flood at the hotel and why she left her there longer than planned." His face began to soften the more he went on. "And then, after leaving the hotel, all I heard about the rest of the afternoon was stories about baking cookies, picking out cookie cutters, and being able to crack the eggs on the bowl and reminding me that I never let her."

I stood there in a state of shock, not thinking this conversation would have gone this way at all.

"I could tell how much fun she had with you. The way her eyes lit up when she talked about baking reminded me so much of how her mother's did when she created a new recipe for the bakery. I looked at her and all I could see was Hope. I think I finally realized that it wasn't a bad thing, and my mom helped me to see that."

I felt my throat tighten a little. I had no idea that Lily enjoyed it so much. I knew that I had, but to hear it from him that she loved every minute of it and that she reminded him of his wife was unexpected.

"I guess what I'm trying to say is thank you." The other half of his smile appeared. The way he talked about Lily made my heart melt.

"I don't know what to say." I was literally speechless.

"You can say that you will let Lily come by again and bake with you. I think she really wants to and I can see the special connection she's made with you."

I wiped my finger along the bottom of my eye, trying to be discreet. "Of course, I would love to. Whenever she wants to come by she's more than welcome to. You have an amazing little girl on your hands. She is truly a gift." I placed the bag of cookies on the table and walked towards the doorway.

"Thank you, she really is. I'll show you out," he said, passing me in the doorway. He buzzed me back through the secured doors and waved to Officer Sheppard as we passed.

He held the front door open for me as we made our way to the parking lot. "Thank you for bringing the cookies by, I'm sure they'll be gone before I get back inside. Officer Sheppard is probably already half way upstairs." We both laughed.

"The next time I bake a batch, I'll be sure to send them your way." I walked passed him on the sidewalk, stepping down from the curb to my car.

He stepped down from the curb and stood in front of me. "I would like that," he said, leaning in and kissing me on the cheek. "Be safe driving home." He opened my car door, closing it after I climbed inside.

I sat there for a moment, wondering if that really just happened. I raised my hand up and touched my cheek, the dampness of his lips still there. It had just happened.

Chapter Fourteen

The next morning, Brad showed up early to the hotel to pick Lily up. He had a hard time falling asleep after his shift, thinking about what had happened the night before. He woke before his alarm and couldn't fall back to sleep. Nancy was already at the front desk hard at work when he walked through the door. The breakfast room had a few early risers but was still pretty quiet.

"You're here awfully early. I don't think Lily is even awake yet," she said, straightening some papers on the counter.

"That's alright, I couldn't sleep so I thought I would come over and grab a cup of coffee and something to eat if you don't mind."

"No, not at all. In fact, I'll join you." Nancy placed the bell up on top of the desk in case somebody needed her and followed Brad into the breakfast area.

He placed his keys on one of the tables and walked straight over to the coffee pot and poured a cup, filling it as close to the top as he could. He reached into the donut case, pulling out a chocolate long john and went back to the table. Nancy filled a cup with coffee and sat down across from him.

"You never have problems sleeping, at least not lately anyways. Is something bothering you?" Her eyes squinted toward him, trying to figure out what he was thinking like she did when he was a little boy. He was rarely able to hide anything from her. Blowing the steam off of her coffee, she took a cautious sip.

Brad took a bite of donut before answering, trying to stall. He swallowed the donut and washed it down with a little coffee.

"Nothing is wrong, really. I just have some things on my mind that I'm not sure what to do about. Every time I close my eyes to try and sleep, I can't stop thinking about it. It's not a big deal; it's just on my mind, that's all." He took another bite of his donut, breaking eye contact with Nancy.

"You aren't making sense. Is it about work? Is it something I can help you figure out?" She looked at him as he stared at the table. She was determined to get it out of him.

"No, work is going fine for once. Not too much goes on at night in this town so it's been pretty low key lately."

Nancy looked at him again, still avoiding her eye contact. "Is it about Lily? Do you need money?"

Brad shook his head and continued to eat the rest of his donut. He wanted to tell her about what happened last night, but he wasn't sure how she would feel about it, doubting that he should be having feelings for another woman. He loved his wife for so long; this was all new territory for him. It was a place he never thought of being in again and it was scary, to say the least.

He fumbled with his keys on the table, getting the nerve to spit it out. "So here's the thing; I got really upset at Cora at the festival about having Lily at the bakery, but you knew that already. But then, when I saw her with Lily and heard Lily talk about her all day and how much fun she had while she was there, I felt so guilty about how I treated her. I know she didn't mean any harm but I went to the defensive thinking she was over stepping with Lily." He stood up from the table and grabbed another donut.

"I understand that; did you apologize to her for the way you acted?"

"I was going to go and find her, but she beat me to it. She came by the station late last night with a bag of cookies for us, and before I could apologize to her, she apologized to me." He sat there looking at his mother, begging her for advice with his eyes.

"That was very kind of her, but she did nothing wrong. Bringing Lily to the bakery the other night was my idea, not hers." Nancy saw something in him that she hadn't seen in a really long time.

"I didn't know that at the time. I told her that I saw how much Lily liked her and loved baking with her and told her she could come by any time she wanted. She seems to have such a big heart, especially for my daughter. And then—"

Nancy sat straight up in her chair, secretly hoping she knew where this story was headed, but wanted to hear him say it. "And then what?"

"And then I walked her out to her car and I kissed her."

Nancy's face lit up, trying with all she had not to leap out of her chair with excitement, trying to contain her smile.

"So, was it a friendly kiss on the cheek or something more?"

Brad's face began to flush. He was suddenly aware of what he was telling his mother, not sure how much more he wanted to say. "It was on the cheek, but I'm not sure yet if it was more than a friendly gesture. I don't even know if I should be having these feelings for somebody. I've only loved one person in my life and when I lost her, I shut off that part of my heart. My daughter is my world now and I'm not sure it would ever be fair to her to replace her mother, ever."

Nancy thought about what he said for a moment. "But would it be fair to her to deny her a mother figure for the rest of her life? Just because you find another person to share your life with doesn't mean that you will be replacing Hope. She will always be Lily's mother and will always be a part of our lives."

Deep down, Brad knew she was right; he just needed to hear it from someone close to him. When he lost Hope, Lily was too young to remember her or anything about the bakery. After making the decision to sell the building, he never found it necessary to tell her about it. He felt as though it was a part of his past that he needed to let go of, when in reality, it was something that he maybe should have been fighting to hang onto.

"You're right, as you always are. I'm not sure how I feel for her right now, but whatever it is, it's the first time I've felt anything like this in a very long time. I feel myself being drawn to her; maybe its seeing her with Lily, maybe it's because she bought the bakery. Whatever it is, I think I need to allow myself to figure it out, to give it a chance." He finished the last of his coffee and tossed it into the trash can near the door.

Nancy stood up and walked over to him, placing her arms around him, embracing him tight. "Follow your heart, son. I think it may be trying to tell you something."

Later that day while out running errands with Lily, Brad couldn't stop thinking about what Nancy said to him. *Listen to your heart.* It was something Hope would have said as she was a true believer in signs. He was the complete opposite when he viewed life, but she always put her heart out there and let it lead her in the right direction. Perhaps it was her heart that led her to him, and now it was time to let his heart lead him to where he was supposed to go; to find those signs she always said were out there instead of resisting the thought of them.

Brad grabbed Lily's hand, wrapping it completely into his, and walked into the grocery store with a short list of items they needed at home. He lifted her into the front of the shopping cart, helping her snap the buckle.

"Can I hold the list, daddy?" she asked.

"Sure, read me the first thing."

Lily looked down at the list in her hand. "Ugh, I can't read yet, silly," she said laughing. Staring back down at it and concentrating, she tried to figure out what the first thing on the list said as they walked passed the checkout registers. "Cora!" she shouted.

Brad stopped pushing the cart and looked around. "Wait, I didn't put her on the list."

"No, daddy, look at that newspaper over there. Cora is on the front of it." Lily was pointing to a stack of newspapers near one of the checkout lines, nearly leaping out of the cart.

Brad walked over to it and picked up a copy. Lily almost instantly grabbed it out of his hands. "Do we need to add this to our list?" he asked.

"Yes please, can I have it to keep in my room?" she asked, hugging the newspaper tight.

"Sure, you can have it after daddy gets to read the story about her. How does that sound?" Lily smiled back at him, still hugging the newspaper. As Brad continued pushing the cart, he stopped in his tracks. Having never given in to signs before, he was beginning to believe maybe they were out there all around him. Was this the first sign he had been given?

"I think you said you were putting bread on the list," Lily reminded him, bringing him back. "There's some bread over there," Lily shouted, pointing to the next aisle.

He pushed the cart over, getting as close to the shelf as he could. Leaning over, Lily grabbed a loaf off of the shelf and placed it into the back of the cart.

"Perfect, what's next on the list?" he asked.

"I can't read, remember?" She took another look at the list, concentrating even harder this time. Suddenly she gasped, "Cora!"

"I thought I already told you she isn't on the list." He grabbed the list from her, reading the next item on it.

"No daddy, Cora is over there; for real this time," she said, pointing toward the milk coolers. "Can we go over and say hi? Please, pretty please?"

He looked down at her, pressing down on her shoulders to keep her from leaping out of the cart. "I'll make a deal with you; you tell me what the next thing on the list says and we will go over and say hello."

"Daddy—"

"Alright, I suppose we can go over and say hello if you please sit down so you don't fall out of the cart."

Lily sat down quickly as Brad walked towards the dairy section. He began mentally preparing himself for what he was going to say. He hadn't seen me since I came by with the cookies and he needed another minute to figure it out. Just as he was running possible lines through his head, Lily shouted out my name, causing several other shoppers to stop and stare.

I turned around quickly to find Lily waving her arms through the air. I closed the cooler door and walked over to meet them. "Well, hello Miss Lily, how are you doing today? Helping daddy buy some groceries?" I shot a quick smile towards Brad and then turned my attention back to Lily, unsure of what to say to him.

"Yep, I get to hold the list and if it's not too high, he even lets me grab it off the shelf." She spoke with such excitement, like grocery shopping was the highlight of her day.

I looked back towards Brad. "That is very nice of you to let her help. I wish I had a helper with me to carry this heavy carton of milk."

Lily raised her hand up in the air. "I could be your helper. Tell her, daddy; tell her how good of a helper I am." She looked up at him with those eyes.

"The best grocery helper in the whole world," he said, Lily smiled and sat back down in her seat.

I switched my basket to my other arm, giving the other a break from the weight of the milk. "Well, if it's okay with your daddy, maybe you can be my helper next time I come shopping for cookie supplies." We both looked over at Brad at the same time.

Brad looked at me, then at Lily, then back to me. He tried to hold his serious face, but it wasn't working for him today. "I think that's a wonderful idea. Lily knows this store very well and can help you find anything you need."

"Yes," Lily cheered to herself quietly.

I looked into the back of their cart. "It looks like you must have just gotten here since you only have one thing in your cart, so I better let you get back to your shopping. I have a lot of baking to do anyways to get ready for the grand opening in a couple of weeks." I held out my basket to show Lily all of the milk, butter, and eggs I had in there, switching arms again.

"No, we have two things in our cart," she stated, holding out the newspaper with the article about the bakery.

I nodded, looking to Brad to see what he thought. "I guess you do, maybe I should pick one up on my way out and see how the story turned out."

"You should, it has your face on it. Daddy said I could keep it in my room after he reads about you. When can I come and help you bake again?" It was funny to me how she could go from one subject to another so quickly.

I looked over to Brad who was blushing. "I just wanted to take a quick look at it, that's all."

"Well, I will either let your daddy or grandma know the next time

I am ready to bake and we will set up a date."

"Please do, I would love to bring her by." Brad cleared his throat, thankful the article conversation had moved on. "Speaking of dates, I was wondering if you had any plans later this evening. I was thinking about going across the lake to the next town for dinner if you wanted to join me." He took a deep breath after saying it all in one sentence.

I looked at him, tilting my head to the side. "I guess I could go with, I don't have anything else going on. I should be finished with my baking by dinner time. Do you have a boat or will we be driving?"

Brad look at me strangely. "Driving; have you felt how cold it is out there today?"

We both laughed. "I wasn't sure since you said across the lake; to me that means in a boat."

"In the summer, yes. This time of year, not a chance. I can pick you up around six if that works?"

I glanced at my wrist, checking my watch. "Six sounds perfect." I set my basket down onto the floor and pulled a piece of scratch paper out of my purse, writing my phone number down on it. "Here is my number, just call or text when you're on your way."

He glanced at the paper and folded it in half, tucking it into his shirt pocket. "I will do that, see you later."

"I'm looking forward to it," I replied, waving to Lily as Brad pushed the cart down the next aisle.

Just before five o'clock, I finished washing the last dish and packaged up everything I had baked. I finished the day with six dozen cookies, four pies, and three pans of brownies. I dried my hands on the towel and wiped the water drops around the sink and double checked that the oven was off before turning off the kitchen lights. I had finished in enough time to give myself an hour to freshen up for my date. As I turned the last light off in the front, there was a knock at the front door.

Checking my watch to be sure it hadn't stopped, it said five o'clock. I wasn't expecting Brad for another hour and Nancy hadn't mentioned that she was going to be stopping by. Living in a small town should be relatively safe, but it still made me nervous as I walked towards the door, the windows still covered in drapes and the sun was almost down. I pulled back the window covering a tiny bit at the edge, trying to see who was out there before opening the door.

As I pulled it open just enough to sneak a peek out without them noticing, I saw an older man and woman standing on the other side. They looked harmless, though neither of them was smiling. I turned the lock on the deadbolt, slowly turning the handle, and opened the door.

"Hi, can I help you with something?" I only opened the door part of the way, just enough to stand sideways in it, protecting the entrance a little.

They looked me up and down and then to each other, deciding who would do the speaking. "Are you the owner of this building?" the man asked, a very serious look across his face.

He intimidated me at first, but I figured I would give him the benefit of the doubt. "Yes, I am, is there something wrong?" I stared back at her, standing there silent on the sidewalk.

"There might be; can we come inside and talk to you for a minute? It's freezing out here and it shouldn't take long."

Reluctantly, I opened the door, motioning them both inside. I closed the door behind them, leaving it unlocked in case I needed to make a run for it. "Please, have a seat. I'll go and turn the lights back on." I walked over to the switch and the room filled with light.

They both pulled out a chair and sat down at the table. She had been holding tight to a manila envelope the whole time, still grasping it as she sat.

"What seems to be the matter?" I wasn't sure if I should pull up a chair and sit with them or keep my distance, standing a ways back.

The man cleared his throat as the woman sat quiet, looking around the room. "I understand you recently purchased this building."

I thought we had already established that at the door, but I went along with it. "Yes, I purchased the building, but I haven't opened for business just yet." I wasn't sure what he was getting at and didn't want to give up too much information.

"Well, the building may not have been available to sell." He reached for the envelope the woman had been griping, opening it up and pulling out a stack of paperwork.

"I'm not sure I understand." I walked closer to the table to see what the papers were that he had.

"Well, this building was left behind by a woman named Hope Harper. Are you aware of that?"

I nodded my head, wondering where this was going.

"Well, when Hope passed away, she left the building to three people: Brad, me, and my wife. Our daughter's wishes were that we decide together how to proceed with the bakery and a possible sale of the property." He paused to look at me and make sure I was following along. "Basically, Brad sold the bakery without telling us."

It was now beginning to make sense, these were her parents. Her mother looked very uncomfortable to be here; sure she hadn't been since she lost Hope. I still wasn't quite sure what he was saying, but I was starting to feel nervous.

"What exactly are you getting at?" I crossed my arms and walked a little closer to the table.

"Well, this building wasn't his alone to sell and we didn't give our permission to do so. We had no intention of selling the bakery and we want it back." He slid the papers across the table for me to take a closer look at.

I began to feel lightheaded hearing what he just said and felt I needed to sit down. I pulled up a chair and looked over the papers. "I'm sorry, but the building isn't for sale. I purchased it legally and I plan to open in a couple of weeks."

"We thought you might say that so we are prepared to buy you out. Name your price and we will buy the building from you and you can buy another vacant building in town." He reached into his dress coat pocket, pulling out his checkbook and placed it on the table.

"I'm very sorry this happened to you, but I am not selling the bakery back to you. I don't know what else you want me to tell you, but the answer is no. This is my home now and I am not leaving it." I stood back up from the table, hoping to appear more firm with them.

He looked at his wife and they both nodded at each other. "Then you leave us no choice. You will be hearing from our lawyer in a few days. We will not give up without a fight." He placed his papers back into the envelope and they stood from their chairs.

"Neither will I," I said, showing them to the door. I slammed it hard behind them, locked the deadbolt and stomped across the room. I'm not an angry person, but the way they just blew in here making demands pushed me over the edge. I'm finally living my dream and I refuse to let a couple of strangers come in and ruin that for me.

Chapter Fifteen

Completely flustered and feeling out of control, I knew there was only one person I could call to help me make sense of everything that just happened. I walked into the kitchen and grabbed my cell phone, pacing the room as it rang.

"Hello?" Nancy said on the other end.

"Hi Nancy, I'm sorry to bother you, but I wasn't sure who else to call. Something strange just happened and I am so confused. Do you have a minute to talk?" I paused at the counter, leaning my elbows on it as I spoke.

"It must be one of those days, something strange happened to me earlier, too. What is going on?" She sounded a little flustered herself, rustling papers in the background.

"I had a couple of visitors a little while ago and it has completely thrown me for a loop. Hope's parents stopped by here very upset that the bakery was sold and basically threatened me if I didn't sell it back to them. What should I do?" I began to pace the room again, waiting for her response.

"I was afraid you were going to say something like that. I checked them in to the hotel a few hours ago. It threw me as well, not at all who I would have expected to come walking through my doors. What did you say to them?"

I paused again, leaning my back against the refrigerator, trying to keep myself from opening it up and stress eating an entire tray of cookies. "They told me Brad should never have sold the building without their consent and if I didn't sell it back, they were going to seek out a lawyer and fight me for it. I'm usually more of a pushover, but something sparked inside of me and I stuck up for myself and fought back. I told them no and asked them to leave, that I would not give up without a fight." I was glad no one could see inside the bakery or they would think I was a crazy person with all of the hand gestures I had flying around.

Nancy sighed. "I'm sorry that happened. I'm sure there is a lot more to the story and we will just have to wait and see what it is. They haven't been back here since we lost Hope; why they chose to come now, I'm not sure. Have you told Brad about any of this?"

"No, you were the first person I called after I calmed down a bit. He will be here any minute to pick me up for dinner. Should I talk to him about it?"

"I don't think that's a good idea. I think you two should go out and enjoy your night, let me worry about them. I'll see if I can find out why they're here and what they're trying to pull."

I worried a little taking her advice again after what had happened with Lily and bringing her to the bakery the other day. But in the end, it all worked out just fine so I agreed. My second line on my phone began to ring.

"I think Brad is here to pick me up; I won't mention it to him until I hear from you later. Thank you for listening." So much for an easy transition into my new life.

I hung up her call and answered Brad's, telling me that he was just down the street and would be here any minute. I raced upstairs to grab my purse, apply some lipstick, and make sure my hair wasn't too disheveled after my crazy kitchen pacing. Peeking out the front window, I saw his car pull up in front of the bakery and went downstairs to meet him.

As I opened the front door, Brad was standing behind his car on the sidewalk. "Would you like to come in for a minute?" I wasn't sure he would say yes, but thought I would extend the offer anyway.

He looked the building up and down, an uneasy look on his face. "Maybe later; if we get to the restaurant too late it will be hard to get a table." He knew that it wasn't a complete lie, but he also left out the truth of why he really wasn't comfortable going inside. A part of him wondered if it still looked the same, or how he would feel walking through those doors again. This night was about getting to know me better and he didn't want to add missing Hope even more than he already was into the mix of emotions he was feeling. One day he would go inside, but today didn't feel like the day.

"Oh, okay. Let me just lock up and I'm ready to go." I turned the lock on the front door, tucking my keys into my purse. He walked out from behind the car and opened my door for me, helping me inside.

The view was beautiful on the drive to the restaurant. The sky was mostly dark now, but the glowing lights along the lake were breathtaking. I made a mental note of the way he took there so I could come back and drive it again during daylight. The trees along the lakeside had lost most of their leaves, giving a great view of the cabins along the shoreline. The night sky was clear, filled with bright shining stars and the moon reflecting off the water, lighting up the lake with its glow.

The restaurant was about half full when we walked in. I followed Brad as he walked over to the hostess to get a seat. After a short wait, we were brought to a table along the wall, the window facing the lake. We both ordered a tall beer on a happy hour special; he seemed impressed with my beverage of choice. An antler chandelier hung overhead, giving off a dim reddish light for an evening feel. Each outer wall had a large brick fireplace, crackling and sending tiny ambers sparks up in the flames.

Brad held up his glass. "To getting to know each other better," he toasted, tapping our glasses together.

"Cheers to that," I said, taking another sip.

The waitress came by a few minutes later to take our order, and we both ordered the house special: a filet, loaded baked potato, and a house salad. He seemed to be pleasantly surprised by me, like I was not at all how he would have expected me to be. He thought it would be more awkward and that I would order a salad and a glass of wine. He did not expect beer and steak to come out of my mouth when I ordered.

There was so much I wanted to know about him, so many questions I had been storing up in my head for weeks now, but was unsure of where to start. Having lived in Maple Falls his whole life, there was so much he could tell me about the town, but I wanted to dig deeper into who he was. Not wanting to get too serious too quickly, I picked a lighter topic.

"Have you always wanted to be a police officer?"

Brad set his beer back onto the table, sprinkling the salt shaker over the top of his napkin to prevent it from sticking to the bottom of his mug. "For as long as I can remember. I used to play with police cars all the time when I was a little boy. I would set up different scenes with my action figures and pretend they were robbing a bank, or had a car chase and they needed help. Most of my high speed chases took place in the kitchen and my mom wasn't very fond of tripping on them after I forgot to pick them up."

I sat there watching his facial expressions and his face light up as he talked about his childhood. He was very animated when he spoke, hand gestures and all.

"I love that you knew what you wanted to be at such a young age. You must be an amazing officer having such a passion for it for all of these years."

"It has its moments, but for the most part I really enjoy what I do. What about you, have you always wanted to be a baker or is it just something you wanted to try in this new life of yours?" He smiled at me jokingly.

"Similar to your story, minus the high speed chases of course. When I was little, my grandmother used to watch me a lot and she would let me help out in the kitchen. We would bake cakes together, cookies, pies, you name it. When we had a shelf full of goodies in the refrigerator, we would pack it all up and donate them to the local food shelf. During the holidays, we would bring some to the local businesses around town, too: the police station, fire station, and the library. I rarely remember being in any other room at her house."

Brad nodded with enjoyment.

"Before I moved, I worked in a bakery for years, but never had the opportunity to bake what I wanted. It was all their recipes and they decided what I made. I wanted the chance to make those decisions for myself so here I am."

"I think Hope was similar to you in that way. She had such a passion for baking, but I could only eat so many sweets at home before I was going to be overweight. I would bring as much as I could to work with me, but there was always something waiting at home on the counter that just came out of the oven. After a while, some of her friends and I encouraged her to look into opening a bakery in town. We didn't have one here or in any of the surrounding towns, so she did." He laughed at the memory, slowly opening up about Hope to me.

"I can totally relate to that. It is that way with any hobby; you love to make all kinds of things, but are not sure what to do with all of the finished products. My grandmother used to make quilts when she wasn't in the kitchen. She would have loved to keep them all, but I'm pretty sure my grandpa would have moved out. She ended up donating them to the children's hospital throughout the year, making extras during the fall and winter. She never wanted money for her creations; she just wanted somebody to enjoy them as much as she did making them."

Our food arrived at the table and we both started with our salads, picking up the side of dressing at the exact same time.

"Your grandmother sounds like a wonderful person," he said, pouring the dressing around his plate.

I nodded, chewing my first bite, not wanting to talk with my mouth full. "She really was. I miss her every day." I lowered my head, taking another bite.

We continued our conversation over dinner, sharing stories about how we grew up, our past relationships, why mine ended and a little more about what happened to Hope. He opened up about Lily and the hopes and fears he had for her.

"After I found out about Lily baking with you, after the anger part passed, I finally realized that she has the passion for baking like her mother did. I am so thankful she got that from her, even though she isn't fully aware of where it came from yet. I know that Hope's plan was to eventually run the bakery with Lily and leave it to her when she was ready to retire, teaching her everything she knew along the way."

The waitress came by and took our plates, leaving the tab in the center of the table.

"It was one of the hardest decisions I had to make selling the bakery. I felt like I was letting Hope down by not giving Lily the opportunity to be there, but I knew nothing about baking. I was trying to figure out how to raise a baby on my own, not wanting to take on learning how to bake on top of that. My mom offered to help out along with the staff we had working there, but it got to be too much." He took the last drink of his beer, setting the empty glass off to the side.

"I can see where that would be hard, but I'm sure that she would have understood. Focusing on Lily was your main priority and by the looks of it, I'd say you've done an amazing job, she is a special little girl." I stopped for a minute, wanting what I was going to say next to come out right and not over step any boundaries. "I would love an opportunity to teach Lily what I know about baking if that's okay with you. I want to make the bakery a place that families come on the weekends, where they buy their birthday and wedding cakes from; a place where I can teach baking classes to children and allow them to find their passion for it. In no way do I want to replace what Hope would have given to her, but if she truly enjoys it, I would love to be able to fuel that fire and let her grow and find her own style in the kitchen."

Brad sat across from me with another one of his hard to read expressions on his face. I hadn't quite deciphered between a few of them yet. Before I said anything more, I waited for him to reply.

"I can't believe you would want to take something like that on." He sat back against the booth, and then sat back up with a little more excitement. "I think that would mean the world to her. I know she loves spending time with you and you are so kind to her."

"I know this may be a bit forward, but I just love your daughter. There is something about her, something that I can't put into words. I've never had any children of my own, but always dreamed of having a daughter to bake with in the kitchen." I stopped to make sure he wasn't going to take off running. "I hope that doesn't creep you out. I'm not a crazy person, I promise."

We both let out a loud laugh at the same time.

"Don't worry, I didn't get that impression. I know how wonderful she is and it's so great to hear someone else have those same feelings for her. You will make a great mother some day; having a daughter is the most amazing feeling in the world."

Grabbing the check off of the table, he reached into his wallet and pulled out enough cash to cover the tab and the tip.

"So, since you're paying for dinner, does this mean that we just had our first official date?"

He thought about it for a minute. "I suppose you're right, unless you don't want this to be a date. Then you can leave the tip."

The more he opened up, the more I was getting to see the other sides of him. He was quite the jokester and it was so nice to see him laughing and smiling.

"I was kind of hoping this was a date."

"Then feel free to put your wallet away."

When the bill was paid, he helped me with my coat and opened the door for me as we left. I had a smile on my face that I couldn't get to go away. Our conversation over dinner was so comfortable, like we had been on many dates before tonight. After passing by the bakery down the main street through town, I realized he wasn't taking me home just yet. A few blocks down, he turned left onto a residential street.

"Where are you taking me?" I asked, unfamiliar with this part of town.

We drove through the neighborhood to the end of the cul-de-sac, pulling into a dimly lit driveway. He parked the car in front of the garage and turned it off.

"Where are we?" I asked again.

"Well I thought after such a good dinner, it was only natural to want dessert." He climbed out of the car and walked around to the passenger side, opening the door for me. "Lily tells me that I make the best ice cream sundaes on earth. I'm not sure if they're that good, but would you like to try one?"

"That's a mighty high standard to live up to," I teased. "I would love to try one."

Brad unlocked the front door and held it open for me, flipping on the light in the foyer. Lily was spending the night with Nancy and Phil so we had the place to ourselves. I slipped my shoes off at the door and followed him down the hallway to the kitchen. I pulled out a stool and sat up at the breakfast bar, resting my forearms on top.

"Do you have a favorite flavor? We have a little bit of everything in the freezer. We make a lot of sundaes around here." He pulled the freezer door open, grabbing four different flavors, setting them across the bar in front of me. As I looked them over, he returned with three syrup toppings, a jar of cherries, and a variety pack of sprinkles from the cupboard above the sink.

"Wow, you mean business around here. But wait, no whipped cream?"

He turned around and opened the refrigerator, pulling a can of it out of the door. "Oh, you mean like this?" he said, holding it up in the air.

"Now you're talking," I smiled.

"So, you have your choice of vanilla, chocolate, strawberry, or cotton candy."

I looked across the bar at all he had out and made my decision. "This may be boring, but I'm going to go with the classic vanilla ice cream, chocolate sauce, and some sprinkles. Oh, and whipped cream and a cherry on top of course."

"Coming right up." He carried her choices over to the center island, pulled two bowls out of the cupboard, and began to make two of his best sundaes on earth, according to Lily.

He put the ice cream back into the freezer and picked up both bowls, carrying them into the living room as I followed behind him. He placed them on a doily that was spread across the wooden coffee table and walked over near the fireplace, flipping up the switch and lighting it. On top of the mantle were framed pictures, stretching from one end to the other. Another group of photographs hung along one of the living room walls. In the center of them all hung a large canvas print of the three of them, what used to be their family.

As I glanced around the room, I tried his famous sundae. "Mmmm—I think Lily may be on to something. You make a pretty mean ice cream sundae. Not too much syrup and just the right amount of sprinkles." I looked closer to see what the shapes the sprinkles were that lay on top of the scoops. "Are those little bones?" I asked, picking one up with my spoon to get a closer look.

"Yes, Lily picked them out at the grocery store a while back. She went through a dog phase and insisted she needed them."

I finished my sundae, placing the empty bowl back onto the table and walked over to the fireplace to warm my hands from holding the cold bowl. I looked closer at who was in the photographs as I rubbed my hands together, trying to regain feeling in my fingers. There was one of Nancy and Phil, some of Lily as a baby, and a couple of their wedding. As I approached the last photo on the mantel, I stopped in my tracks. It was familiar to me, something I had seen when I first got into town. It was a picture of a carving I had discovered on the railing by the lake a few weeks ago. "B + H" I turned back to look at him, still sitting on the couch.

"I saw this," I said to him, pointing at the framed picture. "I was taking a walk out to the lake right after I came to town and was admiring all of the carvings along the path to the lake. I saw this one at the very end."

Brad nodded. "That was from us. We had our wedding ceremony

on the beach and our reception in the ballroom of the hotel. We carved that into the railing right after the ceremony. I remember grabbing my pocket knife that morning, placing it in the pocket of my tuxedo, so that it would be our first memory as husband and wife. There are so many carvings; I'm surprised you spotted ours." He stood up to join me near the fireplace.

"It was all the way to the end and for some reason it stood out to me. It's really special that you have it to go back to and see forever. Something left behind from her that you will always have." I walked over to the wall to admire the rest of the pictures.

"I went to see it a couple of times right after she passed, but haven't been by there for a while. Everyone who gets married on the beach has carved their initials into that railing. My parents built that walkway the first summer they bought the hotel. Theirs were the first ones carved, and now many have put theirs on it since. It has become a town tradition now."

We walked around the room, looking at all of the photos. Some would feel intimidated by all of the photos of Hope still hanging in his home, but I wasn't. It may sound strange, but it made me happy to still see her there, present in their everyday lives. So many times you hear of people packing away their memories after losing someone, but not Brad; he kept her there, right out in the open for everyone to see, making it a place where Lily could go to see her whenever she wanted.

"I love that you keep Hope alive in your home. I'm sure Lily loves being able to see her and how beautiful she was." I looked over at him, staring at the last family photo they had taken together.

"I know she was very little when we lost her and it was something I always wanted her to have. I didn't want her to come to me one day when she's older and know nothing about her mother. She's still young and doesn't ask too many questions yet, but some day it will come and I want her to not be a complete stranger. I haven't told her a lot, like about the bakery, but when the time is right, she will know."

Just then, I got a wonderful idea for the bakery. Brad had kept Hope alive in his home all this time and it was important that I kept her alive in the bakery; to give Lily those memories of both places and let her know that the bakery had once belonged to her mother.

An hour later, after helping him clean up the mess they made in the kitchen, it was time to go home. As we walked to the front door, headlights beamed through the front window as a car pulled into his driveway. When he opened the door, he was shocked to see who was standing there—it was Hope's parents.

"Hello Bradley," she said, the mother doing the talking this time.

Clearly shocked, he was trying to get words out, but was having a hard time forming a sentence. "Why are you here?" was all he could manage to get out.

"We have something we would like to discuss with you, but I can see you are busy at the moment." They looked at him and then over at me, looking me up and down as they had just a few hours ago at the bakery.

My heart was racing, once again regretting that I didn't tell Brad they came to see me. Then he would have at least had a heads up and wouldn't have the look on his face that someone just hit him in the stomach.

"We were just leaving. I suppose we can talk, but I don't want to do it here. Give me thirty minutes and I will meet you in town at the restaurant near the hotel."

They agreed and got back into their car, driving away as we climbed into his. He started the car and leaned forward, resting his head against his steering wheel. After a few minutes of silence, he lifted his head.

"I'm so sorry that just happened. That was Greg and Diane, Hope's parents, and I have no idea why they're in town. I haven't seen them in years."

I wanted to tell him why they were in town and that I had already had my own run in with them, but I didn't want to upset him even more than he already was. The drive back home was quiet, both of us barely speaking. He placed his hand on top of mine and focused his attention on the road ahead; seeming completely zoned out. I didn't want to break it.

He parked in front of my building, climbed out, and opened my door for me, holding my hand to help me out. He pulled me close to him, hugging me for what seemed like forever before letting me go.

"This definitely wasn't how I pictured our night to end, but I had a really great time with you tonight. I hope you enjoyed yourself, too."

I looked up at him, unsure of what to say, but at the same time wanted to reassure him that I did. Looking up at him, he leaned down, pressing his lips gently against mine. Brad was finally beginning to understand what Lily had been telling him all along: there was something special about me, that I had been sent to them for a reason. He started to read the signs around him, knowing that this very moment was a sign that he may be able to love again.

Chapter
Sixteen

The next two weeks were busy; getting the bakery finished so it was ready to open, handing more flyers out around town, and the new drama that came to town in the form of Hope's parents. Last week I received a letter of intent from their lawyer, letting me know that they were going to dig further in to the investigation regarding ownership of the bakery. I read the letter and then proceeded to tuck it back inside the envelope, closing it into one of my empty kitchen drawers. At this point there was nothing more I could do about it and decided to carry on with the opening, even if in the end I lost the bakery. At least I would be able to say that I opened my own bakery, if not for more than a day.

Brad had been distant since Hope's parents came to town. He found out that they came to see me before our date that night and wasn't very happy about it; partly because I didn't tell him, partly because they had threatened to take the bakery away from me. I talked about it mostly to Nancy, not wanting to add to what Brad was already dealing with. She filled me in a little about the meeting he had with them after he brought me home that night, but only what she had been told. She had a feeling that he was keeping most of what they discussed from her, but nothing was going to change that.

Nancy and Lily came by today to help me with the rest of the cleaning in the main dining area. Lily was having a blast with a simple dust rag and some cleaning spray. Most of the tables would need to be wiped again after she did them, but as long as she was having fun, they were perfectly good to me.

When the dusting was finished and all of the glass displays and windows were clean, we went back to our assembly line in the kitchen to make prepackaged cookies like the ones we prepared for the festival. Grabbing her usual spot, Lily pushed a chair to the back and climbed right up at the end of the line.

"Do I do the labels the same way I did them last time, Cora?" she asked, holding the sheet of labels up in the air.

"Yep, just like before." I went to the supply closet and grabbed some more clear bags to package the cookies in and some more ties to close them up with, placing them in front of Nancy. "Would you mind being the middle man again? This order seemed to work pretty well last time."

"Not a problem with me."

I walked over to the cooling rack and pulled out the first batch of cookies. "We're going to start with chocolate chip today; I baked them a few hours ago. I'm going to put three in a package and if there are any extras at the end, you get to be my taste tester."

Lily's eyes widened. "I hope there are lots of extras," she whispered to herself.

The three of them packaged cookies until they were all used up, minus two that were left over. Not needing to taste test any more things I made, I gave them both to Lily. With crumbs on her cheeks and chocolate smeared on her lips, she followed Nancy and I through the front of the bakery, checking for any spots we may have missed while cleaning, making a mental note to pick up the cookie crumb trail she was leaving behind her.

I thought about repainting the walls, but after wiping them down a couple of times with a warm soapy cloth, they came pretty clean. Most of it was dust that had gathered while the building was vacant. Nancy helped me wipe down the built-ins behind the counter, ready for the displays I had built to go in them for the opening.

"Have you heard from Brad lately? The only times I have seen him have been when he drops Lily off or picks her up. No spontaneous visits anymore and he never sticks around to chat like he used to. I think something is bothering him again," Nancy said while wiping some freshly made chocolate finger prints off the front display case.

"No, I haven't and I'm concerned. Ever since Hope's parents came into town, he seems more distant. I feel like he was finally starting to open up to me and now he's pulled back so far. I worry about what they're putting him through and I don't want him to feel like he has to deal with all of it on his own." I walked over to the bucket of water and rinsed my rag and started on the window sill.

"That's how he is; when he's stressed or something is bothering him, he shuts everyone out and tries to deal with it all on his own. I've tried to change that so many times, but I'm afraid he'll always be that way."

I sat down on the floor under the window, thinking about him, wondering what he was thinking and if there was anything I could do to help. "Do you think I should try to contact him? I don't want to be pushy, though."

There was a knock at the door. Nancy and I both look at each other, wondering if it could possibly be Brad. "Do you think?" I wondered, getting up from the floor to see who it was.

"Are you Cora Westerling?" the man on the other side of the door asked, holding a manila envelope in his hand.

"Yes, can I help you with something?" I could see Nancy walk up behind me, wondering who was at the door.

"These are for you, the letter inside will explain it all." He handed me the letter, turned, and walked back to his car parked down the street.

"I am really starting to despise answering this door. Nobody, other than you of course, comes here that I want to see. It's always someone with bad news on the other side." I lock the door and carry the envelope over to one of the tables and sit down, tearing open the top.

"Who is it from?" Nancy asked, pulling up a chair across the table.

"I'm not sure, but I would put money on it that it is from Greg and Diane's lawyer." I pulled the papers out, reading the top cover letter first. Without saying a word, I read all the way to the bottom to understand what it was about.

Nancy sat patiently, waiting for me to finish before asking again. Lily was showing the effects of the two cookies she just ate, running around each of the tables and back and forth to the kitchen.

"Well, it looks like they are proceeding with the investigation of the will Hope left behind. It says here that Brad will have to present it in court if he refuses to give it up to them willingly. It sounds like he has the only copy and they are demanding he give it to them." I slammed the papers down on my leg. "That doesn't sound like something he would do. He doesn't strike me as a type of person to take demands from anybody." I picked the papers back up and read on.

"Definitely not," Nancy agreed.

After reading through the rest of the packet, it was basically stating that the sale of the property may not have been legal, and that

I may lose the property if Brad went against what Hope's wishes were in the will. I sighed, returning the papers to the envelope and walked them to the office, tucking them into the top drawer of the desk.

I returned to the front to find Lily sitting in the middle of the floor, clearly losing her sugar high. "It looks like somebody may need another cookie," I said to her, Nancy giving me a *don't you dare* look. "I'm just teasing, we packaged all that I made so we will have to make more to eat another day." I walked over to Nancy who was finishing up on one of the side windows. "Thank you for your help today, I think we've done about all we can today."

She returned her rag to the water bucket. "It was our pleasure, I'm glad we could be of assistance to you. Do you need us to come by any more before the opening?"

I was mentally checking my to-do list, trying to remember all that was still on it. "I don't think so, maybe the morning of the opening a little early if you can sneak away from the hotel. I could use a little help setting up the decorations and filling the displays with inventory. Do you think that would work?"

"I would be happy to. I may have Lily with me, but if that's a problem, I can certainly leave her with Phil and he can bring her a little later."

Lily stood quickly from the floor where she had been resting. "I'm a great helper, please let me come." She held her hands together up in front of her chest.

"I wouldn't be able to do it without you," I said to her, leaning down giving her a hug.

"Thank you, thank you, thank you," she said, finding a second wind.

"It sounds like a plan then, we will see you in a couple of days. Let me know if anything comes up between now and then that you need help with. Phil is around to help at the hotel if you need me for anything." She grabbed her keys off the table and reached for Lily's hand, walking towards the front door to leave. "Tell Cora goodbye."

She lunged at me, nearly knocking me down with her hug. After they left, I locked the front door, turned off the lights, and headed upstairs to call my next helper.

The following night, Brad opened the front door to the hotel as Lily shot through it at a running speed towards Nancy who was standing behind the front desk. Lily was already at the desk before the door closed behind him.

"What are you doing here? I thought it was your night off. Do I have her again tonight?" Nancy asked, checking the calendar on her desk.

"No, you don't. Lily said she wanted to go swimming so I told her if there weren't too many people in the pool, she could go for a little bit." He pulled the bag with her bathing suit and towel off of his shoulder, placing it on top of the desk. Nancy called Phil on the phone to let him know Lily was on her way down to get ready.

"Grandpa is waiting for you at the end of the hall. Take your bag down there and get your bathing suit on. Leave the rest of your things down there; just bring your towel back when you're ready." Lily dragged her bag down from the high counter and raced down the hall, even faster than her speed when she came through the front door.

"So, why are you really here?" Nancy knew better, he never just stopped by unannounced, especially on his first night off.

"Why does there have to be a reason? Can't I just come by to visit with my daughter without having a hidden agenda?" He tried to play cool, but he knew he wasn't going to fool her.

"Of course you can, but if you did it more often, I wouldn't be so suspicious," she laughed. "So, are you going to tell me what is going on or are you going to hold out on me and make me guess? You know how much I hate playing guessing games."

Before he could answer, Lily came barreling down the hall, dragging her life jacket and inner tube behind her.

"Grandpa told me I could bring these down here, too. I'm all set; can we go to the pool now?" She grabbed his arm and pulled him towards the door to the pool.

Nancy placed the bell on top of the desk and let Phil know she was taking a fifteen minute break to sit with Brad while Lily swam. She leaned down, using her key from a lanyard to unlock the door; the pool was empty. He snapped her life jacket on and helped her step into her inner tube. Walking to the edge of the shallow end, she grasped the railings, slowly dipping her toes into the water to check the temperature. She eased in, one step at a time, letting her body adjust to the cool water. Brad and Nancy grabbed two chairs at a table near the shallow end of the pool, turning them so they could both keep an eye on her.

"So, she is out of ear range. Spill your guts." She leaned back in her chair, crossing her arms across her chest.

Brad took in a slow, deep breath. "I know we've had this conversation, probably more times than I can count, but I'm having a lot of doubts lately about my life. First it was about moving on with Cora, feeling guilty about even the thought of dating anyone else. Now, Hope's parents are back in town and causing me all sorts of problems. Why can't things just go back to how they were a couple of months ago, when all I did was work and take care of my daughter?"

"Is that why you have been distant lately from Cora? She happened to mention she hadn't talked to you much lately. Are you sure you want to go back to a time when she wasn't in your life? I thought you two really hit it off," she asked, narrowing her eyes.

"We did, better than I thought we would, but maybe that's part of the problem. It almost seems too good to be true. She's such a great person and she really cares about Lily. Maybe I'm afraid that if I don't mess things up with her, maybe Hope's parents will. Did you know they're threatening to take the bakery away from her?"

Nancy nodded, not wanting to lead on that she knew a lot already, wanting him to open up about it himself. "I've heard a few things, but I'm not sure what they really want. Every time I see them stroll through the lobby, they never stop by the desk to say hello."

He blew up his cheeks with air, releasing it loudly. "Honestly, I don't know either. I have received many letters from their lawyer with their intent, but I'm not sure they have anything solid to stand on. I've looked Hope's will up and down and no where in it did I see that the bakery was left to them. They are mentioned in there that she hopes they will continue to be a part of it, but I found nothing that says if the building is sold, they need to be contacted first."

Reaching across the table, she gently rubbed her hand on his shoulder. "You have gone through far worse things and came out stronger on the other side. You can handle whatever they throw at you, and know that your dad and I will be right here ready to help if needed. You know that Cora will be, too."

Gently biting his lower lip, he nodded. "I know you are all here if I need you. I'm just not sure that Cora needs all of my drama in her life. I seem to be a magnet for it lately and can't seem to shake it."

"It appears as though nothing has scared her away, yet. What is making you pull back from her so much?"

Brad kept his eyes on Lily who was bobbing up and down in the water without a care in the world. "Fear, I guess; afraid that this might turn into something wonderful. Sounds silly, doesn't it?" He looked over at Nancy who was quietly listening. "Hope told me that she wanted me and Lily to always be happy; to never hold back in life and do everything possible to make sure that she has a great life."

"Wouldn't Cora qualify as something that makes you and Lily happy? I can't speak for you, but your daughter worships her."

He nodded, staring at Lily spin in circles, splashing water across the pool to see if she could reach them.

"You aren't replacing who she was or what she meant to you in your lives. She will always be your first wife and Lily's mother. Cora is just another character in your life's story, not a new person cast to replace the same character. She is her own person and can bring so much into your lives, something I think deep down you want, but are too afraid to see."

Brad sat in silence, thinking about what she just said. She has always had a way of gently stating the truth, making you see what she sees from the outside. She has a way of laying it out in front of you, but is gentle enough to not hurt your feelings.

"I haven't really thought about it the past few years, because I wasn't in a situation where I had to. I never wanted to find another person to share my life with, but ever since Cora came to town, all of that changed. I'm starting to have feelings for someone who isn't Hope and that is really frightening." He paused. "I also fear going back inside the bakery for the opening. I haven't set foot inside there since Hope passed."

Nancy jerked her head back. "You mean all this time you've been seeing Cora, you've never gone inside of her place? Let me ask you this; didn't it feel weird bringing her to your home, the place you and Hope lived most of your lives together?"

"I never really thought about that. It didn't seem weird at all, and she said she felt comfortable there even with all of Hope's pictures I still have hanging up. Perhaps it's because the bakery was really just hers; something that she built from her dreams."

Nancy walked over to the pool and motioned for Lily to come closer to the shallow end. "I supposed I understand that. Have you told Cora about your fear of going inside?"

Brad shook his head. "I'm not sure that she would understand. To her, this is her dream come true, something she is so excited to share with me, but every time I even get near the front door I feel sick to my stomach. I see that shiny glitter sticker on the window of the front door and I remember the day Hope placed it on there. Right after we closed on the building, she insisted on going there to put it on the window, letting everyone know that a bakery was coming soon."

"So are you going to go to the opening tomorrow? I'm guessing she'd be pretty upset if you didn't show up. I know Lily really wants to go and has done a lot to help get everything ready."

Brad knew in his heart that he wanted to go, that he should go, but when it physically came time to walk inside, he wasn't sure he could go through with it. When he sold the building, he assumed that would be it, that he would never have to step foot inside of it ever again if he didn't want to. Never in a million years did he think he would be falling for the woman who bought the building and that she would keep it a bakery, possibly leaving it exactly how his late wife had left it.

"I know that I should go, but can I really do it? Is this really what I want?" Brad turned to face Nancy, his chest tightening.

Nancy spoke in a quiet voice. "You can do this; you know that Hope wanted this for you, and for your daughter. Look at how Lily lights up when she's with Cora! I know that you aren't there when she is, but you've heard her talk about how much fun she has there. She has been so happy since she met Cora, and deep down, I think you are too for the first time in years."

Brad knew she was right. Lily was truly thriving and not a day had gone by that he hadn't heard "Cora" come out of her mouth. The other day he found sketches of cookies she had drawn on some papers in her room.

"I think I am, too, but I don't know how to put aside the other side of those feelings. I don't want to mess up what we have going because of my fears. It's not fair to Lily or to Cora, or to me for that matter."

Lily climbed up the stairs out of the pool and walked over to an empty chair at the table. Brad unbuckled her life jacket and wrapped a towel around her, lifting her up onto his lap. Her teeth were chattering and her lips were a light shade of purple. He rubbed his hands up and down her arms, trying to warm her up.

"I think I have something that may help you. Why don't I take Lily back and get her dressed. You sit in the lobby and help anyone who comes by. I'll be back in a few minutes."

Nancy grabbed Lily's hand and walked her down the hall to her room. Brad went into the breakfast area and poured himself a cup of coffee. He wasn't much for caffeine this late in the day on a night off, but he suddenly felt very tired. His thoughts were going in so many directions that he couldn't seem to keep anything straight. Sitting down in one of the comfy chairs near the fireplace, he placed his coffee on the side table and leaned back, closing his eyes.

Ten minutes later, Nancy and Lily returned, fully dressed with dried, bouncing blonde curls. Nancy was holding something in her right hand, partially hiding it behind her as she walked. Lily went behind the desk to play with the toys she kept in a basket underneath for when Nancy is working. He stood from his chair and made his way towards them.

"I think this might be helpful to you. Please don't open it until you are at home, after Lily has gone to bed. It may have the answers to the questions you're looking for in it." She handed him the white envelope, sealed with his name printed on the front. He recognized the writing right away; it was from Hope.

Chapter
Seventeen

I finished the last bite of my soup I made for dinner when I got Katie's text, telling me that she was on her way over. Of all the new people I have met in this town, Katie is the one I have clicked with the best. We're right around the same age and have a lot of similar interests, crocheting not being one of them of course.

I carried my dishes into the kitchen, placing them into the empty dishwasher. I closed it up, placed the empty pot from the stove into the sink to wash later, and headed downstairs to wait for Katie to arrive. In the kitchen I grabbed a few cookies and placed them on a tray from the cupboard. I arranged them neatly around the plate, going more for presentation than anything else.

I placed the tray on a table in the front, next to the table that was covered in drop cloths, paint, brushes, and stencils. My plan to keep this special project a secret from Nancy, Brad, and Lily had worked. Not that I had much of an opportunity to let the cat out of the bag to Brad. I was hoping I would hear something from him today, still unsure if he would be at the opening or not tomorrow.

With a knock on the door, I sprang forward, eager to let her inside. "Welcome to my new adventure," I said, waving her inside.

"This is beautiful Cora. You have done such a great job with the place, it looks perfect." Her eyes wandered around the room, noticing every piece of it.

"Thank you, but I can't take credit for much, unless you count cleaning glass and dusting. It looked like this when I bought it. Haven't you ever been inside here before?" I was now wondering how long Katie had lived here.

"No, it was only open a short time and I thought I would have plenty of time to check it out. But, when I finally came by, it was already closed." She took off her coat and hung it on the back of one of the chairs. "So, what do we have going on here? You said you needed help painting something, but you were very vague."

"I'm sorry about that, but I wanted to show you instead of trying to explain it over a text or phone call." I reached for my notebook that was placed on the painting table. "This is just a rough sketch, but hopefully you will see my vision." I handed the sketch over to her.

She looked over the drawing, then over at the wall I planned on putting it on. "Where on the wall should we start? I love this idea, I think it will be a huge hit and really mean a lot to everyone."

I climbed up the ladder I had placed near the wall, pointing to where I thought the words should go. "I wanted to center the words here, and then surround the rest of the wall underneath with the frames. Is there an easy way to do that so they don't look too random?"

Katie looked around the room. "Do you have any paper grocery bags lying around?" I ran into the kitchen and grabbed a stash I had tucked under the sink. "How about a pair of scissors and a pen?" Going back through the kitchen and into the office, I returned with both. She cut one of the bags along both sides, spreading it open and laid them flat on the table. "Do you know where you want each of them to hang, or any certain order you want them in?"

I walked over to the frames I had spread out across the floor under the front window. "I kind of have them here how I would like them up there. I'm not sure how to keep them in order, but that is where you're supposed to come in."

Katie grabbed the notebook and pen, turning to a fresh page and tore it out. "Rip this page into a bunch of smaller pieces, numbering them starting at one until each has a number and place one on each frame."

I did as she instructed while she continued cutting the paper bags open, stacking them into a pile on the table. "Finished," I said, walking back over to see what she was going to do next.

"Sorry, but I'm going to need one more pen and a roll of tape. Do you have some?"

"I think I saw some in the desk, let me go check." I went back to the office, returning with a brand new roll that I found in the top drawer. "I hope you're not planning to tape them to the wall; you know I have nails and a hammer for that."

She laughed, cutting open the last paper bag. "Not if you want them to stay up there. Now, go and grab one of the frames, preferably the first one you want to hang on the left hand side of the wall."

I picked up the first frame, returning to the table. Katie placed the frame on top of the paper bag, moving it to the far side to save space for another. Grabbing the pen, she traced the frame onto the bag and then handed the frame back to me, writing the corresponding number on it from the one I placed on the frame. I replaced it on the floor, picking up the next one in the top row.

"This may seem a little tedious, but it will pay off in the end. My mother taught me this when I moved into my apartment and was trying to decorate." She traced the next frame, continuing on until they were all traced onto the bags. "Now, we will cut each of these out and tape them to the wall in the order you chose. That way, we will know what size they all are and how far apart you want them spaced."

I nodded, slowly catching on to what she was doing. We both sat on the floor, cutting away, each taking turns with the one pair of scissors I found. When we were each done with our cutting, we taped them to the wall, trying to come up with the perfect design. Once they were all hung, it gave us a better idea of where to put the words and about how big they should be.

"I picked up some stencils for you to use for the words. Which ones do you like best?" I pulled them out of the shopping bag and held up three different options.

"You want my honest opinion?" Waiting long enough for me to nod, she replied, "None of them."

My mouth dropped open, eyes wide. "What do you mean none of them? They were the only ones at the store; now what?"

Katie held both hands up in front of her. "Now hear me out for a minute. You said you wanted my help, right? Would you be okay with me free handing the letters? I will draw them out in pencil on the wall first so you can approve before I paint them." She raised here eyebrows, offering me a questioning gaze.

Pressing my lips together, I agreed. "But if it doesn't look right, we are going with plan B and using the stencils. I only have tonight to get it right, so, no pressure." Unsure I was able to watch her, I excused myself to go make a pot of coffee, giving her the freedom to create without me hovering around her.

I waited for the pot to finish brewing completely before returning downstairs. I poured two cups and carried them down the stairs, balancing enough to not fall or burn myself. I found another tray in the kitchen, placing both mugs on it, along with some sugar and a small dish of cream I pulled out of the refrigerator. Trying not to look right away, I walked straight over to where the cookies sat, placing them alongside.

"Well, what do you think?" Katie climbed down off the ladder, moving it to the side so I could get a feel for the entire wall.

Sucking in a quick breath, I placed my hands against my chest. "It's perfect."

Katie's head fell back, closing her eyes. "I am so relieved you like it. Can I start the paint now?"

"Yes, please do. I will start placing nails into the paper bags on the wall so when you are finished, we can hang the frames."

Katie got right to work as I stood for a moment watching her true talent come to life. She freely painted, short strokes placed perfectly inside the lines she created. Something I would never have the guts to try, even on a simple piece of paper that could be easily restarted. When she was finished with the first word and half of the second, we stopped for a cookie and coffee break. Pulling up a chair, we sat at the table to relax for a few minutes.

"Have a few cookies, you have certainly earned them." I sat in my chair, admiring the progress we had made. "Nothing like waiting until the last minute. Sorry about that by the way."

"I had no plans, so it was no big deal for me. I haven't painted in a few years so any excuse to get out the brush, I'm all in." She finished her first cookie and started in on her second. "This really isn't on the plan for me right now, but I must be burning a few calories up on the ladder."

We laughed, grabbing for another. "You look fantastic. Tell me a little bit about your wedding. When do I get to meet your fiancé?"

"He should be here tomorrow with me for your opening. He said he didn't have to work, but that can quickly change." She continued telling me how they met, how he proposed, details about the wedding, and what their future plans were. "We haven't done a taste test for cakes yet, would that be something that would interest you? I know you technically aren't open, yet, but you will be."

"I would love to. Let me know when you want to set it up and I will make a bunch of samples for you both to try. It's the best part of the wedding prep, or so I've been told." I placed my head into my hands. "Maybe someday I will get married."

"You will, I can feel it." We each grabbed one more cookie and got back to work.

As she moved on to the rest of the words, making her way down the wall, I started behind her, placing one frame at a time on the wall, removing the paper bags as I went. When she finished the last letter, we worked together, hanging the remaining frames as quickly as we could. As we hung the last one, we both stepped back, admiring what we had just created.

"It looks amazing, Cora; everybody is going to love it."

I stood there, arm in arm with Katie admiring our work, and for the first time in the past couple of weeks, I was starting to get excited about tomorrow.

The streets were nearly empty on the drive home. Brad looked into his rearview mirror, Lily's eyes beginning to get heavy as her head slowly nodded forwards. The street lights shone against her little face each time he drove passed one. By the third street light, she was sound asleep, mouth wide open and resting her head against the side of her car seat. Swimming later in the day may not have been a bad idea after all. With the hour of swimming combined with the meal Nancy had cooked them, she had nothing left.

He pulled into the driveway, placing the car into park, looking over at the seat next to him where the letter rest. Looking back at

Lily, still asleep in the back seat, he wished he could simply snap his fingers and she would be in her bed, pajamas and all. The colder the nights got, the harder it was to keep her asleep while carrying her inside.

He slowly unbuckled her straps, lifting her out of her seat and placing her head against his shoulder. He closed the door with a quick motion of his hip, walking quickly to not wake her up from the noise. Fumbling with his keys, he got the front door unlocked and carried her down the hall to her room. He unzipped her coat after laying her down, pulling out one arm at a time and placing the covers up to her chin.

He closed her door behind him, leaving it open just a crack so the light from the hallway peeked in a little. He unzipped his own coat, placing it on the hanger in the front closet, reaching into his inside pocket to retrieve the letter before closing the door. He placed the letter down on the coffee table in front of him, taking a seat on the couch, staring at it. He had some idea of what would be in there; exactly what he needed to hear according to Nancy, but was afraid to actually read it.

He found comfort in knowing that she took the time to write to him, but was painfully aware that he would have no excuse about moving on with his life once he read it. He tried reaching for the letter three different times, backing away with each attempt.

Rubbing the back of his neck, he stood from the couch and went to the kitchen to grab a glass of water, his mouth suddenly dry as a desert. Slamming down one glass, he held it under the faucet, filling it a second time.

A grimace and a slight shake of his head later, he did one more check on Lily, hearing her snoring before even reaching her door. Confirming what he already knew in an attempt to stall, he went back to the living room, pacing several laps before sitting back down on the couch. There the letter still sat, staring back at him with the intense bright white envelope, as if it were the only thing he could see in the entire room. It almost seemed as though it were glowing, telling him to just open it already. He was waiting for the words "read me" to magically appear on the top. Nancy was clearly given instructions by Hope of when to give the letter to him, and she felt in her heart that now was that time.

He picked up the letter, placing his finger under the corner and sliding it underneath the flap, breaking the seal that she had once placed. He lifted the flap, revealing a hand written letter. It had been so long since he had seen anything with her handwriting on it; it caused a longing so intense it was almost painful. The few things he found around the house with her writing on it had all been tucked away in a box; he wanted to hold on to anything tangible she left behind.

With trembling hands, he pulled the two page letter out of the envelope. Paper clipped to the top of the first page was a photo of the three of them, one they had taken the summer before she passed. He remembered telling her that it was his favorite photo of them together; it was no surprise to him to find it inside. Pulling it off the top, he began reading the letter.

My dearest Bradley,

I thought this letter would be harder to write, knowing that if you are reading this, you are finally ready to move on with your life without me in it. But then I realized that I will always be in it; that half of me is probably running circles around you while you read it. I will always live inside of her and within your heart.

I never wanted to leave you and Lily, that part I know for certain. But God had bigger plans for me and it is my time to find out what it is. I truly believe that I was put on this earth to love you and to bring Lily into this world for you. She needs you just as much as you need her, always remember that. She may never remember who I was, but I hope that you speak of me often and tell her about whom I used to be.

Now that you are reading this, I have to believe that you are ready to move on with your life, that you have found someone special. I trusted Nancy to save this until that time came, and please know how happy I am that you are reading this letter. I wanted nothing more than to be your one and only, your forever, but sadly that was not meant to be. I know that if you have found someone else, that she is sure to be amazing. You always had great taste in women, if I do say so myself.

I ask that she be two things; loving towards you and Lily. That she can show you that you can love again, and show Lily that she can be loved by another woman that isn't her mother, although I do love her deeply. I also hope that she is strong; there will be days that you need to lean on her and Lily will too. I need her to be there for you both when you truly need that support. The day Lily graduates, the day she gets married, when she has babies of her own. She will need to be strong, knowing that Lily will wish I could be there, but know she will be thankful she can be.

Please let her know how truly grateful I am that she has come into your lives, and how welcome she is to be a part of it. I want nothing more than for you and our sweet girl to be happy, and know that it is okay to bring someone else into your lives to make it that way. Know that you are not replacing me as a person, but replacing the role I played in our lives together. Don't be afraid to be excited about your future. She will hold a very special place in my heart for loving my family and for being there when I no longer could.

I love you and Lily with all of my being and felt your love for me every day we were together. Allow yourself to open your heart again, to let her inside, even through the doubts I know you are probably facing. You would only ever choose the most wonderful woman to bring into your lives, so if you have found her, hold onto her tight. You never know where it will take you. Look at all of the wonderful things we got to do in our lives together, even in much too short of time. I wouldn't change a thing in this world about it and hope that you find peace in this and truly allow yourself to love again.

You are an amazing man and the greatest father to Lily, but I'm sure you already know that. I will love you forever, but it is time to close our chapter and start a new one with the three of you. Lily needs it, and so do you. As you know, I was always a believer in signs. Even though you never were, please try to look for them. They will show you which way to go. You will find a moment when you will know that she is the one who is meant for you both.

I love you and will always watch over you both.

Hope

P.S. Please tell her thank you for loving my family for me.

He collapsed on the couch, letting his head fall back, breaking down into tears. So many emotions were hitting him all at once: relief, love, hope, sadness. He knew what her wishes were for his future, but reading it now was exactly what he needed. Knowing it was still going to be hard moving on, he felt that Cora had been sent to them for a reason. Hope took part of his heart with her when she went, but he was starting to find another part inside of him that he had locked up tight, a part the Cora seemed to be filling in.

He still had reservations about the opening tomorrow, but hoped that after a good night's sleep, he would wake in the morning with a form of clarity. He tucked the letter back inside the envelope, wiped his eyes, and carried it with him down the hall, stopping to check on Lily one more time. As he watched her sleep, breathing in and out, he felt very close to Hope, knowing that part of her lived inside their little girl.

He pulled down the box of Hope's things he kept on the top shelf of his closet, adding it to the pile. Replacing it back on the shelf, he climbed into bed, completely drained from the emotions he had felt throughout the day, praying for clarity when he woke in the morning.

When Katie had gone and the downstairs was locked up for the night, I went upstairs to relax, hoping to catch something on TV just long enough to get tired and pass out on the couch. The couch cushions slowly sunk down as I sat, releasing the air inside. I pulled the blanket down that was draped across the back and placed it over my legs. My mail had been stacking up, having thrown most of it on the coffee table over the last couple of days. With it staring back at me, I reached for the top letter, starting there and working my way down. Luckily most of it was junk and I tossed it to the side. A hand full of envelopes down, I came across another letter which appeared to be from a law office.

Clenching my jaw, I opened it, even though I wanted nothing more than to toss it into the junk pile. Unfolding the letter, it was another note stating that Hope's parents were now taking legal action, having not gotten the cooperation of Mr. Bradley Harper. So formal, it stood out to me on the page as though it were written in bold and all caps. I wasn't sure whether I should be mad at them for proceeding or at him for not cooperating. Either way I look at it, I was caught somewhere in the middle of their battle, forced to live in limbo until they decided to play nice.

I ended my mail opening session with that letter, tossing it back on the table, heaviness in my stomach. I wished nothing more than to be able to talk to my grandmother. She always gave the best advice, always supported me no matter what. I'm starting to feel a little bit of that here with the friends that I've made, but nothing will ever compare to her.

In my mind, I feel like I still want to be here, to open my bakery tomorrow and see what happens. But lately, in my heart, I'm having doubts. I haven't slept well all week, lying awake at night thinking about what I really want. Maybe it would be easier to give them what they want, sell the bakery back to them and move on from this. I twisted my neck side to side, trying to release the tension.

Pushing open the coffee table, I reached for Hope's journal, opening to the first page. I read back through all of her notes, her visions she had for the bakery, and also for Lily. Why was I trying so hard to fulfill these things, made by a person I never even knew? Why did I think I could take someone else's dreams and make them mine, to complete these daunting tasks that may affect other people's lives other than my own? Who did I think I was taking on all of this? I closed the cover, placing it back down.

With the journal on one side and the lawyer's letter on the other, it only seemed right to give in. To sell them back the bakery, to leave my new home, the place I hoped to stay forever and start my new beginning. Maybe my life with Chris wasn't as bad as I thought it was. Perhaps I was making it out to be worse than it was, exaggerating the situations more than what they truly were. So he worked all of the time and he wasn't ready to get married. From what I hear, that's common in most relationships and it shouldn't be anything to worry about. If he hasn't moved on, yet, maybe he would take me back. It wasn't my dream life, but as it turns out, what I thought was my dream has slowly turned into a nightmare. Maybe my grass back there was as green as it gets.

Pulling my knees to my chest, I rocked back and forth on the couch, my world beginning to spin around me. I felt more lost than I was the day I decided to pack up my life and leave. All of the signs around me seemed to lead me here, but now I had no idea what they were trying telling me. It was like I was put in the middle of nowhere with ten different signs all pointing in a different direction. Normally I would chose the right one, but now I felt numb, replaying the events over the last few weeks trying to make sense of all that had been happening to me. I felt defeated and was unsure how to overcome that feeling.

I reached for the remote, unable to sit in the deafening silence that pounded through my head. Starting at the local channels, I found one that was airing the news, hoping to catch the weather for tomorrow, praying for a nice day for the crowd I was hoping to find outside my doors.

"This just in; we are getting reports of an insurance company owner being accused of embezzling tens of thousands of dollars from his business. Insurance agent Christopher Warner, is being held on several charges, awaiting a hearing next week, pending further investigation on his case. As of right now, Mr. Warner has pleaded not guilty."

Slamming my hand on the remote, I turn up the volume louder, doing a double take on the photo they were showing on the screen.

My muscles tightened as my hand flew over my mouth, heart racing. Shaking my head, I tried to focus on the words coming out of the reporter's mouth, only being able to focus on Chris's face. I blinked my eyes hard, refocusing on the screen; he was really there and this was really happening.

I tried to process what I just saw as they went to a commercial break. A sudden coldness hit me at my core. Not believing my mind could possibly hold anymore questions, it was now racing full of them. How did I not know he was doing this? If I were ever looking for a sign, I think this one just hit me smack in the middle of my face. How could I have been thinking, just moments ago, to go back to my old life with him?

I paced the room, wandering aimlessly, still in a state of shock. I paused in the window, looking down at the street, completely still below. Tiny white flecks blew passed the street lights, sailing through the air as the wind picked up, sending a chill down my spine and the hair on my arms to rise. I paced the room two more rounds before sitting back on the couch, wrapping myself into my blanket to relieve the chill that had suddenly taken over my body.

Suddenly unable to stay awake, eyelids as heavy as boulders, I force myself to get up and go to bed, still wrapped in my grandmother's quilt. Even though she wasn't here in person to comfort me, having her quilt wrapped around my shoulders felt like the next best thing.

Chapter *Eighteen*

I woke the next morning, still wrapped up in my quilt, hardly having moved from the position I fell asleep in the night before. Taking a moment to adjust to the sunlight, I wiped the sleep from my eyes and pulled my arms out from underneath the quilt. The air seemed crisp in my room and I knew outside would be even colder. Glancing at the clock, I suddenly realized that today was the big day; time to get up and finish all of my last minute things still remaining on my to-do list.

Hardly remembering what happened the night before, I strolled down the hall to the kitchen, making coffee my first priority. I knew I would need at least one cup now and would have to keep it coming to get through the day. Setting the pot to brew, I went downstairs to grab the newspaper from the sidewalk outside. I was never one to typically breeze through the paper, but I was dying to know if there was anything in there about Chris, still not believing what I had seen on the news, wondering if it was all just a bad dream.

The last of the street lights flickered off as the sun began to rise over the horizon. I hadn't seen a sunrise since moving here; being that it was today made it seem even more perfect. I walked back inside, tying my robe a little tighter around me, trying to rid the chill of the morning air against my body. I turned all of the lights on and preheated the oven, having to bake a few more things this morning. The wall we had created seemed even more perfect as I stood back, admiring it once again. It looked even more beautiful in the daylight, the paint glistening on the wall against the sun beams shining in.

I ran back upstairs to shower and get ready, tossing the newspaper on the coffee table as I sprinted past. In record setting time, at least in my book, I was in and out, dressing as I stumbled down the hall to pour a cup of coffee. I filled my cup and went to relax on the couch, making mental notes along the way of things that I needed to check before the opening. Grabbing a coaster, I placed my mug on top and sat back, noticing the three very important pieces of paper staring back at me: the newspaper with Chris's face on the front page, the letters from the lawyers, and Hope's journal.

All of the thoughts I had running in my mind from the night before came crashing back, realizing these things were all possible outcomes for me, unsure of which of them would win in the end. I picked up my mug, wrapping both hands around it, allowing the steam to warm my face. I had three options, all literally laid out in front of me, and now it was my choice which path I wanted to choose. Going back to Chris seemed like the obvious one to take out of the equation, being that he was in jail and I would end up being more alone than I was before I left, if that was even possible.

It was down to two: give in to the lawyers and the case they were putting me in the middle of, or fight back for once in my life. Tell them all that I wouldn't stand for it and this was my dream to fight for. No one else was going to fight for it for me. It was my one chance to keep Hope's dreams alive as well, even though her parent's seemed dead set on me destroying them. If only they would have asked me, allowed me to show them the vision I had for the bakery and how Hope was very much still a part of it.

I took a cautious sip of my coffee, blowing the steam away as it got closer to my lips. From the corner of my eye, a bug flew by me, a rare occurrence this time of year. Most of the bugs went away with the warm air, not typically seeing any this late into the fall. Hearing it crash land, I glanced down at the coffee table, hoping it wasn't something creepy that would make me jump up and scream. Doing a double take, I see a tiny red ladybug, crawling across Hope's journal, fluttering its wings as it landed.

"Where did you come from?" I asked, knowing it was impossible to get a response. I watched it for a moment, crawling on its tiny legs around and around the outer edges of the journal. And then it hit me, my sign had arrived. I sprang up from the couch, careful not to spill coffee on my sweater, and raced down the stairs.

As I got to the bottom, nearly missing the last step, I opened the refrigerator and got right to work. Pulling ingredients from the closet, I mixed a fresh batch of cupcakes to throw in the oven, hoping to get the fresh baked smell to fill the building.

While they baked, I grabbed a stack of fresh linens and dressed all of the tables, draping them perfectly so they hung evenly on all sides. I used crystal vases I found in the cupboard for centerpieces on the table, filling them with fresh pink roses and baby's breath, arranging them as I went, cutting each stem to make them look just right. I pushed each chair in to the table, placing them in the center of each side, never having paid more attention to detail in my life.

I pulled the cupcakes from the oven, placing them on the racks to cool. Reaching in the refrigerator, I grabbed the bins of cookies I had baked earlier and arranged them in fancy glass jars I found in the cupboard. Stacking the same amount inside each of them, I carried them out one by one to the cookie decorating station I had set up near the front window. The cookie jars were placed in the middle of the tables, near the back edge, leaving enough room to decorate them on the table. To the right of the jars I placed three bowls of different sprinkles, and four containers of a variety of colored frosting to the left.

Pulling out each chair a few inches from the table, I draped a child sized apron across the back of each one. I gathered as many spatulas as I could find, placing them in a wide mouth vase. On a small table to the side, I placed a bin to put all of the dirty ones in, giving each child a chance to use a fresh one. I stood back, admiring my work and came to terms that this would be a complete mess with sprinkles everywhere within a matter of minutes of the doors opening. Even still, it brought a smile to my face.

I walked over to the wall, straightening one of the frames, making sure they were all perfect when there was a loud knock on the front door. Through the white sheer curtain covering the window, I could see a little blonde curly head popping up and down as Lily jumped with excitement. I unlocked the door, letting them inside, hardly cracking it before Lily flew passed me.

"Good morning, ladies, thank you so much for coming early to help me with my last minute details," I said, taking their coats and closing the door behind them.

Nancy twirled the scarf off from around her neck, noticing the wall right away. Grabbing onto my arm, she gasped, her breath catching in her throat. "What is this?" she asked, barely getting the words to come out.

"I felt like there was something missing, and I finally realized what it was; it was Hope."

Nancy walked to one end of the wall, slowly making her way to the other side, admiring each photo as she went, running her fingertips along the bottom of the frames. "How did you do all of this? I was just here."

Taking in a deep breath, my posture relaxed seeing how much it meant to Nancy.

"Look grandma! That's me in that picture!" Lily yelled, running over to get a closure look. "And there's mommy and daddy." Nancy walked over to her to see the photo she was referring to. "Grandma, what do those words say?" she asked, pointing to the painted letters up above.

"It says, 'Wall of Hope,'" Nancy said, standing still in that moment.

"Hope? That's my mommy's name." Lily jumped around the bakery, admiring all of the things I had set up around, trying her best not to dive into the frosting. "Grandma, look at all of the sprinkles!"

Nancy looked over at the decorating station. "Don't touch anything; those are for decorating cookies later after everyone else arrives."

"So, what do you think?" I asked Nancy as she turned her attention back to the wall.

"It's beautiful; what made you want to do this?" She made another pass of the wall, looking closely at the photos again.

"After getting to know all of you more and learning about Hope, I began to realize how much this place meant to her; how much she wanted to grow her business and share it with Lily and the rest of the community." I straightened another frame. "Since she is no longer able to do that, I felt like it was up to me to see those plans through; to give other people hope that they can make their dreams happen no matter what. She may not be here physically to fulfill them, but they will happen and I will see to it that they do. This is a way that she can always be here and be a part of the bakery, letting Lily grow up and see her here. And, it's to let everyone else know her spirit will always be here. The bakery started with her vision and I am going to make those dreams come true for Lily."

"I can't even put what I'm feeling into words," Nancy said. "Does Brad know about this?"

I cleared my throat. "No, I wanted to tell him, but since I haven't heard from him for a couple of weeks, I thought maybe it would be best if someday he just sees it for himself. I know he was having a hard time deciding whether or not to come today, I hope this doesn't make him upset."

Nancy looked over at me. "Did he tell you how he was feeling about coming back inside here? I told him to, but I wasn't sure if he actually did."

I shook my head. "No, he never said a word, I could just sense it. Whenever he would pick me up or drop me off, we always said goodbye in the car or on the sidewalk, he never came inside. Do you think he will like it?"

Nancy glanced over at the wall again. "Honestly," she paused. "I think he'll love it. I think it will help him feel more comfortable being here." She glanced down at her watch. "It's getting late, we better get started."

Nancy called Lily over as they walked back to the kitchen to frost the cupcakes. They fashioned another assembly line, this time placing Lily in the middle. I frosted each one then slid them down to Lily, who proudly sprinkled them with rainbow colored confetti sprinkles. When she finished, Nancy was in charge of putting them on the trays, carrying them out to the front, and placing them in the display case.

Thirty minutes later, they were all frosted and beautifully displayed in the glass case for all to see when they walked inside. The three of us stood in front of the case, arms across our chests admiring our work.

Lily nodded her head. "I think we did a great job," she said, running off to do a few crazy eights around the tables after sitting still for the last half an hour.

Nancy checked her watch. "I just remembered something I forgot to do back at the hotel. Would you mind if I left her here and ran back there? It shouldn't take long and I will back for the opening."

We both looked over at Lily, who was doing silly dance moves all around the room. "It shouldn't be a problem; if I need any help she clearly has enough energy to assist me."

"Alright, I'll be back just as soon as I can."

I locked the door behind her and took Lily back to the kitchen to be sure all of the baked goods were accounted for and out on display.

Nancy arrived at the hotel to find Phil working the front desk, checking out the guests whose stay was over. She walked back behind the counter, staring at him until he was finished with the couple standing on the other side.

"Have they checked out, yet?"

"Have who checked out, yet?" Phil replied, confused.

"Greg and Diane; I really need to talk to them before they leave. Have I missed them?" She began frantically pacing the lobby as if that would make her find them sooner.

"I haven't seen them yet this morning. There is still another hour until checkout; maybe they're still in their room." Phil went back to what he was doing, filing guest's paperwork and replacing the plastic key cards into the box where they were kept.

"What room are they staying in?" she asked, slamming her forearms against the top of the counter.

He clicked around on the computer until he found their names, "Room 112." He hesitated a little, not sure what she had up her sleeve. Before he could close their file on his screen, she was already half way down the hall.

Straightening her posture and relaxing her shoulders, she raised her hand up and knocked on their door: nothing. She knocked again: still no answer. Her heart began to race and her breath was darting in and out rapidly. She walked back down to the desk, stomping her feet with the fast pace she was keeping.

"Not in there?" Phil asked, keeping much calmer than she.

"No, they didn't answer. Pull up their file again and tell me what their license plate and car make is, I have to see if they are still here." She walked circles around the lobby, straightening the furniture as she went, which is what she did when something made her uneasy. Stopping by the window, she peered down by the lake, her breath catching in her throat. "Never mind," she shouted and raced out the front door.

She walked faster and faster down the sidewalk on her way down to the lake. The roar of a boat motor passed along the shoreline, her feet now dragging over the leaf covered gravel. When she reached the entrance of the bridge, the pounding sound of her footsteps caught their attention. They both stopped what they were saying and turned towards her.

"I'm so glad I found you," she said, hanging onto the railing and catching her breath.

"Is there something wrong?" They continued to watch her, allowing her to gather her thoughts.

"I need you to do me a favor before you leave town." When they didn't answer, she continued. "You need to stop by the bakery's grand opening today. The doors open at eleven and it's really important that you go there."

They looked at each other, then back to Nancy. "Why on earth would we go there? The next time I step foot in there is when we win it back from her in court."

Nancy couldn't figure out where the anger was coming from. Brad did nothing wrong, and neither had Cora for that matter. "Why are you doing this? Is it so wrong to let Brad move on with his life? Why are you so angry about this?" Her stern face began to soften, trying to sympathize with what they must be going through, but still standing firm in what she believed to be right.

"Our daughter's bakery should not have been sold without our permission. That was the only thing we had left to hold onto of hers and now it's gone. He should have at least talked to us about it first before he made any decisions. It wasn't his to sell and we won't stop until we get our daughter back." She paused, griping her necklace tight, taking a step back.

"It's not going to bring your daughter back," Nancy said softly. She took a small step forward, closing the gap Diane had created. "I'm sorry, but it won't. I wish I could bring her back for you, but that is just not possible. There is still something else you have of hers that you can hold on to; something even more precious than a building." She saw them both release some of the tension they were holding in their shoulders. "You have your granddaughter."

As soon as she said it, Diane fell to her knees and broke down. Nancy reached into her purse, digging for a tissue as tears poured down her cheeks. All of the emotions she had been holding in came flooding out all at once.

"She's still here you know, around all of us every day. She is up there, looking down on us and wanting us to be happy. You should feel comforted that she is watching us, protecting us. Every time I see Lily, I see her mother in her face: her same bubbly personality, her love of life, and her joy of baking. That little girl is more of her mother than you know, and I bet she would love to see you again. And I know deep down, Brad really wants you to be in her life."

As Diane regained her composure, she stood back up on her feet, sliding her arm through her husband's for support. Nancy handed her another tissue, tucking the rest back into her purse. Neither of them spoke as she dabbed her eyes.

"Please just think about it. You need to see that she is still with us." With that, Nancy turned around and walked back to the hotel, leaving them on the bridge in silence. All she could do now was pray that they would listen to what she had said.

Chapter
Nineteen

As the crowd began to gather on the sidewalk in front of the bakery, the fluttery feeling returned to my stomach. I walked over to get Lily who was peeking through the side of the front curtain, trying to see all of the people on the street.

"It's almost time to open the doors. Are you excited for everyone to see the new bakery?" I asked as Lily spun around, releasing the curtain.

"I can't wait to show daddy; I bet he will want to make a cookie with me. He's coming today, right?" She looked up at me with her sparkling eyes, begging for me to tell her the truth, but I wasn't sure what that was.

"I think he's going to try his best to make it. We will just have to wait and see." It wasn't the answer she was hoping for, but seemed to do for now.

I grabbed Lily's hand, wrapping it tightly into mine. Walking to the front door, I grabbed Lily's jacket, helped her get her arms in, and zipped it up. I put mine on next, suddenly chilled with more excitement than nerves. I pinched the edge of the curtain, taking a look at the people gathering outside. There were more people out there than I could have ever imagined and part of me was still holding on to the belief that everything would work out.

"Shall we?" Lily looked up at me, holding out her hand, and gave me a calm nod. Unlocking the door, we pulled it open together, walking outside to see the oversized pink ribbon pinned across the entrance. The air was crisp, blowing my hair back as I stepped forward. We both stood there, taking in the crowd, looking for friends we recognized. I spotted Katie, Alice, and Jackie all gathered near the front of the crowd, waving proudly at me. Mary, Ali, and Linda were standing off to my left, steaming hot coffees in hand. My heart was racing, seeing all of the support I had standing right in front of me.

"Wow! Thank you all so much for coming out today and braving this chilly weather. I cannot believe how many of you are out here, this is truly amazing." I scanned the sidewalk again. "I am so thankful for each and every one of you who came out to support me and this new adventure I have taken on. I've worked really hard over the last couple of months with some help of a few very special people." I looked down at Lily, squeezing her hand. "Before we go inside, there is a very important person here with me today that will need to cut the ribbon first."

I let go of Lily's hand and handed her a large pair of shiny silver scissors I pulled from my jacket pocket. She place one hand on each of the handles, stretching her arms out towards the ribbon. Before pressing her hands together, she paused to look back at me.

"Wait," she said, retracting her hands. "I think we should do it together."

My heart smiled as I placed my hands over the top of hers. "I would love that. Ready?"

Lily nodded and we snipped the ribbon together as the crowd

cheered. Lily jumped up into my arms, excited to show everyone around inside.

"I welcome you all to come inside and enjoy some sweet treats and some fun activities. Feel free to walk around and let me know if there is anything I can do for you." I motioned the crowd inside, greeting each and every one of them as they entered. They were all so friendly, making me feel so welcome and happy I decided to go through with the opening, still unaware of what the outcome would be in the end.

As the crowd diminished and the street began to clear, there were two people waiting in the back: Phil and Brad.

"Congratulations, Cora, I'm so proud of you," Phil said, giving me a hug.

"Thank you so much. Please come inside and find Nancy, you'll probably find her near the cookie decorating station with Lily. I had to try to keep her away from the sprinkles all morning." We both laughed as he walked inside.

"And then there was one," I said, walking towards Brad, still standing back from the door.

"Save the best for last, right?" he replied, pulling me close and kissing me on the cheek.

"I do think I've heard that before." I took a deep breath, hoping he wasn't just here to congratulate me and then leave. As I opened my mouth to talk, he beat me to it.

"I've been thinking a lot about this day for the last couple of weeks and I wasn't sure how it would all play out. But last night, it hit me that this is where I'm supposed to be." He squeezed my hands, holding them against his chest. "I'm so proud of you and cannot wait to see how it looks inside. Lily has been keeping everything a secret from me so I would be surprised today."

I let out the breath I didn't realize I was holding, along with a huge weight off of my shoulders. "I'm not sure what changed your mind last night, but I could not be more excited to see you here now." I leaned down and grabbed the door stop that was propping the door open, closing it behind us.

"Daddy, daddy!" Lily shouted, making her way through the crowd. "Come over here, I have to show you something. We're on the wall!" She grabbed his hand and pulled him forward with all of her strength.

After a few bumps into other people and nearly losing his arm in the process, his gaze lifted, staring directly at the wall. "Oh my goodness," he whispered.

"Look daddy, here I am! And there's you and mommy." She tugged downward on his arm, trying to break his gaze, but was unsuccessful.

"How did you do all of this?" He looked up, reading the painted words along the top. "Wall of Hope?"

"This is her place, a dream she had and she made it come true. I am just here to continue her dreams and help to pass them along to Lily. She will always be here and a part of our lives and I want everyone to know about her. She should never be forgotten and I felt like this would be a great way to keep her memory alive. The Wall of Hope is for her and her family, and for anyone else who has a dream they are chasing, giving them hope that it can happen. Her dreams came true in you and Lily, and also extended into this bakery. I see her same visions and share her same dreams. You and Lily are now a part of them." I waited for him to respond, my heart racing, watching his expression, once again unreadable.

Brad walked the entire wall, looking closely at each and every photo. When he reached the end, he turned back to face me. Shaking his head back and forth slowly, he took in a deep breath, releasing it little by little. "Hope would have loved this. Where did you get all of these photographs?"

I smiled, relieved that he was happy about it. "I found them upstairs in a photo album that must have been left behind."

"I haven't seen some of these in years; so many great memories." He walked up to the frame that was in the center of the wall, running his fingers along the edge of the frame. "And this?" he asked, pointing to a handwritten piece of paper inside, his voice catching in his throat.

"I found that inside of a notebook she had written in. It was with the photo album and it contained so many notes of hers. This is the one that stood out to me the most." We stood there together as he read it; a list that contained everything she wanted in life, starting with marrying a wonderful man, having a family, opening her own bakery.

"I've never seen this before," His hands scrolled to the bottom, to the last wish on her page, written in a different color of ink than the others: "To have Brad find someone to make him and Lily whole again after I am gone."

Nancy appeared behind him, placing her hands on his shoulders. "I think her list may now be complete," she told him, looking over at me.

Brad dabbed the corner of his eye, clearing his throat and turning towards me. "Yes." He looked over to the far side of the wall alongside the pictures. "And what is this over here?"

Grabbing my hand, we walked over near the door. A large cork board hung on the wall, a small container below it containing bright colored index cards and pens. "This is a place where people can write down their hopes and dreams, and hang them on this board for all to see. Believing in you is the first step, putting yourself out there and letting the world know is the next. This gives people a chance to tell others about their dreams and to put it out there in writing. It's not just her wall of hope, it's everybody's."

"I love that," he said, leaning in, pressing his lips gently on my cheek.

Lily came darting through the crowd, cookie in hand. "Cora, daddy, look what I made," she shouted, holding it up in the air, missing a large bite from the side.

"Wow," he said, leaning down on one knee. "Are you sure there is a cookie underneath all of that frosting?" She giggled at him as he tried to steal a bite. "You should come and make one, too."

"I would love to; can you show me around?" Lily grabbed his hand and pulled him towards the decorating station, leaving Nancy and me behind.

"I think this is just what he needed today. You did an amazing job on the bakery. I can't wait to see what you do with it now that it's officially open."

"I could have never opened the bakery without you, I know that for sure."

Looking across the room at Lily and Brad making cookies made my heart smile. As the bell chimed above the door, Brad's expression changed, the look in his eyes intense as he gazed toward the two people he wished he would not have just seen walk in: Hope's parents.

Brad walked across the room towards them, his elbows wide and chest thrust out, a slight flare in his nostrils. Attempting to cut him off, Nancy thrust towards him and stopped him in his tracks.

"Please move aside, mother, they are not welcome here today," he told Nancy, trying to get passed her.

"I invited them," she said, speaking softly, face turned towards her feet.

He turned back to her. "You did what? Why on earth would you do that? They are the last people I want to see and it's not fair to Cora to have them here."

I walked over to Nancy, trying to find out what is going on between the two of them. "Is everything alright?"

"No, it's not; my mother invited them here and I'm trying to figure out what she could possibly have been thinking." He stood there next to me, his frame stiff and his jaw clenched.

"I'm sure she had a good reason, right Nancy?" I looked to her, my lips pressed together and eyes wide.

She looked to both of us, then over to them. "I do have a good reason, please come with me and I'll explain."

We followed her over to where Greg and Diane were standing, just inside the doorway, swallowing hard as we approached. She explained to all of us the conversation she had with them at the lake just hours before the opening, wanting them to come by and see that Hope is still with all of them. She told Brad that she wanted them to see the wall and that she wanted them to come by and see Lily again.

Brad felt a pull on his hand. "Daddy, where did you go? You weren't finished decorating your cookie, yet." Looking up at all of us, she moved slightly behind Brad's leg, unsure of what she had just walked in on. She looked up at him, and then over to them. "Who are they daddy?" she asked, never taking her eyes off of them. "Wait a second." She let go of his leg and ran over to the wall. "You two are on the wall, too." She pointed up to the picture of them hanging near the bottom of the wall.

They looked over at Brad before walking any further, waiting for an approval of some sort. Sighing, he nodded slightly as they moved towards Lily.

"Why are you on the wall? Did you know my mommy, too?" She looked up at them, innocence in her eyes.

Carefully leaning down, Diane reached for her hands. "I did know your mommy. She was very special to me. Do you know why?"

Lily looked at her, shaking her head.

"I am your mommy's mommy. She was my daughter, and do you know what that also makes me?" She paused, letting her process it for a moment. "That makes me your grandma. And do you know who that is over there?" She pointed up at her husband. "That is your grandpa."

Lily looked at her, then at him, returning back to her again. "So if you are my mommy's mommy, is he my mommy's daddy?"

She smiled and nodded, tears rimming her eyes. "That's right honey. We haven't seen you since you were really little so you don't remember us very much. We have both missed you very much. I can't believe how big you are now," she said, holding her hands out, looking Lily up and down. "You must be in high school by now, right?"

"No, silly, I am not that big, yet." She let out a belly laugh, snorting. "So why haven't you come to see me for so long?"

She stood up for a moment, resting her legs. Walking over to a nearby table, she pulled up one of the chairs, inviting Lily to come sit on her lap. Brad moved closer, but allowed her enough space to talk to Lily without hovering. Nancy stood close by, ready to stop Brad at a moment's notice from interrupting them.

"Well, I don't have a great answer for that, other than that I was really sad. When your mommy went to heaven, I got really sad and missed her a lot, just like you and daddy do. But now, I see that you are growing up to be just like her and seeing you here is starting to make me happy again."

Lily laid her head on her grandma's shoulder, listening to her tell her story. She reached her arm up, wrapping it around Lily, her worry melting away that she had been holding onto, worried that perhaps too much time had passed.

"Do you know how happy I am to see you right now?"

Lily sat back up, looking up at her. "If you are so happy, then why are you crying? I thought people only cried when they were sad?"

She wiped her eyes with the cuff of her coat sleeve. "You mean these? These are what you call happy tears; when a person is so happy that they can't control it anymore, they have to let some of it out." Lily nodded as if trying to understand what she was saying.

She jumped down off of her lap. "I know something that will make you even happier. We can go and decorate a cookie together. I know where the table is and Cora picked out the best sprinkles. Do you want to make one with me?" she asked, holding out her hand.

She looked over at Brad cautiously. With Nancy standing at his side, she squeezed his arm, letting him know she wanted him to approve. With a softer expression, he nodded. She stood from her chair, grabbing Lily's hand and began walking towards the cookie station when Lily pulled her back.

"Wait, we forgot somebody." With her other hand, she stretched it out toward Greg. "Aren't you coming too, grandpa? There are enough cookies for all of us to make one. Well, I've already made three or four, but Cora made a ton so it should be okay." Everyone laughed.

As the three of them walked hand in hand to the cookie table, I couldn't help but wash away the tension I had felt for them only a matter of minutes ago. It wasn't really up to me whether to accept them into Lily's life, but from what I could tell it seemed like Brad was opening up to the idea. His posture began to relax and he had opened up his once clenched fists. Watching them all the way to the table, he stood next to Nancy who was eager to voice her opinion.

"I'm sorry I didn't tell you about this earlier, but I wasn't sure they were even going to show up. I was here earlier this morning helping Cora when I saw the wall. I thought that maybe if they saw it, too, saw that Cora wasn't trying to take over the bakery and their daughter's life, they would change their minds about trying to take it back." He appeared to be listening, but never took his eyes off of Lily. "I was hoping once they saw the wall, and once they saw Lily, they would realize how ridiculous they were being and that you hadn't forgotten about Hope; that Lily is part of her and is very much living out the dreams she had for her."

"I guess we'll see." And with that, he walked closer to the table to see that they were alright.

"He'll come around," I said to her, patting her on the shoulder as I mingled around the crowd.

Chapter
Twenty

As the crowds began to fade, I looked around the bakery at the mess of sprinkles on the floor, the cookie crumb-filled tables, and the frosting that looked to have been used as a crayon instead of a decoration at the cookie station. The linens were spotted in coffee drips, chairs arranged haphazardly around the room, and tubs of dirty dishes throughout.

Taking it all in, after working so hard on making today happen, I couldn't help but smile at the success it had become. All of the mess that was in front of me, and the hours it was sure to take to clean it up, was worth every crumb on the floor. Each sprinkle on the floor was a remnant of the many children who had fun today decorating their own cookies. Every coffee mug left on a tabletop, needing to be washed, was a sign of friends gathering around, sharing stories, and enjoying each others company.

When the doors were opened this morning, it was a place I wanted friends to gather and catch up, for families to have celebrations at, for locals to stop by on a daily basis for their morning treat. All of my visions had come true today, seeing so much of that here in this room.

Brad was near the door, saying goodbye to a few of his fellow officers as they left for their night shift, shaking their hands as they walked out the front door. Walking towards me, he leaned on the counter near the register where I stood.

"Well, I do believe today turned into a great success," he said, placing his hands on top of mine, glancing over to one of the tables where Lily was sitting, still visiting with her grandma and grandpa. "There was definitely a twist in the day that I didn't see coming, but it seems to have turned out alright."

"By the looks of the place, I would have to agree. I think everyone who came by had a great time and there are sure to be a countless number of children running around their homes with an insane sugar high."

Brad laughed, seeing some of that in his own daughter, watching her as she danced in front of the table, showing off all of her new moves. "How many cookies do you think she had today?"

"I don't think it's about the number of cookies as much as it is the amount of frosting piled on the top of them. She probably has enough sugar in her body to keep her awake until next week." I laughed, watching her begin to spin in circles.

Brad checked his watch. "My mom should be back any time to pick her up. She had to run a quick errand and then offered to take Lily home with her so I could stay behind and help you clean up this mess."

"You don't need to do that, I'm sure I can handle it on my own if you want to take her home." Looking around again, my heart began to race at the sight.

"Sure you can, if you ate as much frosting as Lily had today. Maybe we should let her start and burn a little of it off before my mom picks her up."

A few minutes later, Nancy came through the front door holding a gift bag. Lily was still dancing around as the last of the guests were putting their coats on, getting ready to leave.

"Well I can see she hasn't slowed down one bit since I left." Nancy joined us at the counter.

"I think you could come in here tomorrow and she would still be going. The sugar high has got to come crashing down soon, I hope." He looked over at Nancy. "Were you able to find what you needed?"

"It's all in the bag," she said, handing it over to him.

I looked at each of them, back and forth. "What are you two up to?" I asked, getting nothing but two smirks in return.

"I better get Lily ready to go." He placed the bag on a table and walked over to where she was still twirling. She resisted him at first, not wanting the night to end. After three attempts, he finally got both of her arms into her jacket sleeves and managed to get the zipper halfway up before she tried to get away. The beginning of the crash had definitely begun.

"I think I'll go see if he needs some help," I said, excusing myself. When I reached her, she perked back up and was able to stand on her own again, far from the limp noodle she had just given her dad.

"Tell him you want me to stay. Pleeeease?" she begged, cupping her hands together.

"I am so happy that you had so much fun here today. I was wondering if you wanted to come back tomorrow to help me get things ready for our first official open day on Monday."

Lily's face lit up. "Can I, dad?" she asked, looking up at him, using the eyes she used to get everything she wanted.

"Only if you go with grandma now back to the hotel and get some rest. Bakers have to wake up very early in the morning and need to get a good night's sleep." He looked up at me for backup.

"He's right; we need to be up bright and early in the morning to bake all of the fresh pastries. Do you think you can get some sleep and be ready to help me tomorrow?"

She jumped up. "Grandma it is time to go. If I get a lot of sleep tonight, Cora said I can come back in the morning bright and early to help her bake." She turned around and gave her grandma and grandpa a hug goodbye. "Will I see you tomorrow, too?"

They looked up at Brad and Nancy. "Well, I think if your grandma has a room free, we will probably stay one more night. Maybe we can have breakfast together in the morning."

Nancy nodded. "I think your room is still available tonight. We would be happy to have you another night."

"Then it's settled, we have a breakfast date in the morning."

"Okay," Lily told them, "but it will have to be pretty early. I am a baker now and I need to be back bright and early to bake." She ran to the door, waiting for Nancy to catch up.

"Well I guess that is my cue. Cora, it really was a wonderful opening day. A lot of fun memories were created for sure. Brad, have fun cleaning up and don't let Cora work too hard. Greg and Diane, I'm glad you decided to come by today. I think it was good for everybody to have you here. I'll see you all in the morning." She waved goodbye, joining Lily at the front door.

"How many blocks do you think it will take before she is out like a light?"

The four of them laughed. "My guess is less than one." He grabbed Cora's hand and walked her over to the table where he left the gift bag.

"Ah, yes, the mysterious bag. Do I get to see what is inside or are you going to keep torturing me and make me wait until tomorrow. You will learn very quickly that I am not one who can wait when it comes to surprises."

"Well, as good as this place looked today and as much work as you put into it, I noticed that there was still something missing. So,

I kindly asked Nancy to run to the store and pick that something up for me." He lifted the handles of the bag, handing it over to me.

I pulled the tissue paper out of the top of the bag cautiously, waiting for something to jump out at me. Under the tissue paper revealed a wooden picture frame. Grabbing the edge of it, I pulled it out of the bag.

He grabbed my hand, walking me over to the cork board hanging on the wall where many people had placed their hopes today. "I realized that of all the wonderful memories on the wall were memories from my past, and there weren't any yet of my hopes for my future. So, I wrote out a card with my hope on it and added it here." He smiled, wiping his finger across my cheek, drying a tear I was trying so hard to hide.

"How did you do this? You just took this picture a few hours ago." I stood there staring at the frame; a picture of Brad, Lily, and me decorating cookies together.

"I gave my mom my phone and told her to go and have the photo printed at the store and buy a frame for it." He grabbed my hand again, walking over to where the other pictures hung. "And there just so happens to be an empty space right here to hang it. Right beneath the photo of Brad, Hope, and Lily, he placed the photo of the three of us.

"My hope is that our future will be amazing as long as you are by our side. Hope knew that there was someone out there that we were going to find to continue our lives with. I have no doubt that you are that person and that she sent you to us. Lily needs you in her life, and so do I."

Tears were flowing down my cheeks faster than I could wipe them. "I need you both, too."

"Hope wrote me a letter and gave it to Nancy, instructing her to give it to me when she felt that I had met someone special. Last night,

Nancy gave it to me, and after reading it, it became clear how much you meant to me and how much I wanted you in our lives."

Clearing his throat, we realize Greg and Diane were still in the room. There they stood, standing near the table where Lily had been dancing. She wiped a tear, holding her hands up to her chest.

"I'm sorry, I forgot you were standing there," Brad said as they walked over near us.

"Don't be, I'm glad we were here, to see how much she means to you and to see everything here today." She reached for my hand, holding it inside of hers. "Cora, you have done a wonderful job with the bakery and I cannot express into words how much these beautiful photos mean to my husband and me." She looked over to him, and then back to me, grabbing on to Brad's hand, too. "I wanted to let you know that we have decided to drop the lawyers and not fight you for the bakery. We know that it is in wonderful hands and it was something we just had to see for ourselves. And if it's alright, we would like to be a part of yours and Lily's life again."

Brad thought about it for a moment, looking over to me. It was something I was open to, but as a new person in their lives, I didn't have as much to overcome as he and his family did. It wasn't my place to tell him what to do, so I simply smiled, letting him know I was fine with whatever he decided.

He looked over at both of them. "I think it will take us a while to get there, but I'm certainly willing to try. I would love it if you both would be in Lily's life. You have missed out on quite a few years of her life. She is a pretty amazing little girl."

"We could see that in the first thirty seconds of seeing her; so many similarities to her mother, her love of baking being one that stands out to me." They both hugged Brad, and then came to me for one as well.

I felt like after all they have put us through, it was a quick forgiveness, but it wasn't something I wanted in my life anymore. After going through all I had in the last few months, I was happy to move on from it and continue on with my life, now assured that I would be able to continue with the new one I was building.

"We won't keep you any longer. Thank you for letting us come and enjoy today with all of you. I owe a lot of that to your mother, so if I don't see her back at the hotel tonight, please be sure to thank her for us."

We walked them to the door, following them outside to where their car was parked on the street. Saying our goodbyes again, we both stood there, watching them walk down the street to their car. As they got in a pulled away from the curb, I couldn't help but feel so thankful for them. They were the two people who brought Hope into this world, and without her, I wouldn't have Brad and Lily in my life now. She was the one who brought hope back into my life when I didn't have much left. For them I will always be grateful, for raising such an amazing daughter who loved with all she had, and for allowing me into their lives to continue from where she left off.

"So, after all you have been through over the last couple of weeks, and especially today, are you sure you want to be in our lives? Things tend to get a little crazy every now and then." He stood behind me, wrapping his arms over the top of my shoulders as I lay my head back against him, breathing in his scent, watching them drive away.

"I now know you're the reason I was brought here to this town, and now I can never imagine myself living anywhere else, or with anyone other than you and Lily. Every day may not be easy, but I know in my heart that it will be worth it. There is just one more question I have for you that I don't know the answer to, yet." I turned around to face him, holding one of his hands in each of mine. "Do you prefer to wash the dishes or dry?"

He laughed as I ran back inside, chasing closely behind me,

locking the door behind him. We both stood in front of the wall, staring at all of the photographs hanging in front of us.

"For the first time in a long time, I can finally say that I am excited for my future." Turning off the lights, we walked hand in hand back to the kitchen.

"Me too," I agreed, resting my head against his arm.